Enjoy the
adventure
the stars may
fall.

—Riley Adams

ASHES TO ASHES

RILEY ADARIS

ASHES TO ASHES

©2023 Riley Adaris

ISBN 979 8 35091-901-1

eBook ISBN 979-8-35091-902-8

PART ONE:
ASHES AND DUST

CHAPTER ONE

"You fucker! Wake **up**, goddamnit!"

"Ma'am, you need to stay calm, help is—"

"I'm calm enough!" I shouted into the house phone, the speaker button lit orange. I was panting, pushing, waiting.

Come on, baby, come on. Don't do this. Don't leave me.

"One hundred!"

Check for breathing. Don't waste time looking for a pulse. Just worry about breathing.

"Nothing. Fuck, baby, come on."

"Ma'am, are there any medical issues we should be aware of?"

"No, no, nothing." *Push, push, blow, blow. When it stops, nobody knows.*

We had just redone our staff certifications at the bar a few weeks ago, and the wry words of the instructor came back to me now. The instructor, a tiny blond with a stubby ponytail, said it becomes a rhythm. I watched that rhythm happen as if from the doorway: a too-pale, short-haired woman lying on the floor, hastily pulled-on boxers bunched up, a woman in yoga pants and tank top leaning over her, long braid falling in her face and getting tossed back. The scene unfolding around them showed signs of the panicked situation—the bed askew, the old braided rug bunched up behind the cedar chest at the end of the bed.

"Up here! Up the stairs, all the way down the hall!" she—I—yelled at the noise coming from downstairs. Heavy boots announced the arrival of first responders. I dropped back in, falling out of the rhythm and back into myself, in the scene of anger and confusion and the kind of fear that turns your belly to ice. Scuffed black boots stepped into my line of sight as I looked down at my wife's pale legs.

"What's going on today, ma'am?" The clipped words assumed control of the situation. I didn't stop pushing.

"I don't know. My wife, Nan—Nan Montgomery-Shaw. She slept in, and she wasn't awake yet. I came to check on her. She'll be thirty-seven in March." My own voice was lead, each word dropping to the floor, emotionless until the last; it faltered as gloved hands reached over mine, taking over.

Another uniform came through the doorway and took the phone from me. "Miss, how long has it been since you've seen her?"

I must have responded. Another question, another answer. I floated in and out, my body staying put but wandering around, getting lost, watching the scene I had practiced. It didn't seem real; it wasn't supposed to look like this. This wasn't a plastic mannequin; there wasn't an outdated DVD paused on the directions. I watched the crowd of bodies as firefighters arrived to assist, boots stomping down the hall. I heard something that sounded like a dentist's drill and saw the paramedic push something into Nan's leg, below her knee.

"I've got access. Hand me an epi." His hair looked grayer than it should have been for his age. He didn't flinch at how intrusive he was being to the person who lay in front of him. A voice called out from the black-and-yellow box: *Analyzing. Do not touch patient.* The voice was so mechanical, the paramedic so composed, I wondered if he had made the order himself.

All movement froze. Only the paramedic showed any sign of life, drawing the plunger back to load the next syringe, one icy-blue eye on the needle, one on the box. A momentary, collective breath was held.

No shock advised. Resume CPR. Blue-gloved hands fell to her chest and pushed and pushed and pushed. With half an ear, I heard the muffled snort of one of the paramedics, the low conversation that ensued. I didn't follow. I thought I heard something about chicken, but I wasn't trying to listen. I watched the gray paramedic, firefighters in suspenders and big brown pants, and a group of people kneeling all around Nan. Most of the faces crowded around her looked like kids, kids whose eyes were already shuttered, who seemed too young to be so brusque in an emergency. Of course, they weren't kids. I knew that. But what did it take, to do CPR to someone around your own age? Nan was barely older than me. I had felt her ribs crunch under my hands and my stomach had recoiled at the sensation; these people were talking about food.

More questions were asked. I gave more answers.

"Please, please, please take her to the hospital. She needs a hospital. Please, you have to take her!" A woman's voice broke into a sob. I didn't recognize it as my own.

Analyzing. Do not touch patient. Freeze. Hold. Lift the needle on this record.*No shock advised. Resume CPR.* Drop. Push. Watch. Beg.

Analyzing.

No shock advised. The scene started to fade away, losing color and definition. The urgency slowly drained. I moved down the hallway backward, my eyes on Nan's cold, cold feet, visible through the open door. She needs socks, I thought dimly. They need to put socks on her.

I sat when the back of my legs hit a chair.

They started to file out of the room. I saw the gray paramedic on the phone, a little gray notepad in hand. I could hear someone's breath huffing out with exertion as CPR continued. The medic paced, kicking up dust from where the rug had lain for so long. His voice drifted down the hall.

"All right. Thanks, Doc. Time? 9:47. Got it. Send you the report when we connect up. Yeah, next of kin's on-site. Will do." A pause. "We're done here, guys. Thanks for your help. Jeanne, will you disconnect? I'm going to go talk to the, uh, girlfriend."

He walked out of the bedroom and came down the hall toward me. I heard his boots get closer; I stared past him before he obscured my view. I looked up and saw his eyes already distant, already putting space between himself and the bad news he was about to deliver. He pulled up the small footstool that stood in the corner and sat. He had no sooner begun to offer his first condolences and ask his last questions than I heard myself start screaming.

CHAPTER TWO

I had always been good in a crisis. If other people were freaking out, I could always be counted on to hold the line. It wasn't a conscious thing for me; it was just handling whatever came next. Probably a remnant of childhood, when one or both of my parents would disappear for days at a time and someone had to keep up the appearance of a normal family. This wasn't the same, I thought. This was happening here, to me, to my wife. I couldn't settle. I still sat on the chair in our little library, the rest of the people in our house leaving me alone. My hands still shook in my lap. The silence was laced with trepidation.

The firefighters had left loudly and quickly while the paramedics packed up, some mumbling condolences on their way out. The gray one who'd run the show was hanging around until the state police arrived.

"It's technically a crime scene, I'm sorry," he explained with a shrug. "I can't leave you alone with the body."

The body. The body of my wife, my love, my world. I took a deep breath. "Wife," I reminded him without looking up.

He wasn't paying attention. "Pardon me?"

"Wife," I said tersely. " 'The body' is my wife." Our marriage certificate hung above the couch, where any idiot wandering around the living room could see it. It was framed and matted between two Supreme Court decisions, the hard-fought cases that had finally conferred the rights of marriage to same-sex couples nationwide. I wasn't going to let some asshole demean it. "I'm her wife. I'm not a friend or a girlfriend," I continued, getting fired up. The anger leapt within me, snarling at the usual calmness that accompanied me in crises. I thought of the parable of the two wolves and struggled to tamp down the near-violent emotions. "It's legal, you know."

You fucking Neanderthal, I added in my head.

"Uh, yeah." He looked uncomfortable and bored. He didn't want to be here. "Well, I can't leave you alone with her. The cops will take over when they get here."

"Yeah, I got that. You good if I make some phone calls?" I stepped away without waiting for an answer and walked downstairs to an empty kitchen.

Nothing looked different. The coffeemaker was on; the sink had a few dishes in it from last night's dinner. My book lay open, spine-up on the couch, where I had put it down when I heard Nan snoring funny. I had walked up the stairs—why hadn't I run? Why hadn't I gotten there faster, known what was happening sooner? What the fuck had even happened?

I took a fresh mug from the cabinet, poured coffee, and dumped sugar in. I eyed the bottle of bourbon that I had used to mix some spiked cocoa the night before. It was ten o'clock in the morning.

What the hell, I thought, and tipped some into my mug. For a moment, I thought about offering some coffee—straight—to the paramedic. I'd been raised on Southern hospitality, after all; it would be rude not to offer. I sighed and did the mature thing.

After grabbing my coffee and a hoodie, I stuck my middle finger up at the stairs and took the phone outside.

It was warmer than usual for January. There was no frost left in the sunny areas after shrinking back to the shadows. I sat for a little bit. I might not have been exactly calm, but I did know a lot of the steps that had to come next. Nan's ex-girlfriend had passed away—passed away, she fucking died, stupid not to say it—the year before and Nan had been distraught, not having known that she had been sick. Between that and handling the arrangements for my grandmother when I was sixteen, this wasn't my first rodeo. The calls came first. I had a mental list going: Nan's mother, her brother, my parents. Her work, my work. Fuck.

Family came first. I rearranged the list in my head, then dialed the office number for the bar from memory. It rang and rang. Six rings in, I hung up. I looked at my watch; it wasn't even eleven. I dialed again, punching in the extension that would go to Cleo's phone. He answered on the second ring, laughter in his voice.

"Hello?"

"Cleo."

"Del! Wait. What's up?" The humor disappeared from his voice immediately.

"Hey, uh, it's not good. It's bad. It's the worst kind of bad, man."

"Hey, you okay? What's going on?" I heard him murmur something to Johnathon.

"Uh—it's Nan. Nan's . . . gone." I ran my hand over my hair, wrapping it around my braid and pulling, as if that slight pain would keep me tethered to reality.

"What do you mean, 'gone'? She run off on you, honey?" Cleo demanded.

"No, no. She's—she's dead. She died. Oh, Christ. She's upstairs, and she's dead."

"What the fuck? Girl, you call 911? What are you talking to me for? We're on our way."

"No, they've already been here. She's gone. She's just . . . gone." I took a shaky breath. I could hear Johnathon in the background, his voice frantic even from a distance. Why that of all things steadied me, I didn't know. "But yeah, if you could come, I'd appreciate it."

"Of course, of course. We'll be there right soon as we can. Oh, Jesus wept. You sit tight, honey. We're coming." Cleo shouted something to Johnathon as he hung up.

I lowered the phone. Nan was dead. Those were words that had come out of my mouth, and they were true. My Nan—gone. Not gone. Dead. I drank half my coffee and wished for something stronger than the bourbon.

I had to look the next number up in my cell; Nan's mother, Gloria, and I weren't exactly friends. I dialed quickly, wanting to get it over with, but hit "End" as I saw the police car swing into the curve of our driveway a little too quick. I took another gulp of coffee and steeled myself to deal with more uniforms when the door popped open and the friendliest face I'd ever seen jumped out.

"Del! Shit! What? What the fuck!" She walked to me quickly—Officer Angela Sirois wouldn't run on scene. She grabbed my hands. "Not Nan. Not Nan," she said, her eyes begging for the truth to be anything but that. I nodded. She threw her arms around me and rocked from side to side, saying, "Shit, shit, shit. Jesus. Shit."

For some reason, it got me to smile, just a little bit. She might be in uniform today, but Ange was forever herself, a chatty redhead with the mouth of a sailor.

"Oh, Ange. I'm so glad you're here." I hugged her back. "The paramedic—he won't leave. He won't let me stay with her unless he's right there. But you're here now."

She held on. She was Nan's roommate from college, but we had forged our own bond over the past few years. "I'm here. I heard your address tap out for the medical, and I was just over across town. I'd hoped you'd fallen off the porch or some damn fool thing. I texted Nan. Jesus fuck, I texted her, then next thing I know, I heard them call for the coroner. I jumped the call. Easy to do—no one likes these. Dealing with family after death sucks." She drew out the last word, then slapped her hand over her mouth. "I mean, in general. Shit. Not you. You know what I mean. Oh, damn it. This sucks, though. Are you sure? Of course. They wouldn't call the coroner if—fuck. *Fuck*."

"Yeah. Can you come in now? There's coffee. I didn't offer any to the paramedic," I admitted. She snorted, then pulled back and straightened up, all five feet and one inch of herself. I was still nearly a head taller. She gave her uniform a quick tug, and I opened the door. The paramedic was already coming down the stairs.

"I saw you pull up, Officer, I—" He stopped when he saw me.

"I'll take your report. Mrs. Montgomery-Shaw, would you like to wait somewhere more comfortable?" The woman who had just rocked me, sworn the air blue, and snorted at my manners was briskly all business now. I found I had to smother a smile of my own. There was humor in the surreal, it seemed.

"I'll be in the parlor, then," I heard myself say, with some sort of affect. What was I saying? I felt almost giddy going back out the door. I nearly tripped on my coffee, choking with laughter. Crazy. I was going crazy. *This has done broke my brain,* I thought and coughed to cover the laugh.

I sat down hard on the steps, dropping my head into my arms. Maybe I *was* going crazy. Or maybe I was dreaming. Maybe none of this was happening, and it was all a bad dream. It had to be. Any minute now, I'd wake up and Nan would be right there, her glasses on the nightstand, her arms and legs flung around, her skin warm and soft. I could see it. I knew exactly how she would look. And it was Saturday—we were both working tonight, so she'd make us brunch and we would read the news to each other on our phones while we drank coffee and ate too much bacon because she could never make half a pack, and we'd both complain about how full we were after, and I'd tease her, my chef wife, that it was always her fault that we were so full, and if she'd just stop cooking so damn well—

The pain in my arms stopped my thoughts from spiraling further from reality. My fingers dug in, nails leaving crescents deep in my skin. My hands hurt from the pressure. *Pinch me,* I thought. *Not a dream.*

Not a dream.

I didn't hear the door open, but I lifted my head when I saw the scuffed black boots appear.

"I'm sorry for your loss, ma'am," the paramedic said stiffly.

"It's not a dream. Not a dream." My voice was now dull, the rising hysteria swept away once again. I didn't look at him, and he didn't answer. He walked away, up the drive. Out of the corner of my eye, I noticed the ambulance pulled over on the side of the road in front of the house. I hadn't noticed it before.

Angela sat next to me on the step with her own cup of coffee. "Jaded motherfucker," she said simply. We sat there a moment, then she rubbed a hand on my back. "You can go to her, honey. You can't move or change anything, but you can be with her."

"Is it really a crime scene?" I asked.

She sighed and dropped her hand before responding. "Technically, yes. Because it's an unattended death, we have to treat it as a possible crime scene. Because it might be homicide"—I snorted at that—"or suicide."

"What? Ange, come on. You know it's not." I was immediately so incensed that I jumped up and stood, ready to fight anyone who'd say differently.

Ange didn't get up, only took a long sip and shrugged.

"Yeah, honey, I know it's not. I mean, *I* know *you* didn't do anything, and I seriously doubt that Nan would have offed herself. But in my world, you never know. You have to go through the steps, gather the evidence."

"Evidence? What evidence? Like, a note? Was there a note?" I demanded.

"No, no, baby. That's not what I mean. There was no note. I mean in general, it's what you do. I mean—we. It's what we do. What we have to do whenever someone who wasn't supposed to die turns up dead." She sighed again and lifted her coffee, running the hot mug over her forehead. "Fuck, Nan. What the fuck."

"So, what—if I go to her, I'm a suspect or something?" I asked, still angry and incredulous that anyone—friend, officer, asshole paramedic—could think that Nan had killed herself.

"No. You're not a suspect. Unless you move her or change things around her to make it look different."

"Why would I do that?"

"Fuck if I know, Del. Jesus Christ, do you want to see her or not?" Irritation and raw grief leaked through the professional facade as she looked up at me from her seat on the steps. I nodded, unable to speak over the lump of rage and fear and who-knows-what-else in my throat. "So, go. Touch her, but don't move her."

Not knowing what else to say, I started up the steps. I reached down and touched Ange's shoulder. Her other hand came up to mine for a moment.

Then I went inside to sit with my wife.

CHAPTER THREE

Death and dealing with the aftermath of it was utterly surreal. A few days after Nan took her last breaths, I found myself leaving the local funeral home with all that was left of my life in this world. I didn't know how to transport ashes—excuse me, cremains. What a creepy word. I stood there staring at the passenger seat of my truck for several minutes before I ended up placing the box on the bench seat and buckling it in. It felt strange, but it made me smile as I clicked the belt into place. Before every Thanksgiving, Nan would buckle the turkey in as if it were precious cargo, as if she weren't about to pull out its innards and smoke it or whatever other kitchen magic she did.

I blinked the memory away. What I now restrained so carefully was no turkey. It was far more precious.

The container I had chosen for the ashes was not really an urn. Nan wouldn't have wanted that, to be in something so ostentatious, its unmistakable shape yet another reminder of the dead inhabitant. And expensive—holy shit. The strangely tall funeral director had told me I could bring anything that fit a certain measurement and had a fitted lid. I had scoured the house for the perfect vessel, not wanting her ashes—fuck *cremains*—to end up in a coffee can, as she had joked about for years. I'd be damned if I was going to let that happen. With my luck, I'd stumble into the kitchen and try to brew a pot of her some early morning.

I'd thought of one of her favorite stockpots or ordering something online, but the whimsical or nostalgic didn't feel right. I managed to find something that fit the funeral director's specs that wouldn't be as jarring as having her stuck in random housewares.

It was old wooden box, a find from an antique shop we had passed on our travels. Nan loved to poke around stores that were little more than junk, mostly leftovers that nobody wanted from estate sales going back generations. She always had a plan to repurpose this or refinish that, make an art project out of scraps of wood and twine and who knows what else. I didn't know which shop it had come from or what journey it had taken, but I remembered Nan talking excitedly about rewiring it as a lamp. *It would be a reminder on dark days that there was still light,* she had said.

The box stood a little more than a foot tall, maybe six inches wide on each side, the craftsmanship evident. Pale gold wood underlaid intricate swirls of mahogany at the corners; thin strips in the same deep shade reinforced the edges. The domed lid was carved in the same patterns in solid mahogany; even the ring on top was made of the smooth wood. It fit snugly, a little more so during the humid summer months. Only the tiny brass hinges and ornate latch were metal. It had held a bottle of wine as a gift in its day, or at least, that's what Wikipedia said, as Nan had reported.

Whatever it was, it was beautiful—and with its intricate carvings and natural aperture, it was perfect.

I realized I was still half inside the truck, staring at what had become the urn. I scrubbed my hands over my cold face and walked around to my side. I had refused all company, all the offers from well-meaning friends with tears on their cheeks. I wasn't the only one feeling lost without Nan right now. Our friends and family were devastated, and I felt like they were all looking to me. They were waiting for me to say that things were going to be all right, that this was hard—fucking impossible—but we would continue to live on for Nan. It was what she would've wanted, she'd be happy to know, she wouldn't want us to be sad, and on and on with the bullshit words that are put in the mouths of the dead. I couldn't take the pleading eyes asking for this to not be true, to not be real. I couldn't take the futilely bunched fists of her brother, looking to fight an enemy that didn't exist, or the constant disapproval of her mother, waiting to strike but currently masked by grief.

So here I was, alone, driving along our winter roads with half of us a pile of dust. The radio murmured; I wasn't sure what station was on. I hit a frost heave I wasn't expecting and the truck bounced. Instinctively, I looked over at the container. It stood just the same. Steady as she goes, as Nan would have said.

I gasped and instinctively hit the brakes as the pain shot through me. Her voice, happy, practically dancing over the words, was so clear to me in that moment. I looked over again, thinking that maybe, somehow, I don't know—she'd be there. But all I found was the urn.

The blare of a horn yanked my wandering attention back to the road and the task at hand. A heavy truck swerved around me slowly, its snowplow lifted, and I noticed that I had not lifted my foot from the brake since my immediate stop. I shivered once, the potential danger of the moment sinking in. With a deep breath, I eased off the brake and onto the clutch and kept going. All I had to do was get home, then I could fall apart. Again.

I pulled into the driveway after what felt like hours. The threat of snow in the forecast was enough to keep folks off the roads, and the long drive-way was blessedly empty. No one was waiting for me to say something to make them feel better; no one was offering me a shoulder, then crying on mine instead. They all had the best of intentions, every one of them, but it was exhausting. I parked, got out, and slowly made my way over to the other side of the truck, trailing my fingers along the sea-green paint. The hood was warm in contrast to the cold, gray February day, but I felt as if I was moving through thick, icy mud. Every step was a burden. Every inch was closer to the truth that this box of ashes and dust was all that remained of my love.

I unbuckled the seat belt and lifted the urn. In total, it weighed maybe seven pounds, for box and contents. Cradling it in my arms, I kicked the truck door shut and carried it inside the house, through the door that Nan had been carried out of days before. I wished that this moment could be the undoing of that one, like hitting rewind on an old home video. The picture would get all scratchy and streaky, obscuring the events but for the basic motions and color. The thin bars of the metal stretcher would disappear; the heavy gray of the zipped bag that held my wife would disintegrate; the sheet that shrouded her would fall away. Her lifeless limbs would become supple; her pale skin would bloom again with the rush of blood through uncollapsed veins. Her still chest would lose the leftover adhesive, the IVs would fall from her arms, her ribs would knit together and expand under her breasts to draw in breath, and finally, as I crossed the threshold into our bedroom, her eyes would open, their soft hazel full of life and empty of fear. There would be no blur of people in uniforms, no irritating paramedic, no mechanical voice saying that there was no hope left.

The daydream rushed through my ears as it ended. I sat alone on the edge of our bed, holding the small, ornate coffin. It was so perfect in its shape, the lines clean. The dust that had collected had been carefully wiped away. The stillness was broken when I jolted suddenly, an unbidden mem-ory firing through my body: Nan at a haunted house a few years back, where the room we were in began to close in around us. She had panicked as the wall moved closer to the path we were on, and she pushed up against me to hurry me to the exit door. Her claustrophobia was nothing I wanted to fuck with, not then, not now.

I lifted my hand, shaking as I pressed the little latch, popping it open so the domed lid was no longer sealed. I opened it no further; I couldn't bear to look inside. I didn't want the image to replace any I had of her, and I was terrified that if I saw what her body had become, I would never see her as I remembered her again. This was enough. I was content that she was not somehow trapped inside the closed box.

Evening was approaching quickly, the darkness slowly creeping into the room. I hadn't turned on any lights when I came in, my hands full of precious cargo. I sat there on my side of the bed as the gray day slid into a dark night.

"Now what?" I whispered, waiting for some answer from the utter silence. Outside, the snow began to fall in fat flakes from a deep purple sky.

PART TWO:
EMBERS AND COALS

CHAPTER FOUR

"DEL, GO HOME."

Byron wiped down the long bar of the Hub 'n Spoke. I had been off shift since eleven; last call was still twenty minutes away. I lifted my glass. "Still got a little left, man," I said, swirling it around and taking a sip. I didn't really want it, but I didn't want to leave. "Anyway, it's not home."

I had been living at the apartment for a little over three months. I was pretty much unpacked because of course I was; Nan used to tease me that I had to unpack everything we brought in every hotel room. It helped that I hadn't held on to a lot of stuff from the house—books, mostly. I had kept

Nan's dresser—moved it still packed full of her clothes—and a few boxes of things. Gloria, never a candidate for Mother-in-Law of the Year, as far as I was concerned, had demanded a lot of stuff back. Pack rats, the lot of them, I thought. I didn't care that it was unkind. Her mom could have all the shit she wanted. It wasn't going to bring Nan back or make her not marry me or not be gay or absolve whatever sin she felt her daughter was.

"Let her bury herself in it. Whatever. What the fuck do I care. She just doesn't want me to have it," I said, raising my voice.

Byron kept cleaning and didn't respond.

"I said this already, didn't I?"

At that, he nodded.

I threw back the last of the whiskey, pressing the back of my forearm to my mouth to keep it in at the sudden rise in my throat. I swallowed hard and set the glass down. "All right."

I stood from the barstool, a nicely padded version of a wide, noseless bike saddle. I immediately found myself on the floor when my legs gave way. "By-y-y!" I whined, drawing out the vowel. It took a moment for him to appear in front of me, the beads at the ends of his braids clicking as he crouched.

"Not driving," he and I said together.

"Jinx!" I shouted, laughing. He shook his head again as he helped me back up to the barstool. "You owe me a Coke."

Back behind the bar, he dipped in the ice chest, grabbed the nozzle, and slid the soft drink over to me. "Give me ten," he said and went into the office.

I raised my glass to him and sipped. I hadn't intended on getting drunk, but then, I didn't usually intend on it. It just seemed to happen these days. And why the fuck not? I thought to myself. It wasn't like I had anyone to answer to. And it wasn't, like, *all* the time. Some nights sucked. Days were usually okay, I mused; I could get through most days all right. Sometimes the grief got through. I wouldn't even notice it before that sneaky bitch would tie my shoelaces together and I would find myself facedown on the floor, crying before I'd even gotten my coffee, but during the day, she mostly left me alone. I knew where all those little reminders were, all the tokens and clues and memories. I avoided them. Closed my eyes. *If I can't see you, you can't see me.*

But nights? The nights were hard. I drained the Coke, temporarily settling my stomach even as I wished it was something stronger. I couldn't stand the darkness. Nan had been my light, my guiding star. She had kept me going through the worst moments. Now I was left aimless and alone—alone with my grief and anger, at their devastating mercy. I was terrified of what would happen as the nights grew longer, as the darkness extended at both ends of the day.

I startled and nearly fell off the stool again at Byron's hand on my shoulder. He simply moved with me, shifting his grip to my arm to steady me. I slid down and threw my arm around his shoulders; he was several inches shorter, so this worked naturally. He let me lean on him wordlessly, even as hot tears filled my eyes. Grief took the reins from the whiskey that filled my head until I couldn't take another step. My feet were rooted as the first sob broke through, shaking my body out of its stupor. Byron took the opportunity to guide me out the heavy doors to my own truck. The old door creaked open as he helped me into the passenger side and creaked when it shut. I curled up in the seat—Nan's seat—and let the tears come. Not like I had much choice. Once that tap was turned on, I had to let it run.

Byron knew this. He had been there for me; we'd been friends for as long as we'd been manning the bar here in Halfway. We had bonded over a love of good whiskey and James Baldwin novels. He said ten words to every hundred of mine, but his insights were incredible. He was quiet by nature. He never saw a need to fill the silence in a conversation. Patrons might've raised an eyebrow over the soft timbre of his voice, but they loved him for how he listened and how his experimental drink concoctions always hit the spot. I loved him because he was family and, after Nan, my best friend. He was one of three—shit, two now—people who knew everything about my past.

I cried as he stowed his bicycle in the bed of the truck. I kept going the whole way back and cried still more as we sat in my driveway. The radio was barely on, strains of *BBC Newshour* filling the space between sobs. Byron waited until my breathing leveled out some, then simply touched his hand to my shoulder again.

"Ready?" he asked.

I dragged my arm across my face, a futile effort to sop up some of the tears. "Yeah, all right." He handed me my keys and got out, coming around for my door. "A gentleman and a scholar," I mumbled. He grinned. I couldn't even return it, not with the familiar feeling of failure tapping me on the shoulder. "All right. Just get me to the door," I said. He didn't let me fall as I got out of the truck. He walked me to the door under a yellow light, where flies buzzed around. I managed to get the key in the door on the second try and stumbled inside.

"Del," he said, and I turned around in my dark living room. "It might not be home, but it's a good place to stop a while. Just until the light comes back."

I couldn't speak or I'd start crying again, so I nodded. He dropped my keys on the table inside the door, then reached in and flipped the lock on the knob before pulling the door shut behind him.

I stood in the dark a minute, two minutes. I don't know how long. The whiskey and tears had intertwined, a glorious but painful release. I wondered if euphoria could be heavy or if I was being stretched between my spinning head and sinking stomach. I wanted to lie down now. I stumbled toward the bedroom, detouring at the last moment to make it to the toilet in time to be sick.

The tears were back; they leaked out of my eyes as I vomited. The still-thinking part of my brain that would not fucking turn off reminded me that no one was here, that I was alone. Nan wasn't coming to hold back my hair and bring me a cool drink of water, murmur to me, and take me to bed.

Exhausted, I pulled myself up to the sink. Mouthwash would have to do, seeing as I lacked the coordination for anything more. I left the top of the bottle off, wherever it had fallen to. The moon was bright enough that I didn't stop to think about turning on the lights. I pulled myself into the bedroom using the doorway, trying to stay upright. There was a little desk inside the door that held Nan's ashes, glasses, and my favorite picture in a simple frame. I kissed my fingertips and tried to touch them to the antique box, the way I did every night.

I completely misjudged the distance, I realized with dull horror, as my hand stretched out and found nothing but empty air. I fell forward, my hip bouncing off the desk and sending everything on top wobbling. I tried to grab hold and steady myself, which only gave the precious items another hard rattle. Everything seemed to be happening in slow motion. I finally landed mostly on my ass, one arm tangled in a blanket, the other outstretched in a desperate attempt to catch the wooden urn as I watched it, the top unlatched and opening, finish its descent to the floor.

It landed with the sharp sound of wood striking wood, and the ashes of my love spilled out to lie on the moonlit floor right before everything went black.

CHAPTER FIVE

I woke in the semidarkness, curled up on blankets that I must have finally succeeded in tugging off the bed. I tapped my watch: nothing. We didn't have an alarm clock, so I had no idea what time it was. The hangover was already making itself known; I was groggy, my mouth fuzzy and tasting of whiskey gone stale. I pushed myself up, leaning on one arm while I half scrubbed my face with the other. As I tried to blink away the dryness in my eyes, I noticed the bright light from the moon streaming in, making the pile of—was that sand?—on the floor glow almost white.

I looked out the window. The moon was a bit past a quarter in size, but you wouldn't know it from the room, which practically pulsed with an almost ethereal glow, as if the moon were inside the room, filling every corner. How was it making so much light? Looking at the sand, I wondered if I had already gotten the vacuum back from the repair guy, and where on earth I had put it. But wait, no—the vacuum had gotten tossed during the move.

Get a new vacuum, then. When had we moved? Where was—

I reeled back as if I had been slapped across the face. *We* hadn't moved, *I* had. Nan was gone. Died. Cremated and everything. The wail started from somewhere deep inside, rising, tearing out of my throat as what happened struck me full force.

Cremated. As in ashes. It was ashes, not sand, that lay spilled on the floor. I reached out, then snatched my hand back. My wife's ashes were . . . definitely glowing now?

Hallucinating. I really had lost it, I thought, as I scrambled backward as quickly as my spinning head allowed. With my back to the wall, I grabbed the windowsill above me as the ashes, impossibly, began to float.

What the fuck?

Like starlings, I watched the ashes come together in one continuous form rather than tiny particles, and the glow started to shimmer from within, white and yellow and hints of flame blue. There was a hum in the air, rising decibel by decibel. The ashes began to bubble up like lava, and I wondered how a pile of dust could act so like a liquid, but even that physics-related train of thought couldn't derail what I was witnessing with my own eyes, my room lit up like a fairground by moonlight.

The hum grew louder around me. The shimmer grew stronger, until I found myself shading my eyes from the brightness as the ashes fell away, curling into themselves like smoke until none were left. In their place crouched something I could never even dream up.

The bird was large and sleek, shaped rather like a swan. Its large wings were open, half outstretched. The head displayed the same sort of topknot as a quail but was much larger. The tail was long and fanned out, the two outer tail feathers extending at least an additional foot beyond the other pinions. It was pure white but for pale golden streaks down the feathers on the thighs, leading into the two long feathers. Those, along with the topknot, were a shade of blue I felt like I couldn't understand, a shade that managed to be both deep and bright. The curved beak was a much darker gold, its legs as thick as my finger. Claws, short but razor sharp, tipped the toes. The eyes were dark, clear, and full of power, two glittering sapphires set against a backdrop of snow.

Looking over its shoulder, the glorious bird met my incredulous stare with an expression of scorn. The creature emitted a resonating cry that seemed to hold in it all the world's tears. I heard the roar of worlds rushing past us to bring us to this moment, a cacophony of sound that crescendoed and dropped into crystal-clear silence.

Then the connection broke. The bird looked up briefly and rose on no more than a single wingbeat. Time flexed against the walls of the room and slowed down as the bird neared the ceiling, once again looking at me. It inclined its head toward me, then arrowed up, wings and tail tightly spiraling inward at the sudden burst of white flames. There was a flash of light so bright and silent, I thought death had come for me as well.

Then, just as quickly, the light faded. The magical, mythical creature was gone, as were the ashes; there was no trace of them left in the low carpet. The box lay on its side, open but undamaged, at the feet of an old man standing stark naked and looking very confused.

CHAPTER SIX

"What in the hell is going on here?"

I pressed the heels of my hands to my eyes and leaned forward, suddenly queasy.

"Who the hell are you? Explain yourself, missy! Why are you in my room and on the floor? And where are my pajamas?" he demanded.

"I—I don't know. Am I still drunk? Jesus, how much did I have?" I muttered to myself, still refusing to open my eyes.

An exasperated sound came from the man, who could not possibly be real and here and in my bedroom. "Ah, forget it. Just get me some damn clothes," he said. He? It? Was it some sort of apparition, a ghost of grandfathers past? He flapped a hand in my direction. "Hello?"

The annoyance in his tone would have been funny, had I heard it in any other situation. He sounded like he belonged on a sitcom set in a nursing home. I slowly lowered my hands and opened my eyes.

The night was dark again, as it should have been all along. Still, the thin light from the moon added to the yellow glow of the neighbor's back-porch light, and I could see enough to know that, yes, there was an old man standing at my dresser. I blinked. Yup, still there. His skin was pale and a little loose, like a suit that didn't fit quite right in certain places. His butt sagged over skinny legs and I could see bruising on his arms, despite the diminished moonlight. He had a short cap of hair that I assumed was gray, based on the rest of him. He muttered to himself as he ran his fingers over the edge of my dresser.

"This isn't my bureau. They moved things around on me again. Where's that nurse? She can't keep moving my things. How'm I supposed to find anything?"

I stood slowly, mindful of the effects of tonight's whiskey. The room spun halfway around before settling where it belonged. My head pounding, I pressed the heel of one hand to my temple and held onto the nightstand with the other.

"Um. Sir. Hello. I'm Del. Well, Delilah, but everyone calls me Del. And you are . . . ?" I wasn't sure what I was expecting, but it was definitely not for him to turn, face me full-on (yup, definitely naked), and stick his hand out. Automatically, I put mine in his, and with much more vigor than I'd anticipated, he covered it with his other hand and pumped it in welcome.

"Name's Maltby, Naylor Maltby. Friends o' mine used to call me Salty Maltby, back in my Navy days. Nowadays, most folks call me Nelly. Nice to meet you, Del. You must be new around here. Are you one of the nurses? The light looks different in here. And why was my bureau changed? I don't remember a thing about it. In fact, the last thing I remember—" He paused, mouth still open, as if the word was waiting and he'd run out of air to push it out. He dropped his hand and pulled back a little bit, straightening up slightly. "Why, I don't remember what the last thing was."

"That's okay, Mr. Maltby. We'll, uh, figure that out later. For now, let's get you some clothes, okay?" I moved around him to Nan's dresser. It stood in the far corner of the room, the top of it empty. It had been that way since some well-meaning friend had cleaned it in the days following her death, all the loose earrings, matchbooks, and pocket flotsam packed away somewhere else. It still felt like hers, so I was loathe to put anything of mine on it, and so it remained, blank but for the collecting dust.

The drawers, however, were still packed tight. Nan had liked her clothes. I pulled out a T-shirt and some sweatpants, ignored the way the hair on my arms bristled at riffling through her clothes so carelessly when I hadn't even seen them for months. I turned and thrust them at the man. "Here you go. Why don't you get dressed, and I'll make some coffee?"

"Ha, you must be new." He chuckled. "I haven't been able to get dressed on my own in some years. Aren't you going to help me?"

It finally dawned on me what he was thinking, waking up and not finding things, calling me a nurse, the bruises on his arms and the backs of his hands.

"Do you know where you are right now, Mr. Maltby?" I said carefully. He looked up from testing the waistband of the sweatpants, surprised.

"Well, sure, Del, don't you? I'm in my room right here at Twelve Elms." His eyes, blue except for a tiny band of brown around the pupil, narrowed. "What happened? You didn't call that damn ambulance again, did you? I don't remember falling, I'm not bleeding from anywhere . . ." he trailed off.

"No, no," I said. "No ambulance. Uh, okay. Fuck. All right, let's get you dressed."

He took that as a cue to sit on the edge of the bed and lift one leg.

"I usually wear Depends," he reminded me.

"Sorry, fresh out. We'll get you some more in the morning." I crouched and guided his foot into the pant leg and back to the floor, then repeated it with the other leg. I held out a hand to help him up; he grasped the inside of my arm, near my elbow, and I returned the grip automatically.

He pulled himself up. Down went the pants.

"You're a sturdy thing, aren't you?" he commented as I averted my gaze and reached down to tug the sweats up around his waist, tying the drawstring before letting go.

"Yes sir," I said. "You have no idea. You got it from here?"

He waved a hand. "Go on. You're making coffee, you said? I hope you're better at it than that other nurse—what's her name? Frannie, Frankie, something." I left him muttering at the shirt and backed out of the bedroom. When I flipped on the light switch, I heard his satisfied, "Ah!" I leaned against the wall, out of view for a minute.

That had really happened. I had helped an old man dress in my dead wife's clothes, I thought to myself. What the actual fuck was going on here? Where did he even come from?

Twelve Elms, I remembered. Twelve Elms was a nursing home somewhere across town. I took the few steps into the kitchen, absently pressing the button on the coffeepot. I noticed the sky going gray outside and finally looked at the clock. 4:55. Perfect, I thought. Guess it's time to get up. My alarm wouldn't be singing for another five hours. I reached automatically for my pockets, looking for it, realizing I was still dressed from the night before. What had that been about again?

I pulled a cup from the first half of the brewing pot and dumped in sugar and a single ice cube. I stood in place as I swallowed it down. When the coffeemaker beeped its job well done, I refilled—sugar, no ice this time. The first jolt on board, I grabbed what was always the second mug. I hadn't made morning coffee for anyone since Nan. I stopped midpour; I couldn't give this grief-stricken hallucination of a man this mug. My mind flashed to Nan's fingers wrapped around it, warming them awake on the red ceramic.

I closed my eyes on the memory. It could have been any morning, October to May, or even summer sometime. The way her hand fit, her finger up against the lip of the mug—

"That for me?" Like a bubble popping, I found myself back in my kitchen. This strange man I had never seen before expected coffee.

"Uh, no. Hold on. How do you take it?" I grabbed another mug at random and nearly toppled it upon seeing him in my wife's clothes.

"Black, please."

"Yeah, okay. Have a seat." My mind racing, I poured the coffee and set it down on the counter. "One sec." I grabbed a bottle of magic headache pills and some vitamins before joining him back in the kitchen, where he stood, looking around. I pulled out the two chairs at the little table and tossed whatever clothes and magazines were on it to the floor. "All right, Mr. Maltby." I handed him his coffee.

"Call me Nelly!" he said cheerfully. "Say, new mugs? These aren't the usual. You know, I didn't even know there was a kitchen back here." He took a sip. "Hot damn, that's coffee!"

I stared at him. This man had to be a caricature. He couldn't possibly be real.

"Mr. Maltby—Nelly—I, uh, don't know where to start."

"Try the beginning," he suggested with a wink.

Jesus. A wink.

"Ha. Yeah. Well. It doesn't quite work like that, I don't think. All right. Um, all right. So. My name's Del—I guess we've established that. But I'm not a nurse, I'm a bartender. And this isn't Twelve Elms. This is my house— my apartment," I corrected. I still wasn't used to being back in an apartment, rather than our house. "You're in my apartment, and I'm not really sure how you got here, or why you're here."

He was watching me, his old eyes squinting under the kitchen light. "Am I on some television show?"

"What? No, no. You're in my house, somehow, across town from Twelve Elms. You just sort of . . . appeared in my bedroom." I couldn't bring myself to say how; it was too incredible. I looked down and realized I was still holding the pill bottle. I shook out two of the red caplets and added a couple of the vitamins for good measure while he sat, trying to digest this information.

"Could I have my pills, please? I'm ready for breakfast now," he said, much more hesitantly.

"I don't have any pills for you. These are just for my hang—my headache. And I don't have anything for breakfast, really. But I know a good diner."

"We can go out?" He brightened immediately. "My treat!"

CHAPTER SEVEN

The sun was breaking over the trees that ran down the center of Hyde Avenue when we pulled into the parking lot of The Hot Plate. The pitched canopy laid atop a dozen-and-a-half poles that showed their age in rusty, white-and-orange relief. The old diner had passed through several sets of hands throughout its history; it was the type with black-and-white tiled floors, leather-topped stools, and tabletop jukeboxes at every booth. The tables were sticky with humidity, and the floors looked like they hadn't seen a good mopping in some time, though I knew they had. The owners, Jack and Mary Mason, were from out west, retired from the corporate life in some city in Michigan. They had been traveling the country for six months before seeing the diner, which had been a failing pizza place;

they'd sold their RV and bought it outright. They still sat for breakfast most mornings at six, though now they had their own booth with a plaque and everything. There was talk of handing the reins to one of the grandkids, as they were fast approaching eighty, but there had been talk of that as long as we'd been going.

I parked and walked around to the passenger door. Nelly had his seat belt off by the time I got there, and he held onto my arm as he gingerly stepped out of the truck. His brow was slightly furrowed as he looked at the diner.

Nan and I had come here for years—as girlfriends, as newlyweds, after a long night at the bar. We came here the morning of the Supreme Court decision for marriage equality. I thought about how we had been chewing our nails to the quick, waiting at home for the verdict on NPR. Anxious and sick with it, we decided we'd feel better at the diner; it didn't change anything, and we'd sat on the stools, coffee going cold while the radio coverage played. When the decision was read, even the correspondent's calm voice broke a little, and I started crying while everyone else around us burst into applause. Jack and Mary had hurried over from their kitchen booth as Nan grabbed me by the shoulders, kissed me hard, then declared to the world at large, "I'm going to marry you, Delilah Shaw!" Jack had slapped her on the back and proclaimed himself the best man, to which Nan had laughed and told him, "You're the best man we know, Jack Mason!"

The memory of her voice faded as the bell jingled, and a couple strolled out with go-cups of coffee. With his free hand, the man tipped his hat at Nelly, who reached up to do the same, a move clearly seared into his arm's muscle memory. When his fingers didn't find a brim, his eyes filled with annoyance, then panic. He stopped short and looked around and finally down at himself. Slowly, he brought his hands up, gently tapping his spread fingers into his chest, as if feeling for substance. He looked at me and startled slightly, as if he'd forgotten I was there.

Before I could ask if he was okay, he narrowed his eyes. "Del."

"Yep."

"Something's fishy."

"Oh yeah, for sure, Mr. Maltby." I took his elbow and guided him up the two small steps.

"I can't put my finger on it," he said slowly, looking intently at the doorway to the diner. Layers upon layers of red paint on the trim showed where it had chipped since the last coat, like rings in an old tree.

"We'll work it out," I muttered as we entered. The air was already warm from the ovens, and the complete joke of an AC unit clunked on at the end of the counter. I threw a nod to Wendy at the stove and waved at Amy and Justine filling coffees as I steered the old man down to our preferred booth: exactly where I had sat with Nan most often. I think we had sat at every seat over the years, but there was one she'd liked in particular. It had the best angle for people watching, she'd say.

Mr. Maltby hung onto my arm as he lowered himself into the seat, then inched his legs under the table.

I slid in across from him. "Mr. Maltby—"

"Del, please, call me Nelly, won't you? You're making me feel old and decrepit with this 'Mr. Maltby' crap."

"Yeah. Okay. Nelly."

He beamed. "See? Not so hard. We're friends now."

"I—all right. Hard to argue with that. But right now—"

Justine appeared at my elbow, pouring her pot of coffee into mismatched mugs. "Heya, hon. Nan's side today, eh? Ah, Christ, what a thing. What can I get you? Who's your friend?" She nodded at Nelly as I added my two packets of sugar.

"Well, hi there, darling," Nelly said. "Aren't you picture pretty."

Justine's right eyebrow raised so high, it practically disappeared. I waited for the snappy response, but she grinned.

"Aren't you the charmer," she said, planting a hand on her hip. "You been here before? You have a familiar thing about you."

"Don't think so, ma'am. Wait a minute—isn't this old Jack Mason's place?" He suddenly sat up a little straighter, looking around, as if just realizing it was familiar territory.

"Sure is. I'll let him know you're here if you'd like. What's your name, honey?" She pulled her pen and pad out of her apron.

"Ah—yes. If you please. You tell him—ha, you tell him old Salty's here. He'll know. But you can call me Nelly. Most everyone does," he told her, sending me a wink. "Even Del here, now."

"Okay then, Nelly, what'll it be for ya?" The pen and pad vanished back into the pocket without a mark; I had never seen her write down an order, let alone seen it served incorrectly.

"Poached egg on toast with some of those little sausages sounds about right."

"You got it. Del?" She turned to me and clucked her tongue. "Don't you look whipped. Rough night again? Gotta let go of that bottle now and again, girl. All right, anyway. Let me get your order, then I'll bring you over some more coffee." She waved the empty pot in her hand.

"Thanks, Justine. I'll take my usual sugar."

"Okay, sweetie." She rubbed my shoulder before she disappeared. She touched everyone she met. It had taken Nan some time to get used to that.

Across the table, Nelly drank his coffee, looking around for a minute before I saw his eyes light up. "Vicky!" He started to push himself up from the table.

I turned to follow his line of sight to a young woman sitting a few booths behind us as I fumbled my way out of the seat to help him. The brunette's head jerked up, and her eyes went wide before she said something in a low voice over the table. She slid out of the booth and was out the side door before I could get Nelly on his feet. Once he stood, he said her name again, now confused.

Another woman's head popped out, older but also brunette. Her expression was one of pure shock, then her face set into angry lines, her mouth thinning further upon seeing us. She disappeared a moment, then rose from the booth gracefully. Her pale yellow blazer set in place with a single tug and she marched over, low black heels clicking on the tile. She stood in front of him, back ramrod straight.

"Jacqueline! Honey, I didn't—"

The words died on his lips as she cut him off sharply.

"I don't know who put you up to this, but this is not funny. My daughter thought you were her grandfather when she saw you, then you call her name? Is this some sort of joke?" "No, Jackie, I—"

"And my name! I don't know who the hell you are, but if this is some sick practical joke, you"—she jabbed a finger close to his face—"you can just tell whoever sent you that my father is not only dead, but he's dead to us." She zeroed in on me. "And to whoever your . . . accomplice is, maybe instead of setting up ridiculous pranks, my father should have handled his own affairs." She spat the last word out with venom, then threw up her chin and turned on her heel. Every movement was perfectly controlled as she leaned into the booth, picked up a leather purse the same color as her blazer, and walked out.

I found myself wondering what a woman with such confidence and self-righteous anger did for a living, a game I often played during the slower hours at work. Power broker, maybe? Yeah, she'd drive down from the city, come into the bar on a Friday after closing bell, and order a dry martini to shake off the week.

The storyline in my head crumbled as I felt Nelly's hand shake in mine.

"Here—sit. Wow. What the hell was that?" I wondered out loud before taking my own seat. I reached for my nearly empty coffee. The old man sat, staring in stunned silence, toward the space the two women had occupied. "Nelly?" I leaned forward. "Nelly, what the holy hell is going on?"

He looked up at me slowly. "I—I don't know." He looked devastated.

"Who were those people? Did you know them?" I asked, gently sliding his coffee back to him.

He wrapped his bony, thick-knuckled fingers around the smiling ceramic cow. "The one who ran away—that was Victoria, my granddaughter. The angry one?" A ghost of a smile. "That was my daughter, Jackie. She's always had a sharp tongue on her." His eyes narrowed and met mine. "What did they mean by me not only being dead but being dead to them, Del? What did they mean?"

I shrugged, at a loss. "I don't know. I really have no idea. I mean, you're not dead. You're here. You're sitting right here, aren't you?"

"As far as I know."

"Okay, well—"

"Here ya go, honey." Justine appeared again to fill my coffee, dropping some extra sugar packets on the table before topping off Nelly's cup. "I'll be right back with your orders. Wendy's finishing them up." She moved away.

I turned to see her bussing the table where the two women had sat. Her expression didn't change. I hoped they had at least paid before taking off like a couple bats out of hell.

I looked back at Nelly. "You okay there?"

He shook his head slowly. "I don't rightly know, Del. I don't have a clue as to what is going on today. The world didn't seem so strange yesterday, when I . . ." he trailed off, staring back into middle distance. "What did they mean?"

There was a clatter at the kitchen doors, and I looked up to see it swinging behind our waitress, tray in hand. She stopped and lowered it, resting the edge on our table as she transferred plates.

"One egg, poached, with white toast, side of sausage. Short stack of strawberry-banana pancakes with whipped cream, extra syrup on the side. You good on coffee? Good. Holler if you need anything, all right?" Tucking the tray under her arm, she patted Nelly's shoulder and moved away as the door chimed open.

I watched as Nelly unrolled his paper napkin, unfolded it, and tucked it into the neck of his T-shirt. Mechanically, he began to eat, but his eyes were far away.

"The hell it is!" Angry words coming from the direction of the kitchen broke the silence. I looked up to see Jack Mason, stocky and with a head full of steam, bearing down on us.

When Nelly turned his head, Jack stopped short. The color drained from his face, and he leaned heavily into the end of another booth for support.

"The hell it is," he repeated, much quieter now. "I'll be damned. It is."

"Hey there, Jack." Nelly smiled nervously. "Been some time now, hasn't it?" Jack said nothing, just stared. Nelly's smile faded and he cleared his throat. He looked down at his plate and hurriedly tugged the napkin off. "I, uh, had hoped to see you before this. Never made it here, though. 'Specially not so early. Not much of a morning person myself. But this—this is great . . ." he trailed off, still pinned under that stare. "Look, Jack, I'm happy to see you, and I'm sorry if you aren't the same. I'll be taking my leave after I finish this breakfast Del here took me for, and you won't have to see me again. I promise you—hey!"

Jack cut him off by leaning over and poking him hard in the shoulder. Twice.

Jack sat back hard in the booth across the aisle from Nelly, never blinking, his gaze never shifting. Justine and Amy had come out of the kitchen, Wendy watching from the pass-through. For a fleeting moment, I hoped she would warm up my pancakes, which were rapidly going cold, untouched on my plate.

"Damn it, Jack. What's wrong with you?" Nelly burst out, his cheeks flushing red after noticing the small diner was focused on them.

"You're supposed to be dead." Jack said slowly, his eyes still never leaving Nelly's face. "How can you be sitting in my diner if you're supposed to be dead?"

"Ah, Jack, not you too! Why, my daughter just—" Bewildered, Nelly looked over at me. I could do no more than shrug and shake my head. "What do you mean, I'm supposed to be dead?"

Jack jerked upright, as if the movement needed the comfort of oil to operate smoothly. He pulled his wallet out of his back pocket. He opened the slim, worn leather and pulled out a piece of paper slightly larger than a business card. He laid it on the table with trembling hands.

Naylor "Nelly" Saltalamacchia Maltby, a little younger and smiling in a light blue button-down, looked up from the picture. Underneath the picture was script that read, forever in our hearts, with two dates: 3/9/1941 – 1/28/2018.

Jack cleared his throat. "I went to your funeral. It was almost six months ago, Salty. What the hell are you doing here?"

CHAPTER EIGHT

The old man's eyes met mine across the table, bright with fear and confusion. My own head was roaring. It felt like all the air had gone out of the room. I couldn't sit there any longer. I shoved myself up from the table and practically ran for the door, the checkerboard floor pitching underneath me, the voices of my friends buzzing indiscernibly. I made it outside, falling to my knees at the edge of the awning's long morning shadow. My chest burned, my heart thrumming in my ears.

I felt a hand come down on my back gently. I sucked in a breath, and the gray around the corners of my vision disappeared. My stomach tried to right itself again.

"Honey, honey. Del, you okay? You all right?" Justine rubbed small circles between my shoulders, leaning over me. I couldn't speak; I shook my head. I felt her hand run down my hair.

I pulled in another breath, slower this time. I could feel the warmth from the summer sun creeping over my fingers as the shadow receded.

"Is this really happening?" I wondered aloud.

"Well, I don't know what's happening, but something sure is," Justine agreed. "Who is that sweet old man? Where did he come from? And what on God's green earth has Jack all fired up like that? And where is Mary for all of this?" Justine chattered on, flustered, as she tried to help me up.

I stood there, staring at the gravel in my palms. Yes, this was most definitely real.

"Girl, I hate to tell ya, you look like shit. Are you sure there's—"

"That was Nan's—that's the day Nan died." It was still hard to make those words come out; they still didn't make sense to me. I brushed my hands against each other, then dragged one over my hair. I felt the grit in my palm as I tugged on my short ponytail. I had chopped the braid off maybe a week after Nan's death. "That was Nan's birthday."

Something clicked in my brain. Nelly. Salty. What was his name?

Naylor Saltalamacchia Maltby.

"NSM," I murmured.

Justine looked at me kindly, but not without suspicion. Hell, she was right to be. Maybe I had finally gone 'round the bend.

She patted my shoulder. "All right, let's get you sitting down out of the sun. There, now, that's a good girl." She slipped an arm around my waist as if waiting for me to lean on her and we turned toward the diner. Just for a moment, I tipped my head to her shoulder and closed my eyes.

"I miss her so much, Justine. So fucking much. It hurts."

"I know, sweetie. I know. Come, now, I'll get you some water."

I shook my head. "Just a couple coffees to go, if you don't mind. Nelly's not a fan of my brew." It wasn't a full lie; he hadn't wanted more than a few sips.

She chuckled as we made our way inside. "If you didn't make it as thick as mud to hold up a stick, he might."

"If I want brown-bean water, Justine, I just come for yours." She smacked me on the back of the head. "Ma'am." I grinned because she wanted me to as she pretended to huff off.

The commotion had died down. Mary now sat at their usual table, chatting with Wendy while keeping an eye on the two old men sitting across from each other. Jack was in what had been my seat. They stared at each other in silence, each holding their coffee in their right hand, left hand on the table as if to protect it. Jack scowled while Nelly managed to look both melancholy and indignant at the same time. The funeral card had been tucked away, and the newspaper had disappeared. I approached, unnoticed.

"Nelly, let's head out." No response. Not even a flicker of a glance. "Nelly." Nothing. I knocked twice on the table and both men looked up, startled. "We should go," I said.

He cleared his throat. "All right. Jack, I'll see . . ." He reached his hand out and almost touched Jack's, then yanked it back as if it were fire. His shoulders slumped. "I'll see you around, Jack."

Justine passed me a carry tray with two go-cups and a brown lunch bag. She looked pointedly at the bag and said, "Share, honey," before turning her attention to Nelly. "Now, you come back, all right? You make our girl Del here bring you back to see us soon." She rubbed his shoulder again, pleased when he patted her hand with his own.

"I'll do that," he said. He took my arm as I reached for the door with my other hand. The jingle of the bell almost covered Jack's low, gruff question.

"You gonna come back, Salty?"

He stared at his coffee from his seat in the booth—Nan's seat. I felt the memory slice through my heart.

His eyes came up at the silence. "You gonna come back this time?"

Nelly let out a shaky breath. "Far as I know, Jack. But I suppose we'll see." He walked out, all eyes on our departure. When I opened the door for him, he snapped, "I'm not your damn date. Go on."

I was a little taken aback; I'd figured he wouldn't mind, since he didn't before. When we got to the truck, I glanced back and saw everyone—Mary, Wendy, Justine, and Amy—staring out the windows, everyone but Mary practically pressed up against them. Jack watched from right where we'd left him.

I stepped back and let Nelly maneuver himself in before walking around to my side. The sun had reached under the awning, nearly to the door of the diner, as I eased out of the parking lot. We drove back to my place in silence.

We pulled up to the house and I cut the engine. We sat a moment, then Nelly cleared his throat again.

"Del, uh . . . do you smoke?" His voice was sheepish. "I haven't had a cigarette in too long to count. This seems like a good day for it, and, well, I'm not sure you're a nurse. I'm not sure of much right now, though." He trailed off and gazed out the window.

I didn't smoke, but I kept a couple packs of American Spirits on standby for my folks at the bar. Nan had quit years ago and didn't want them in the house, so I kept them in the truck, along with a couple of cheap lighters. I opened the console and dug them out, handing them over to Nelly before getting out with the coffees. He tapped the pack a couple times and pulled one out. As he raised it to his lips, I knocked on the window and shook my head.

"Not in the truck, Nelly. Come on."

He nodded once and opened his door. He got out of the vehicle with absolutely no problem.

"It was different in my day, Del. You could sit and smoke and talk in the car, watching the world go by through the windshield, just like a movie. Pick a spot with a view and kick back." He gestured before lighting the cigarette and taking a deep drag without a single cough. For a moment, his face showed nothing but pure pleasure.

"We can sit out back," I said, stepping to the concrete path that led around to what the landlord generously called a patio.

Under his own power, as if I hadn't been helping him around all morning, Nelly joined me.

We walked around the side of the apartment to a six-foot-by-ten-foot concrete slab that held two camping chairs and an old paint can, a couple of abandoned beer bottles huddled together on it. The cheap awning above filtered the morning sun through green plastic, casting an eerie tinge over us.

Nelly sat closest to the back door. I took the other chair and handed over his coffee. I peeked in the bag Justine had given me: plastic-wrapped donuts, likely the ones that hadn't sold yesterday. I put the bag down, not quite ready to eat. Instead, I looked at the tangle of shrubs and woods behind the house. The small lawn needed mowing. We sat in silence until most of Nelly's cigarette was gone.

"So, Del, what the hell do you think is going on?"

I laughed humorlessly. I didn't know what else to do. I fleetingly wished that I could smoke, just to have something to do with my hands and mouth.

Remembering I was still in last night's pants, I reached into the front pocket for a toothpick. The ones from the bar were little plastic swords in bright colors. I ran the tiny cutlass through my fingers.

"Well, shit. I don't know where to start." I blew out a breath. "You showed up in my bedroom."

"How? How'd I get there?"

I lifted my hands. "I don't know, honestly. You sort of . . . appeared, you know? In the middle of the night. You—"

"Closer to morning."

"What?"

"I think it was closer to morning."

I shook my head. "Okay, whatever. But you—"

"Well, don't you think the details are important?" he demanded, taking a last drag and tapping the cigarette into one of the empty bottles. "I do."

"Okay, but this isn't a full account, for Christ's sake. Let's line up the facts first. Can we do that?" I heard the annoyance in my voice, but seriously?

He didn't reply.

"So, you show up in my room in the middle of the night—but *closer to morning*, okay—naked, where my wife's urn had spilled on the floor. Suddenly, her ashes are gone, and then there you are." He opened his mouth to speak but must have caught the look on my face because he closed it again. I barreled on. "Then you're calling me *nurse* and wanting coffee and your medication. Okay, I can fix one of those things. We go to the diner—somewhere you say you've never been before—somehow piss off two women in your own family, and at least three people think you're dead!

"Then—*then*—I fucking realize that your initials are Nan's initials. Your birthday is her birthday. Different years, obviously, but fuck." At some point, my tangent had become a rant, and I had started pacing. I didn't remember getting up. "The day you supposedly died is the day *she* died. There's a funeral card with your name and picture on it and Jack Mason sitting in her seat, scowling at you. So, I don't know, Nelly—Salty, Mr. Maltby, whoever you are and whatever you're called. I don't know what the fuck is going on here."

I dropped into the chair heavily, holding my head in my hands.

"I'm a bartender with a fucking hangover. I'm a goddamn widow, not some . . . I don't know, mystery detective or whatever. My head hurts, I've barely slept, I have no idea who you are or why you're here. The sun is barely up, and I already want a fucking drink." Tears stung. The silence stretched out—one minute, two. Longer.

His continued lack of response had the heat of embarrassment creeping up my neck until I could feel my ears burn. I glanced over and saw him staring off at the heavy greenery in the small yard.

"Nelly, I'm sorry."

He looked surprised. "Sorry for what?"

"I'm not mad at you about all this. I just—"I broke off as he chuckled a little, then a little more, louder, until he was full-out laughing, nearly doubled over in his chair. "What?"

"Ah, Del, I know. I know when a woman's mad at me," he said when he recovered. "You don't get to be my age and married to the same woman for over forty years and not know when you're the target and when you're just standing a little too close." He patted his chest and looked down for a moment before wiping the corners of his eyes with his fingertips.

"Okay, well, still. I'm sorry," I said, spent.

He waved a hand and took a sip of his coffee. "Nonsense. Nothing to be sorry for. Now, young lady, you come with me." He heaved up and out of the chair with more range of motion than I felt like I could muster up.

"Where are we going?" I asked wearily.

"Not 'we,' Del, you. And you, my dear, are going to take a nap." I stared at him. He smiled and held out a hand. "Come on, now." When I stood, I couldn't deny the wave of exhaustion. I was used to late nights, but I hadn't seen the sunrise in some time. He took my arm and smiled at me gently. "My Annamaria would lose her temper right quick when she was tired. She said it was the spicy side of her." He chuckled again, more to himself. "Yeah, she was one hot ticket, that's for sure. She could run on all day and half the night. But sometimes, y'know, she'd hit that wall. Looks like the same wall you're hitting right now," he said, patting my arm as I let us in the unlocked back door, fumbling it shut behind us. We crossed the small kitchen and stopped at my bedroom door. "Go on, now, Del. You need it."

I opened my mouth on some feeble protest, my bed calling my name.

"No, no, not a word out of you. Go. Get some sleep. Don't worry about me. I'll amuse myself with your bookshelf."

I nodded and went into my bedroom. Nelly reached in for the door and pulled it shut behind him. I picked up the blanket off the floor and wrapped it around my shoulders, laid down in its protective shell, and instantly fell asleep.

CHAPTER NINE

I awoke with a start, sweating and tangled in the bedspread, the sun streaming in. Nan. Nelly. Wait. Nelly was here; Nan was not. I checked my watch, only to discover it was not on my wrist. I struggled out of the blanket, digging for my phone in my back pocket. I had six unread messages, but I didn't care about that right now. It was just after 3:00 p.m. I looked around my room, at the angle of the sunlight through the open curtains. Okay, that made sense, at least. I stood and shook off some of the desire to pull the covers back over my head. I dry-swallowed two more of the magic headache pills to keep ahead of the hangover.

Then I went out to find Nelly.

My mug from this morning was still on the kitchen counter, along with my half-finished coffee from the diner and the bag of donuts. I gulped down both cold coffees and grabbed a donut, unwrapping it as I walked to the front room. I found my visitor in the old armchair, head tipped back and catching flies. He had a well-used paperback on his chest, thumb tucked into the pages—one of Truman Capote's collections of short stories. It made me smile a little to see one of my favorite—and, by most accounts, queer—authors keeping him entertained. A small plate with crumbs sat on the armrest. I grabbed it, then shoved some stuff over and settled down on the couch. Holding the donut in my mouth, I dug a notebook and Sharpie out of the pile. All right, I thought. Let's figure this out.

I took another bite and put the donut on the plate, wiping my hands on my shirt before uncapping the pen. *Things we know*, I scrawled across the top, then paused. I took another bite and started writing.

Came home after work

How had I gotten home? I'd been in no shape to drive. But my truck had been parked in the driveway. I flipped the page and started a new list, titled *Questions??*

Question: How did I get home?

Know: Woke up on the floor

Know: Nan's urn was on the floor, ashes everywhere

I let out a shaky breath.

Question: How did the urn end up on the floor?

Know:

I paused. Did I really *know* anything that had happened? Everything I'd seen had seemed like a dream, one of those terrifying ones where you can't escape but you can feel everything. I didn't know how it was real—how it could possibly be. I shrugged and added to the title of the first page, so it read, *Things we know/saw.*

Saw: The ashes became a bird

Question: Did that fucking happen?

Question: What bird???

Saw: Bird became a naked man

Question: WHY was he naked?

Know: His name is Nelly

Know: He is supposed to be dead

Know: He didn't know he was supposed to be dead

Taking comfort in sugar, I stuffed the rest of the donut in my face before continuing.

Know: He has the same initials as Nan before she was Montgomery-Shaw (NSM)

Know: Same birthday (3/9, 1941/1981)

Know: Same death day (1/28/2018)

Know: He doesn't know what's going on any more than I do

Question: What the fuck is going on?

Know: He knows Jack Mason

Know: His family thought he was dead, and they're angry

Question: Why are they so angry?

Question: How does he know Jack?

Question: How the hell is he so calm about all this?

Question: Why is this happening?

Question: If Nelly is here, why can't Nan be here?

Question: WHERE IS NAN

My breath caught up to my scrawling across the paper. If people came back from the dead, where was Nan? Why did I have this old guy? I mean, Nelly seemed great, but they were Nan's ashes, so why—

A thought tickled around my brain when I heard Nelly cough. I looked up from the messy couch. He was gazing around, confused, blinking the sleep from his eyes. I didn't say anything. I wanted to see what, if anything, he remembered. Slowly, he focused on me.

"At least I didn't wear my birthday suit to the party this time," he said. We smiled at each other. He sat up straighter. "Well, you don't live neatly, Del. And you don't leave much in the way of a map."

"What do you mean?"

He gestured around the small room, filled only with the couch and chair and a wall of shelved books. Stacks of books rose from the floor, stalagmites I could skirt around in the dark. The couch was covered in what had been in a desk, once upon a time: notebooks and office supplies, magazines, printouts of recipes. Shoeboxes—anything with Nan's handwriting on it, or anything I'd felt some connection to her with, I had kept and tucked into shoeboxes. I must have a dozen.

"Well, I didn't want to pry, so I didn't open anything. But you don't have any pictures out, none at all. You could start your own store with your books, there's so many different kinds." He paused. "I might not know what's going on right now, but I'd like to get to know you, Del," he said quietly. After a beat, and with a forced laugh, he added, "Hell, you've already met some of my family!" His smile faded. "Where's your family, Del?"

I looked down at the notebook, the thick lines that spelled out *WHERE IS NAN* staring back at me. I closed it carefully, leaving the marker tucked in the pages. "Arkansas, mostly. We're not close." I took a breath to steady myself. "It was pretty much just me and Nan."

"Nan." He nodded. "The one who made you a widow," he prompted gently, at my silence.

I blew out another breath and looked down. "Yeah. Nan is—was— my wife." I looked up at him, immediately defensive. "Anything to say about that?"

"Should there be?" he asked easily.

I sat and waited, my stony silence daring him to say anything. He watched me right back, patient as a cat. Finally, I shrugged.

"Sometimes folks got a problem with that. Mostly back in Arkansas, not so much here. Some, though—anyway. That's all." I brushed it off.

He watched me.

"No, I don't think that's all, somehow, but all right. No, I've got no problem with that, none at all. In fact, well . . ." he faded off, staring out into middle distance. They glistened with love and pain before he shook it away. "That's neither here nor there. I'm glad you found your love and that she found you. She must've been a hell of a woman. I'm sorry for your loss."

Why those five words, words I had heard over and over for six months, suddenly took on new meaning coming from Nelly, I couldn't say. I could barely speak over the knot in my throat. I nodded and managed to whisper, "Thank you."

"It's a hell of a thing, to lose a wife. That woman by your side. My Annamaria, she's been gone near fourteen years—fifteen? What year is it again? 2006. No, no—twelve. Twelve years, come October."

I fidgeted with the pen in my hand, nodding along with his calculation. The easy math made it possible to speak again, somehow. "How'd she die?"

"Heart attack. Was fine, then"—he snapped his fingers—"boom. Dropped dead right in her little herb garden she was so proud of. Good thing, too—she'd've had a right fit if she'd squashed her own petunias. The herbs were 'eartier." He chuckled. He spoke easily, the dark little joke shared often enough to take out the sting. "We had a lot of life together left, we thought. I had retired a few months before she died. We were going to travel, like we did when we were young. Go to Mexico, to where her family had lived. They're not there now, of course, but the town's still there. Take her to Cancun." He wiggled his eyebrows suggestively at me, and I couldn't help but laugh. "She was a fine-looking woman. Still turned heads, only most of them were gray now." This time, we both laughed. He was quiet for a few minutes, lost in memory—or maybe not lost so much as just visiting. I knew the feeling. Sometimes I felt like I could drop back into some treasured moment and stay a while, watching her fall asleep in the hammock, listening to a podcast; chopping and throwing brightly colored chunks of vegetables into a soup; that time she had come into the bedroom with only her chef's coat wrapped around her, dropping it with a flourish and proclaiming, *Bon appetit*!

I blinked and squinted as I shook my head and landed firmly in the present, Nan-less moment. I watched Nelly come back to himself too. We had both been off in our own worlds long enough for the sun to reach around and stab in through the side windows.

"We should think about dinner soon," I said.

"You just ate a donut."

"And?"

He laughed. "Did you say you're a bartender?"

"Yeah, why?"

He shook his head. "Every barkeep I knew was divorced or widowed, and all of 'em ate like crap."

It was my turn to laugh. "Yeah, that fits." I paused. "Hey, uh, you wanna see my bar? I mean, not *my* bar, but the bar. My job. The bar where I work." I wasn't sure why I was stumbling over that like I was asking him on a date, but there you had it. "I'm not on the stick tonight, but I'll make sure you get something good in ya."

He lit up like Christmas morning. The man liked to get out, I thought. Who could blame him?

He started to speak, then paused, looking sheepish. "Uh, do you think I could borrow some, uh, other pants?"

I realized then that he was still wearing the sweats I'd helped him into about twelve (absolutely fucking surreal) hours ago. I nodded, curious to see how this would go.

"Of course. Be right back." I went to the bedroom and steeled myself against the onslaught of emotion at handling her clothes outside of that adrenaline-fueled moment this morning. I pulled out a pair of jeans she had barely had the chance to wear. I found him standing in front of one of the bookshelves, his back to me, running his fingers along the worn paperback spines.

"Your own shop, I'm telling you," he said softly. "I always wanted to be able to read more than I did. Puts me to sleep, as you can see. I do love a good story, though. My Anna—" His voice broke a little. "My Annamaria would read poetry, of all things, out loud, right out on the porch. I was not much one for poetry, but she—she changed it. She made it make sense. She had a way of making things make sense to me." He pulled a collection of Pablo Neruda's poems off the shelf and held it gently. "That's what a good teacher does, right?" He looked over at me. "That's what she did. She was a teacher. English with a kick, and Spanish, of course." He looked around at the shelves. "She'd've loved this." He nodded, still panning. "Yeah, she would've. Oh, pants. Thank you kindly." He took them from me and walked to the bathroom—a little slowly, maybe, but perfectly steady.

I stood outside the door and listened. He wouldn't be the first guy I'd had to chaperone and escort from their seat to the head and back. I heard the muffled sounds of clothes being changed and nothing else. I firmly blocked my thoughts of asking about his wife's teaching career. I needed the buffer of a drink before opening that mind's door.

I heard the knob turning and scooted away quickly, not willing to be caught listening for the sound of a man peeing, though I could justify that I was only listening to make sure he was okay.

He looked more relaxed in the jeans. Younger, somehow. Maybe it was the combination of the band T-shirt and the denim, or the grin plastered on his face. "Do you know how long it's been since I've had a pair of these on?" He swayed his hips slowly from side to side, then turned around to show off the butt. "Baby's got her blue jeans on!" He cackled, turning back and slapping his hands together at his own joke. He wiped his eyes with his fingertips. "Hoo boy, I tell you." He shook his head as he caught his breath, eyes shining. "So, Del, you got dancing at this bar of yours?"

CHAPTER TEN

It was still daylight when we pulled up to the bar, the shadows just starting to get long. I hesitated before parking. I always parked around back, even when I wasn't working, but I didn't want Nelly walking through the dark back hall. I chose a spot not too far from the door and eased the truck in headfirst. Nelly continued the lively chatter he had kept up the whole ride.

"Do you know how hard it is to actually get a handicap parking pass? I'm old! I'm more than seventy-five years old. I've walked a lot! I can park a little closer, y'know?" His voice was animated, more telling a story than complaining. I figured it was a conversation he'd had before, too, maybe with some of his cronies at the assisted living place. He was out of the truck the same as me, mobile as you please. I shook my head behind his back as we walked up to the bar, before I reached out and pulled the heavy wooden door open.

From afar, the faded brick and black-painted wood advertised it as a tough-guy place. It wasn't until you got closer that you could see the almost delicate rendering of an antique bicycle, the kind with the giant front wheel, on the grainy wooden sign that hung above the door. The vanilla-white paint had soaked into the wood, giving it a vintage look before the name of the bar, the Hub 'n Spoke, was even written.

It had been an Irish bar for years, passing through several owners and families in the process. It stood on a block of old storefronts—the barber-shop, laundromat, recruiter's office, and ice cream shop remained behind panes of glass too old to ever really look clean again. New businesses were taking over the empty locations; gentrification had begun to make its way to Halfway. A vintage record store, tattoo and piercing parlor, and boutique handicrafts store had already staked their claim. A local insurance broker was moving out after selling his practice and clients to one of the big companies; word on the street was that there was a bidding war between a smoothie joint and fancy pet store for the corner store location.

On our side of the street there were only three buildings. In the middle sat the bar, which was more of a tavern. On the second floor were rooms for short-term rent, more often used for folks who couldn't safely drive home after imbibing. I had stayed there for over a month after Nan died. After a few weeks at the house, I couldn't stand to go back to our house in Pinesburg—not without her there, not to sleep. I had tried; I couldn't get in our bed. I had just sat up all night, touching her things. I'd opened and closed the top of her body wash so many times, it had broken off in my hand. The next morning, I'd packed a couple overnight bags and moved in here.

To either side of the bar were old warehouses, both converted about eight years ago. The one on the left had been completely gutted, then paved and turned into an indoor skatepark. Pretty neat idea for the kids to have somewhere to go, since all the local businesses had signs posted about no skating in the parking lots. The same people bought the one on the right and created a combined bike-and-skate shop, complete with sales, rentals, and repairs. Nan and I had gone to a series of classes there to learn how to take care of our own bikes, fixing flats and so on.

The bar changed hands again about five years ago. The new owners had ditched the Irish theme and completely revamped the interior. Using spare parts and castoffs from the businesses on either side, they'd taken the idea of a biker bar, replaced Harleys with Cannondales, threw in some vintage art and a state-of-the-art tap system, and created a bicycle bar. Everything from the lamps to the coasters echoed the theme. The barstools were cushioned with extra-wide, custom-leather bicycle seats; a shiny bike chain in thick, clear resin edged the bar itself. The lazy Susans that held Tabasco, salt, and pepper were made from old gears, and the door chime was a vintage bell. The friendly chirp announced our entrance.

Letting Nelly in ahead of me, I let the door fall closed behind me as he looked around, taking it all in. He looked at the near-turquoise-blue walls above the slick-black wainscoting, the jumble of art on the walls, the black booths around the walls and the few high-tops in the middle. The new owners had kept the lighting the same; it was soft and dim, making the whole place look sleek and easy, in what could have easily been horrendously garish in electric blue and chrome. I jerked my head up in greeting to the tall blond behind the bar. Mina had been a swimmer before becoming a cyclist, and those broad shoulders made her appear even more of an Amazon. Closing in on sixty, she had retired early to move up to Maryland with her son and his husband from Atlanta. They may have been the owners, but it was Mina who managed.

She flashed her wide grin at me.

"Good to see you upright, Del. Wasn't sure you would be for long last night. Who's your fella here?" She may have moved from Atlanta, but there was no way you'd know it from her voice. It was pure Chesapeake, through and through.

"Mina, this is Nelly. Nelly, our house manager, Mina. It's her boys that own the bar."

Nelly, standing nearly four inches shorter than her, stuck out a hand as he looked up at her.

"Pleased to meet you, ma'am. I can't say I've ever seen this place before, but I think I would have liked to."

Mina smiled. "Pleased to meetcha, too, Nelly. All right now, Del. You need a fix?"

I nodded.

"Coming right up."

I slid onto a stool, lifting my fingers in greeting to the old man at the end of the bar. He nodded in acknowledgment and looked keenly at Nelly. Roy was one of our regulars; he came in when we opened at four, three days a week. His wife took an exercise class at the YMCA and would then go for drinks at what Roy described as "some girl bar downtown." He had been coming to this bar, whoever it was run by at the time, for nearly twenty years.

A pint-sized Mason jar slid in front of me, holding a murky-brown liquid, a lemon wedge stuck on the rim. Mina's hangover cure smelled like an out-of-control herb garden and tasted just as botanical. It covered most of the molasses and apple cider vinegar and who-the-hell-knew-what-else that also went into it. I didn't ask questions. I downed the concoction in three gulps, then bit down on the lemon.

"In my day, if you got yourself hungover, you just drank till it went away again," Nelly offered, finding his purchase on the stool easily.

"Yeah, well, that's next. Whiskey?" I asked.

"That'll do nicely."

I caught Mina's eye and held up two fingers. Within moments, two short glasses of whiskey, neat, sat in front of us. Nelly picked his up, swirling the amber liquid in the glass. "Sure been a year or two since I've had a glass of the good stuff." He sipped, closing his eyes, the pleasure evident on his face. "Smooth as you please," he murmured and sipped again before setting the glass down and opening his eyes.

I felt sort of proud that he liked it, that he seemed comfortable in the place where I spent most of my time. And since he'd made himself so at home in the apartment, well, either he was ridiculously easy to please or he and I were more similar than I thought. I downed half my glass and looked at him.

"We're good to talk here," I told him. "Mina and Cleo and Johnathon— that'd be her boys—they're solid. They're cool," I explained.

Nelly nodded. "All right, then, let's talk," he said.

I pulled my notebook out of my shoulder bag, opening to the page of what we knew and had seen.

"Okay, so we've figured out that you are supposed to be dead, or at least have died, the same day as Nan. You have the same initials, birthday, yadda yadda. You were probably most recently alive at Twelve Elms, since that's the last thing you remember. We know your family isn't happy with you, and you know the diner Nan and I went to. You know Jack." I snorted a bit, the whiskey making that a little funny to me. "So, we got a lot of questions left."

"How did I die?" Nelly demanded. "Write that one down. And if I'm really dead and buried, what in the hell am I doing here?"

I nodded and flipped the page, writing his questions under mine. "Keep going."

"Why were Jackie and Victoria so upset? Were they afraid because I'm dead? Do they think I'm haunting them or some fool thing? Where's my wife? Where's my Annamaria?" He paused as his voice caught on her name. He quickly finished his whiskey. "If I'm here, where's your wife, Del? Where's Nan? And above all," he said, his voice rising, "what the hell is going on here?"

Roy looked over as Nelly's fist hit the bar.

"That's what we're trying to figure out, man," I reminded him. "Right now, I think we have more questions than answers. I'm not sure what to do about that."

Mina appeared with the bottle. She refilled our glasses, then leaned on the bar, reading my scribbles in the notebook. "Y'all trying to solve a mystery?" she asked, eyes brightly curious.

"Yeah, after a fashion," I responded. "Actually, we could use some outside perspective."

She cocked her head to the side. "Well, you're in luck. The boys will be here in a moment."

Right on cue, Cleo and Johnathon made their entrance. Cleo was Mina's son; he stood nearly half a foot taller and was a carbon copy of her. Broad shoulders nipped into a waist most girls only dreamt of, sitting above thick legs that had propelled him across the country on his bike. Nan had called him Stretch, as in Armstrong; he'd laugh and stoop and sweetly kiss her cheek. For all his size, he was the gentlest soul.

His husband, still dressed for work, could not have looked more different. Topping out at five-foot-ten, a full head shorter than his beau, Johnathon looked sleek in a light gray suit, navy shirt, and shimmery gray tie. He hailed from Louisiana but had worked to remove nearly all the accent out of his voice. His parents had fled Haiti for the American Dream when they'd discovered they were pregnant and unwed. Johnathon was a masterful storyteller; it was a swashbuckling tale of one narrow escape from gators and bandits to the next until his parents made it on foot across the Louisiana line. Now working as a successful real estate agent from a firm in Richmond, he had discovered the bar and warehouses that flanked it. He had turned the sale of the warehouses into a franchise opportunity for the firm and was now based here in town, running the branch and serving as co-owner of the bar.

Which, we heard, needed a, "Damn espresso machine already, not this home-store latte-in-a-pod monstrosity," with enough heat in Johnathon's voice to know the discussion was ongoing.

"You're, like, the only one who drinks coffee in this bar, J. Hey, Del!" Cleo went from rolling his eyes to brightening up. "You're not on tonight. What's up? Heya, Ma," he continued, leaning over the bar to kiss his mother's cheek. Nelly watched this play out curiously as Cleo took a seat and Johnathon moved behind the bar. Mina handed him a cup of black coffee with a wink as he kissed her in turn.

"Del, how's it going? Ah, Mr. . . . . Maltby, right?" Johnathon asked after a brief pause to search for the name.

Nelly looked surprised.

"Call me Nelly," he said. "My apologies, I can't quite seem to remember if—uh, how we met." He shook Johnathon's offered hand.

"I helped sell your home on Ashton Street a few years back," he said. "I work for Lawson Realty."

"Of course, of course," Nelly said. I could tell he was being polite; he wasn't having the same ease of memory as Johnathon was. "How's business these days?"

Johnathon smiled and gestured around him. "You're looking at it. This is the bar we own, me and Cleo. And you've met Mina, my mother-in-law, and delightful Delilah."

I winced. "No one calls me that, Johnathon."

"I do," Cleo piped up. I rolled my eyes, and he patted my shoulder and kissed my cheek, too, before holding out a hand to Nelly. "So, whatcha doing here on your night off?"

"They got a mystery on their hands," Mina said, wiggling her eyebrows. "A riddle of some sort, it looks like."

All six-foot-whatever of him lit up like Christmas. "Count me in!" He popped up on the stool on my left and rested his chin on his hands. "Tell me more."

I could feel the nerves radiating from Nelly in waves. I put a hand over his on the bar and spoke quietly. "Hey. It's okay. These are my people. No one's going to be mad here."

He nodded, and as he caught my hand between his, patted his assent.

I looked up to the three of them—Mina, Cleo, and Johnathon—all staring at me. I took a deep breath. "Would one of you mind pouring some more whiskey?"

CHAPTER ELEVEN

It took time to tell, since my voice faltered and my unreliable eyes teared up at every turn and Nelly added quiet, detailed interjections. Thirty minutes and three shots later (except Johnathon, who'd kept it to one), the five of us were squeezed into one of the rounded booths. I was still wedged between Nelly and Cleo, the latter of whom held my hand in both of his. The only sound was the rapid clicking of the pen as I tapped it on the paper, waiting for someone to speak.

Mina finally broke the silence. She blew out a breath and looked at Nelly.

"Well, you sure look good for a dead guy," she said lightly, reaching forward for his hand.

Surprised, he jumped a little before holding hers.

"Yeah, well." He cleared his throat. "Guess that whole adage about sleeping when you're dead is about wrong as you can get."

Mina laughed.

"Del, love, are you doing okay?" Cleo asked. You could always rely on his gentle, genuine concern.

I answered as honestly as I could. "I don't know? Sort of. I mean, for not knowing what the hell is going on right now, talking with the living dead, and not knowing where Nan is anymore—sure, I guess I'm doing fine." The whiskey smoothed the sting like it always did.

Johnathon, his dark eyes clouded with worry and disbelief, shook his head. "This is no living dead. My maman told me stories of the zombies raised by voodoo powers. They do not speak, and all they seek is to do their master's bidding so they can return to rest."

I rolled my eyes. "I didn't mean that kind of living dead, Johnathon. Just that he's supposed to be dead, and here he is."

He held his hands up, palms out. "No offense—"

"None taken," Nelly replied.

"—but there is something strange going on, obviously. Not voodoo, but something not of this world." He tapped two fingers on the table, where Mina and Nelly still held hands. She didn't seem to question the reality of his presence at all. That was one thing I loved about her. She was a rock. Johnathon looked back up at me. "Are you sure you told us everything?"

I nodded. "Yes. Everything."

He pressed, "You told us every detail?"

Tired and annoyed, I rubbed my hands over my eyes. "Yes, Johnathon. It's not like I'm hiding anything here."

His eyes cut to Cleo, then back to me. Cleo murmured, "Enough."

"Something is missing," Johnathon insisted. "Everything, Del. Everything you saw and thought and smelled and tasted and heard and felt—think about it."

"Yes, goddamnit, I told you—" I stopped abruptly. It came back to me in a flash. "Wait."

The four people around me leaned forward. The air was so charged, it felt like it could crackle any second. Everybody jolted when the chirp of the door opening broke through the silence.

Byron entered the bar with his bike and disappeared around the corner to the hanging rack. When he came back around the corner, helmet unbuckled but on, his eyebrow rose a fraction, his only sign of surprise to see the bar unmanned with the owners crammed into a booth with us. It was going to get busy soon, but he nodded to us all and went back to the office. We were silent as we waited. He came back out and over to the table.

"Folks want another round?" he asked.

Everyone looked at me. I shrugged. Why not?

"Actually, By, can you pull up for a minute?" He looked around the table, then wordlessly went behind the bar. He nodded to Roy on the way back, who was getting up to go.

"Been over there a good half hour," Roy whispered audibly. "Dunno what's going on. Mina, honey," he called out louder, "just settle me up, it's all here for ya."

Mina thanked him as he walked out. Byron came back to the table with a fresh bottle of whiskey and an additional glass. After pouring the round—Johnathon included this time—he pulled over a chair from a nearby table.

"Thanks, By." Dark eyes on me, he nodded again. Nelly seemed a bit uneasy again. Maybe it was Byron's silent manner, or the act of another person joining, but I saw Mina squeeze his hand again. We were all used to our taciturn philosopher, but his near silence sometimes rubbed people wrong.

Or maybe it was his smaller stature and softer features, especially compared to the other two guys at the table. "All right. Basically . . ."

Nelly didn't jump in at all this time. I wondered if he was getting tired. It seemed like time had stopped inside the bar.

"So . . . yeah. That brings us here. I asked Mina and the guys for their opinion or help or whatever, and now you."

"Del was about to tell us something she left out," Johnathon said, eyes cutting sharply back to me.

"Forgot, then remembered, for crap's sake, Johnathon. I'm not fucking leaving anything out on purpose."

Maybe I was the one getting tired. I rubbed my hands over my face.

"I saw something. Or thought I did. Maybe it was a hallucination, but shit, I thought Nelly was, too, and he's real."

"In the flesh," he said with a half smile. "Or something."

"Or something," I agreed. "Anyway. Yeah. When the ashes spilled, right before Nelly showed up, it was like they were glowing. Not, like, lit up, but from inside, you know? Bright from the inside, and so white—white as snow. Then they sort of . . . swirled up." I paused and looked down at my whiskey. I took a deep breath and threw the shot back.

It sounded so crazy in my head. This is where they haul me off to the looney bin, I thought. Maybe I *was* cuckoo. I snorted, whiskey swimming in my mind. I felt a jab in my shin and realized Johnathon had kicked me under the table.

"Look," I said, spreading my hands out and shrugging. "It sounds fucking insane, even in my head. I don't want any of you thinking I've lost it any more than I already have."

"We're already sitting here with a dead guy who showed up in your bedroom," Mina reminded me mildly.

"There was a bird," I blurted out. This strange news was absorbed with barely a blink as they all sat there, staring at me, waiting for me to go on.

"Fuck. Like, a big bird. Nothing I've ever seen before. All white, with two long, blue—bright blue—feathers coming out of its tail. The ashes were gone, and then it was just Nelly." That tickle in my mind was back, but I still couldn't place it. "I felt like it knew me. It looked right at me. It was breathtaking," I said, my voice softening. "Beautiful. It looked right at me, and then it was gone. And Nelly was standing there, fucking stark-ass naked, right in front of my dresser.

"That's what I saw. That's what I remember." I looked down at my glass and found it empty, so I snatched Cleo's and tossed it down too. My head spun.

" 'When heaven shall call her from this cloud of darkness / Who from the sacred ashes of her honor / Shall star-like rise, as great in fame as she was, / And so stand fix'd,' " Byron said quietly. We all looked at him. "You saw a phoenix. It rose from Nan's ashes, showed itself to you, and became Nelly. You're on a quest." I shook my head and reached over for the bottle, which he moved away from me. "And you're cut off."

"Come on, man," I said, reaching out again. This time, Cleo put his arm around my shoulders.

"He's right, honey. You need to take a pause on this."

I tried pulling away from him, but his grasp, while gentle, was like iron. "No, I need to figure this shit out. A phoenix? A quest? What the fuck are you talking about?" I looked over, appealing to Nelly. "Are you hearing this?"

He looked troubled but smiled kindly. "Maybe we could all use a little change of topic," he suggested. "Or some food?"

"Oh, bullshit. You just want this to last longer so you don't have to go back to being dead." The words pounced from my mouth. "You get a nice little trip with drinks and cigarettes and what-the-fuck-all-else instead of lying around in a grave, and what happens to Nan, huh? You're here. Where the fuck is my wife?"

Tears, hot and angry, did nothing to soothe the scorched earth that lay before me. Nelly radiated hurt. His mouth trembled open; his eyes welled up. He gripped his hands together as Mina slapped hers on the table to shove herself up.

"Delilah Anne Montgomery-Shaw, you are officially too drunk to continue this conversation. Go on upstairs and sleep it off."

"The hell I am," I said.

She pointed.

"It's, like, six o'clock," I protested.

Her eyes only narrowed. "Go."

Rolling my eyes and huffing out a breath like a teenager in full temper, I did as I was told. I didn't want to admit she was right. I can hold my liquor, I thought to myself. The fuck do they expect, with the day I've had.

I heard Cleo behind me as I got to the staircase outside the main room and began to weave my way up the stairs. "I'm fine," I mumbled, hearing the petulance over the lack of enunciation. He took my arm; I yanked it away and nearly did a face-plant halfway up. He caught me around the waist.

"Sorry, honey, Momma said," he apologized even as he lifted me, pulling me up like a blushing bride being whisked away.

I couldn't keep my eyes open anymore. They closed as I dropped my head against his chest. "She's not my momma," I muttered defiantly.

"I heard that," Mina called. "Put her in six, honey, and leave her some water. Put up the DND tag and come on back down."

The fight was leaving me, washed away by a fresh river of tears, dragging me down into the depths of my darkest grief.

"I just want Nan back," I sobbed as Cleo laid me down gently. He tugged up the blanket, and I rolled over on my side. "I just want Nan back."

I felt his hand on my back, rubbing circles over my shoulder blades. "I know, honey. I know."

At his quiet voice, I let myself fall into the black again.

PART THREE:
SPARKS AND TINDER

CHAPTER TWELVE

I woke up in the dark. The red dots of the alarm clock blinked against the black. I had no idea what it read in that moment, my vision too bleary to make out numbers. From the sounds of it, it was well into the evening. The bar was hopping downstairs, the bass reverberating through the floor and my skull. Whatever time it was, I was already hungover. Fuck.

I yanked the little chain for the bedside light and squinted. There was a glass of water and a glass of Mina's fix with three ibuprofens on the nightstand. I scowled and took my medicine, breathing through my teeth until I was relatively confident it wouldn't all come right back up.

Shame washed over me and turned my stomach again, sending me facedown on the bed. I remembered everything. I couldn't believe my acid tongue. How could I have said those things to Nelly? What kind of monster was I? I pulled the pillow over my head until I couldn't stand my own breath. I lay there miserably for I-don't-know-how-long until I felt my body sink back into sleep.

The next time I woke, my head was still pounding, but the room around me no longer pulsed with music. I pushed up, letting my feet hit the floor. I sat hunched on the low bed and felt like a prisoner in a jail cell of some old movie, staring at the floor. I no longer felt sick, but the shame weighed heavily on me. I was trying to berate myself into standing when there was a soft knock on the door. As it creaked open, I threw a hand up to guard against the hall light.

"Hey." Still suited up, Johnathon crouched in front of me.

I focused on him for a second. His deep brown skin was almost aglow in the yellow light, and his eyes were clear. I caught myself before a sneer took hold and something else nasty fell out of my mouth. Instead, I dropped my head back in my hands.

"Nelly?" I mumbled.

"Mina's new bestie? Passed out in the office downstairs. How are you holding up?"

I groaned. "I'm a shitty person, Johnathon."

He nodded. "You definitely let your bitch flag fly. You can be a mean drunk, girl."

"Fuck. I know."

"Is that something you think you need some help with?"

I looked up into his eyes, which were intent on mine but held no judgment. I remembered that he had helped one of his college buddies get into rehab; they were still friends, and his friend had been sober for some years now. I thought he might've even come to the bar once or twice, but it was hazy. I sighed.

"No, thanks. No. I haven't been that bad in . . . I dunno, a while. Actually, I don't remember if I've ever been that mean."

Unfolding from his position, Johnathon joined me on the edge of the bed. The mattress dipped so we bumped up together, and he put his arm around me. "There was the time you bit me and called me an arrogant, capitalist asshole who was going to—how did you say it? Lead the patriarchy right into your queer little village."

I grimaced as he chuckled. "I forgot about that."

He tapped his other hand to his collarbone. "Got the scar to prove it. My in-Del-ible mark," he teased.

I sighed again and let my head rest on his shoulder. "You're trying to make me feel better about being an asshole."

"No, I'm reminding you that even though that happened, we got through it, and I love you."

"I love you too." We were quiet for a minute. "Not for nothing, but I think being visited by the dead and trying to figure out what the fuck is going on with my own dead wife is reason enough to drink."

"Sure it is, baby. You just gotta be better about cutting it off. By my count, you were eight shots deep in little over an hour. I was a little scared to see what *Exorcist* shit I'd find when I came in."

I snorted out a laugh. "Nah, I kept it down somehow. Someone brought me some fix"—I nodded toward the table—"and some meds. Helped."

"We were checking on you every couple of hours or so."

"Thank you for that." I took a breath and held it a moment. "How's Nelly, really?"

Johnathon was silent. The dark made the quiet stretch out, the chirp of crickets barely making it past the hum of the air conditioning system.

"You know, I met Nelly a few years back," he finally said. "Been thinking about it all night. He wasn't in good shape then. He was all bruised up on one whole side of his body. He was in one of those old wheelchairs you see at the ER, you know the ones.

"He had been released from the hospital and was supposed to be in rehab. Not drinking rehab, but like a nursing home where they help old people recover from shit. He had fallen in his house, the one I was selling. He'd tripped coming down the stairs and taken a header the rest of the way down. He lived alone. His daughter found him the next day. I guess it was close to thirty hours that he lay on the floor. He'd been in a bad way— angry, belligerent, not making a ton of sense. The daughter—uh, Jackie or Jacqueline, I think—cried a lot when she was telling me all this. He'd taken a swing at her, something he'd never done before. She couldn't get him to listen, couldn't get him off the floor. He'd, you know, soiled himself because he couldn't get up for so long. It wasn't a good scene. So, she called the fire department, and they got an ambulance over there to take him to the hospital.

"The family decided he couldn't live alone anymore and that he had to move to some sort of assisted living facility or something. He wasn't happy about it. He wanted to be home, in his home, where he'd lived with his wife for thirty-something years."

"His Annamaria," I said quietly.

"Yeah. He put up a hell of a fight, according to the daughter. Mentally, he was with it, so they were limited on what they could do without him, and he wanted no part of it. He just wanted to go home. Finally, he agreed to sign the papers to sell the house if he could see it one more time. That's when I met him. He wasn't steady on his feet, and he was going back to the facility after we were done. He couldn't go inside, and he was arguing with his daughter about that. He started telling this story about his days in the Navy, and how this wasn't the Navy, so she couldn't tell him what to do. She got frustrated and walked away for a bit. Then he turned to me—this bruised old man who had been rambling on about the brotherhood and orders and all that—and he grabbed my wrist hard. He was a lot stronger than he looked."

Still is, I thought as I pulled my legs up on the bed and crossed them. Johnathon was in storytelling mode. I rested my chin on my fists and listened.

"He pulled me down to him a little and said to me, 'Son, I need you to do something for me. Not right now, because she'll come out and then the gig's up. But when we leave, I need you to go into the garage. There's a red metal toolbox. Under the tray are some envelopes. They're old, mind you, and smudged up. I need you to bring those to me. Get them out of my house before you sell it, and get them to me at whatever prison they're sticking me in. Can you do that for me?'

"I told him that he was my client and I'd do my best by him. I told him I didn't have any control over anything inside the house, just the building and the grounds, but he dismissed that. 'Just take care of that for me, will you,' he told me before launching into another rambling story. I looked up, and the daughter was heading toward us. She said they were leaving, and that she would be in touch to handle the transfer of paperwork. I helped him into the car for her, and he shook my hand hard. He seemed satisfied." He paused, his hands stilling in his lap for a moment. He let out a little sigh, then continued, "I waited until they'd turned the corner, then I went into the garage. I had the keys, anyway, so it wasn't like I was breaking in, but I was worried it might look like that anyway."

I nodded. His credentials and the suit he wore wouldn't have mattered if someone had gotten a bug up their butt to call the cops.

He continued, "The daughter had talked about an estate sale but said I was free to check it out for whatever I needed to do to make it ready. I looked around – the table where he'd said, the shelves, even behind some stuff, but I never found the toolbox." He lifted his hands in a shrug. "I looked around a little more, but didn't see any envelopes or mail or anything like that. I figured, hey, I'd done my due diligence. I'd looked and hadn't found anything. I locked up and left and forgot about it 'til now."

"Did you go see him? Tell him?" I demanded.

He shook his head, and his shoulders sank a little. "No. I should have, but I sort of just figured, hey, I hadn't found anything, so why bother."

"I wonder what he was looking for." Johnathon shrugged again.

"I dunno. He said it was envelopes, so I figured pictures or something. Or letters, maybe. I tried to stay out of family business like that. I gave the daughter some names of folks who could help with estate sales and all that, and it never came up again. The whole thing only sticks out to me because I hadn't been here for but a few weeks, and it was one of my first independent sales for Lawson.

"Seeing him tonight, he looks a world better than when I met him, ironically enough. I don't think he remembers me. I haven't told him any of this—wasn't sure if I should. Truth be told, I didn't really remember it all that well until I saw him, and then . . . well, we didn't want to upset him more after you came up, so Mina sort of took over. You know her, she did her thing. They sat at that table, telling stories like old friends, most of the night. When the music turned up at ten, she brought him back to her office. Last I looked, he was knocked out in the chair."

"Not that hunk of junk. Can you even call it a chair anymore?" The recliner was one holdover from previous owners—and the ones before them—that had been kept for something like sentimental value. The stained yellow-and-brown upholstery suggested it had been purchased alongside a disco ball and some platform boots.

"Held us plenty of times," Johnathon smiled, bumping against me. When I kept staring at the floor, he sighed. "He's hurting and confused. He doesn't seem to know what's going on better than any of us—or you, for all that."

"It's the weirdest fucking thing, man. He's here, but he's not alive. He gets tired, but he moves around like he's not seventy-something years old. He drinks but doesn't get drunk. He eats, but I don't think he's used the bathroom once. People see him, notice him, even recognize him. You can touch him and hear him and see him. He's not a hallucination or some woo-woo manifestation. I'm not in some dream state or psychotic break—though who knows, maybe that's next. I keep waiting for something to happen, I dunno, like he disappears into thin air or gets cut and doesn't bleed or something. I don't know. This is all such a fucking weird thing. And I can't stop thinking about her, J. I want Nan. I can't help it. If Nelly gets to come back, why can't she?"

I was getting choked up again. Johnathon's arm came around me and he pulled me into his shoulder. I pulled back, not wanting to lean against him anymore. He didn't move; he let me decide where I was going to go, which soothed me—that simple allowance in a moment where he could have held onto me tightly until I broke. I sighed, my sobs at bay, and leaned into my friend.

"I'm so lucky to have you guys."

Now he squeezed me. "You always will, Del."

The light from the hall disappeared as Cleo filled the doorway. "Just wanted to check on y'all," he said, leaning on the doorjamb.

"Just getting sappy." Johnathon smiled at his husband before turning back to me. "So, what's the next step?"

"I . . . have no idea," I admitted.

"Why doesn't everyone get some sleep, and we can reconvene in the morning? Bar's closing, and Byron can get you and Nelly home," Cleo offered. Johnathon nodded his agreement.

"Actually, I think Nelly and I will crash here. I'm already used to the mattress again, and we've got the room tonight. I can go rustle up breakfast in the morning too."

"You might should go talk to Momma first," Cleo said, a gentle warning in his voice. "She's been protective of your friend there."

"You're right." I scrubbed my hands over my face again, trying to bury any lingering anger. I'd already fucked up enough; it wouldn't do to try to go a round with Mina right now. I gripped the back of my neck, squeezing until I felt the bristling subside. Johnathon rose, causing me to sink into the mattress more as I tried to push up to my feet. He caught my arm as my head pounded with the change in elevation.

"Steady out," he said. "There's a girl."

"I'm good," I replied.

"Oh, and Del?"

"Yeah?"

"That other thing—if that changes, let me know. We take care of each other, hmm?"

I nodded and patted his shoulder as I followed him out. We went down, the old wooden steps creaking audibly over the music, which had been turned back down to background noise. Byron was behind the bar and gave us a nod as we came in. One of the guys nudged me forward. I got the message and moved back behind the bar.

"By," I began, but he cut me off.

"We'll get there, but you talk to Mina now. Kettle's on." He reached behind me and unplugged the electric kettle. "Kettle's ready." I looked over and saw he had already put the tea bag into a thick mug emblazoned with the bar's logo.

"You're the best," I murmured. I filled the cup and headed back toward the office.

The door was open. Nelly was sitting in the chair as he had in my apartment, asleep, an old *National Geographic* in his lap. Mina sat at the desk, looking over receipts and checking them against her iPad. I tapped on the doorjamb.

Her gaze cut straight to mine and locked in, and my shoulders wanted to hunch. I felt like a teenager, somehow. She held up a hand to stop anything I might have said, pointed to Nelly, and put a finger to her lips. I nodded and stepped back to wait.

I sat on the steps outside the office and waited. Dunking the tea bag in and out, I played with it until I nearly jumped at Mina's hands reaching for the mug. The woman moved like a damn ninja, I thought. She took the mug and jerked her head toward the bar. I followed her over to the same table where tonight's events had gone down.

She spoke first. "Well. I'd like to hear what you have to say for yourself?"

My chagrin intensified. There was never any beating around the bush with her.

"I'm sorry, Mina. I was completely out of line. I shouldn't have said any of that. Not to Nelly, not to Byron, and not to you. It was wrong and selfish and unfair." Under the table, my fingers twisted uncomfortably as I held her unwavering gaze. "And I shouldn't have said you're not my momma." She hummed a little and nodded. "You were right, I was too drunk. For the conversation, the company—too drunk in general. I'm sorry."

I finally broke, looking away from her inscrutable face and down at my hands.

"You hurt some feelings tonight, girl. My girl," she said softer, and I looked up. "We're family. You know that, maybe better than anyone in this place. Family forgives when we fuck up." She sighed and sipped her tea. "Not a one of us hasn't been too drunk here, of all places. It's a bar for a reason, not some fancy coffee shop." She raised her voice on the end of the sentence, and I laughed when both Johnathon's and Cleo's hands flew up in the air. She shook her head and smiled. "What's the plan for now, honey?"

"Crash here for the night. I'll pick up breakfast for everyone in the morning and . . . maybe we can pick up where we left off?" I shrugged a little as I trailed off. "I don't know what was said after I left, and it seems like there was some stuff I should."

Mina nodded. "Why don't you go on up, then. No point in trying to patch things with that sweet old man in the middle of the night."

I bowed my head, shame and gratitude stopping any response.

She leaned forward and rubbed my shoulder. "You'll make it right, Del. Tomorrow." I nodded in agreement, face hot. "Go on now. Get yourself another glass of fix." I looked up to meet her arched eyebrow. "And go on to bed. I'll take care of getting Nelly set up. You need anything else?"

The bathrooms were stocked with cheap wrapped toothbrushes, toothpaste, and the complementary soaps hotels carried. I shook my head, suddenly choked up again at her tenderness.

She was right. We were family, and harsh words weren't going to break that bond.

She gave my shoulder a squeeze as she rose. I took a minute to compose myself again. As I stood, Byron came around the corner with his bike, his highlighter-yellow helmet on and unfastened. He touched two fingers to the shade brim. As I opened my mouth to speak, he held up a hand and interrupted me for the second time that night—and maybe ever.

"Tomorrow's good enough," he said simply. "You go get some rest. 'Night." I watched the blink of the light above the back tire flash as he quickly made his way out the door.

CHAPTER THIRTEEN

Despite everything, my eyes popped open at the lovely hour of six o'clock. I had neglected to pull the shades before collapsing back into bed the night before. The sun was strong and beginning to light the floor. I rolled over and pulled the pillow over my head before I remembered that I'd promised everyone breakfast, and I sure as hell wasn't cooking. On a groan (better than a whimper), I got out of bed and tugged on my jeans. I grabbed my hat and tiptoed downstairs, hurrying over the boards I couldn't quite avoid creaking in the silence.

Keys, I thought. Someone would've taken them at some point. As I patted my hands against my hips, the absence of the key ring on my belt loop confirmed my theory, and I went back to the office. Mina kept a cupboard for the keys of both patrons and staff who wouldn't be going home that night, shaped like a kid's drawing of a house. She had printed a picture of a sad-looking basset hound and written "in the doghouse" right on top. There was no way to not feel at least a bit sheepish when you knew your keys were in there, and sure enough, mine were.

Mornings were not usually my best time, but here I was for the second day in a row, firing up my truck and heading to the diner at sunrise. I left the radio off. I might've just slept close to ten hours by myself, but I hadn't really had much of a minute alone since Nelly . . . arrived? Appeared? Whatever.

Since Nelly.

Nan had been a morning person. She would get the coffee rolling, and at least a couple times a week, she'd cook up something new for breakfast in the oven or the skillet. I thought about her crepes, how the delicate dough had cradled the fluffy, seasoned eggs or strawberry jam and mascarpone. Whether she went for sweet or savory, eating them was an experience: the balance of filling to crepe; tender mouthfuls of incredible flavors, her hungry eyes watching my mouth as I tried to take it slow, to take my time and savor every morsel. The way that one lock of unruly hair never stayed behind the thin frame of her glasses. The light dusting of flour she left on my cheek when she leaned in and laid her hand on my face, moving in to share the taste of the last bite before she took—

The truck jolted slightly as it bumped into the parking lot. I looked around in surprise. I had been so deep in memory that I had lost track of my driving, yet here I was, safely at my destination. It had been a while since that had happened. The first few weeks after Nan, I'd almost stopped driving because of it. I parked under the awning, still in the shade; I could see the girls' cars out back, but I had no company in the front lot. I patted the dash and murmured thanks to my old truck for keeping the passage safe, and then I went in.

As soon as the bell jangled, Justine pulled me into a hug. "Oh, honey, I'm so glad you came in. Now, maybe someone can tell us what all is going on around here! First you come in with that sweet old gentleman caller and Jack gets all het up about it, then he storms off, leaving Mary here, poor girl—Amy took her home shortly after. Not a word from either of them today—Jack and Mary, I mean—and you know that's not like them," she continued, ushering me up to the counter. "Now, before we get into all of that, what'll it be? The usual?" She poured a mug of coffee and placed it down, grabbed two sugars from her apron, then stuck her hands on her hips and faced me full-on. "Well, don't you look like steamed crap, Delilah Shaw—'scuse me, Montgomery-Shaw—and you ain't said a word since you walked in here."

I started to laugh. I couldn't help it. Mother Hen Justine's barrage of words made it just roll out of me. I saw the shock on her face, then saw it turn to concern when I continued laughing hard enough that my eyes sheened over with tears. I dropped my head into my arms on the counter and felt my whole body shake with it. It took me a minute to calm down.

Finally, I raised my head, wiping my eyes on my shirt sleeves as I let out a long breath. "Oh, Justine. Shit, you don't know how much I needed that. And no, not the usual," I continued, gathering what was left of my composure. "I'm picking up breakfast for a meeting at the bar."

"Well," she said slowly, eyes never leaving my face. "All right, then. You want I should tell the girls to do something up for you? 'Bout ten of ya?"

"Six, I think, but yeah, I trust y'all to take care of us."

She nodded and escaped into the back. I lifted my coffee, smiling until the terrible brew hit my tongue. I could hear the murmurs of her rapid-fire report to the cooks, then the bustle of her coming back out the swinging doors.

"So, where's your friend?" Justine asked, wiping a perfectly clean spot on the counter before sliding her gaze up.

"Oh, he's back at the bar," I said casually.

"The bar? He's not one of them *entrepreneurs*, is he?" she sneered like it was a dirty word. "He was far too much of a gentleman. He's not looking to put Mina and the boys out? Why, I—"

"No, no. Nothing like that," I assured her before she could really get indignant. I hid my smile behind my coffee as she planted her hands on her hips again. "Don't go getting all worked up. Everything's fine."

She sniffed. "I know a lie when I hear one."

"How're the boys? Season must be about to start," I said brightly.

Her eyes narrowed. "You're changing the subject, don't think I don't know it. But you look like you were dragged backward through last week, so I'll let ya. Jason made varsity . . ." She started rolling silverware up in paper napkins as she talked, telling me about her twins, one of whom was in marching band, the other on the football team. I listened and shook my head at her offer to refill.

Somewhere in the middle of homecoming plans, the bell at the pass-through rang. Justine brought over three wrapped aluminum trays.

"Okay, honey, you got your scrambled eggs and your grits, your sausage and bacon and toast—all white, hope that's all right—some beans, oh, and this whole thing is pancakes, all the fixings in there too. You want some help getting it to the truck?"

"No, that's okay. Just let me know how much, and I'll take care of that while I'm here."

She waved me off. "Mina's got a tab and a deal with Jack, don't even worry. Now, you'll come back and tell us everything when you can, right, honey? And maybe get some sleep in between now and then?"

"I will," I promised and, on impulse, kissed her cheek. "Thank you for taking care of me."

She blushed a little. "Well, now, of course. You're part of the family, after all. Family takes care. Let me get the door for you." She held it open as I maneuvered the trays out and walked me to the truck anyway.

"Would you let me know when Jack's around? Got something I want to talk to him about."

Her eyes sharpened. "Sure thing, honey, I'll let you know. I'll be sure to shoot you a text when they show themselves. Oh, let me get your door, now, too."

I slid the stack of trays in, then turned and gave her a tight hug.

She patted my back and laughed a little. "Go on with you, now, don't let that food go cold. I added a little something in there for you, too, honey. You enjoy, now, go on." She stood in the lot as I hopped in and started the truck, waving as I pulled away.

As I turned to go back to the bar, I saw her wipe her eyes before she headed back inside.

Family takes care, I thought. She was the second person to mention family in the past few hours, and the second to claim me as one of their own. I tried to remember if Justine or anyone at the diner had done that before. I had felt the connection, absolutely, but it was different at the bar. I hadn't worked at the diner, and neither had Nan. We had just sort of been absorbed, become regulars. We weren't there the same days, but at least once a week, you could find us in the people-watching booth. I went more after Nan died, needing to be near her, needing to feel like there was something to bridge the chasm between a world with love and light and color and a world without her in it. I'd gone with Angie, with the boys—even Byron a couple times, sharing his near silence, just being there.

I pulled up to the bar and parked, then paused before opening the door. Was that it? Surely I'd brought more people there—Nan too. I remembered another friend of Nan's, Jess or Jessica or something; she had come through town once. But no, come to think of it, we hadn't gone. Nan had turned down my offer of taking her to the diner, so we'd grabbed sandwiches at the Wawa and found a spot on the bike trail. We had surely never taken her sour-faced mother or brother there.

Nearly five years, and only folks from the bar and one shared friend. No one from my past, no one from the restaurant two towns north, where Nan had worked. It struck me that we had only brought the most important people to the diner. Everyone went to the bar, but the diner? If we took you there, you were a part of us. The diner was just for family.

A knock on the window by my face made me bite back a scream. I just about hit the roof of the truck, I jumped so high.

Johnathon looked at me quizzically, black brows drawn together, the slightest shadow of a wrinkle between them.

I pressed a hand to my pounding heart and opened the door with the other.

"Figured you could use some help. Wasn't trying to startle you," he said. "You good?"

I let my breath out with a little laugh. "Yeah, yeah, I'm good. Got a little lost in thought, I guess."

"I guess," he repeated, looking down at the stack of silver foil on the floor. "So, you need that hand?"

"Sure. Everyone else up?"

"Just about. Nelly's still looking shaky and sad as hell. I wondered if y'all hadn't talked yet?" I shook my head, and he shrugged. "Figured as much. He was up when we got here. Cleo's still working on becoming human. Mina too." I handed the heavy tray full of pancakes to him and slid out the last two trays. "Byron's on his way. Second round of coffee is on."

I kicked the truck door shut with my foot, and we headed toward the bar. The door swung open to reveal Cleo, a giant mug clutched in his hand.

"Need help?" His voice was still a little gruff with the early morning. Johnathon kissed his shoulder as he walked by, complimenting his timing.

"Just that's perfect."

I followed him in, bringing the trays to one end of the long beer-hall-type table. Someone—Johnathon, if I had to guess—had already put out a stack of plates and some silverware. We set the trays up buffet-style but waited to open them. Johnathon pulled out the serving spoons and tucked them into their trays. Satisfied, he looked up at me across the table and gestured behind me.

I followed his gaze and saw Nelly sitting at a booth, his hands wrapped around a mug. "Actually, can you help me with one more thing first?"

"Of course."

"Can I borrow your handkerchief?" He raised his eyebrows at my request. "Come on, I know you've got one. Just 'cause you're in jeans doesn't mean you're leaving home without it. You'll get it back," I said as he handed me the folded white cloth. "Probably. Or I'll replace it."

"Don't worry about it. I have enough."

"Thanks, J." Taking a deep breath to steel myself for the humbling, I crossed over and sat opposite of Nelly. "Hey. Uh . . . sleep well?" I mentally slapped myself for such bullshit opening small talk. "Nelly, I—""Before you say anything, Del, I'd like to, if you don't mind." He finally looked up from his coffee, and his eyes were quiet and sad. "I don't know what's happening or why I'm here. I don't know where I was . . . before. I guess I went and died six months ago, and I don't remember anything about that. I remember going to bed the way I always did in my room and, next thing I know, waking up in your house." He paused and took a shaky breath. "I don't know where your wife is. I don't know where *my* wife is. If I did, I'd sure as hell be trying to get back to her. I don't want to be away from her for another second if I don't have to. But I'm not keeping any secrets, Del. I just don't know." He looked back down at his coffee. "And that's what I have to say on the matter."

I felt about six inches tall. "Nelly, I'm so sorry. I can't begin to tell you how sorry I am that I said those things. It was cruel—and not even true. There's no excuse. I'm sorry I hurt you, and I'm sorry I made you wonder if I trusted or believed you. This is on me. We're going to find the answers, and . . . I guess we'll figure it out from there, because I know about as much as you do about all this madness. Precious fucking little. But I'm so, so sorry I hurt you." He nodded, eyes still downcast. "I don't expect it'll be easy to forgive me. I don't know if you'd even want to. I'm not saying you have to, even. I'm just—I'm sorry."

He nodded again, and I saw a tear slide down his cheek. He cleared his throat and patted his chest. I laid the handkerchief on the table between us. He looked up at me quickly before he took it and dabbed at his eyes.

We both remained, the silence uncomfortable. Nelly stared down at the handkerchief, rubbing the embroidered letter *J* with his thumb. "My Annamaria, she believed in forgiveness. She taught me that too. Not everyone believes in that, you know? Same way not everyone believes in God or the Devil or Heaven or Hell. I'd never given it too much thought, but I've always thought there were lines a man couldn't cross—hell, a woman either. Don't matter. And I figured, well, once one of those lines was crossed, that was it. There was no going back. But my Annamaria . . ." He shook his head slowly. "She didn't hold that for a second. She was all heart. She had a memory on her a mile long, though." He chuckled a little. "She'd forgive, but damn, she'd remember. And ooh, you'd have to really light her fire to get her to bring it up. She kept her tongue, mostly, but she had a way of looking at you where you just knew that *she* knew that she had that edge. She never lost it, but she did forgive." Finally, he raised his eyes to mine. " 'Course I forgive you, Del. I can't not. I know you're hurting, too, and angry and confused, and probably a bit scared as well." I didn't reply. "I want to figure this out. I want to—I want to go home, whatever that means right now. And I wish that will mean you get Nan back. I just don't know."

Silence fell again.

I was hesitant as I reached across the table to touch the corner of the handkerchief. "You kept patting your chest like you were looking for pockets. I've seen plenty of guys here at the bar do that, looking for their cash or cigarettes. But then I remembered seeing someone in my family do the same thing when they were looking for their handkerchief."

Nelly's face registered surprise, and then he smiled. He put his hand over mine on the table, the edge of the soft cloth between us. "Friends?".

I met his eyes with a smile of my own. "Yeah. Friends."

He gave my hand a final pat and was nearly halfway out of the booth before he pulled his hand away. "Good. I'm starving, and I can smell those little sausages from here."

CHAPTER FOURTEEN

Twenty minutes later, we were all assembled at the table. Coffees had been freshened (doctored, in my case); the banter was peppered with laughs and groans—the overlapping, simultaneous conversations made the six of us sound like at least a dozen. Mina sat across from Johnathon, next to Nelly, who was next to me; Cleo took his spot at Johnathon's side, and Byron ended up across from me. I had found the folded-foil package of strawberries and half-melted chocolate chips with the pancakes, courtesy of Justine. I couldn't help but get choked up as I added them to my stack, tears pricking my eyes as I looked around at all these amazing people.

Nelly was discussing football with Cleo as Johnathon recounted something to Mina that had him rolling his eyes and her bark of laughter ringing out. Byron smiled when our eyes met, but it quickly faded from his face.

"Del?" he asked. The table fell silent but for chewing.

"Nothing. I'm fine," I said and sniffled a tiny bit. No one had to voice their disbelief for me to know it was there. "I was just thinking . . . you guys are my family. You were the first people I called when Nan died. I didn't even call my parents or Gloria for a few hours. You guys—I called you and you came right away. You were there for me. You've always been there for me. And you were there for Nan too. I don't know if we knew how much. This morning, at the diner"—I felt Nelly stiffen beside me—"I realized that too. Y'all have been there. Nan and I didn't really take anyone else to the diner."

"Well, to be fair, we've been here a bit longer," Mina said, digging back into her pancakes and eggs. "We've got our own thing there, a business relationship, what have you."

"No, I get that, but like, the diner became our spot. I guess we were the closest things we were to regulars anywhere. We brought everyone here— anyone who visited or new friends we made—but we only took family there. We only took you guys." I looked over at Nelly. "And you. I took you. It didn't cross my mind to go anywhere else. More than friends, Nelly"—he looked up at me—"we're family."

His eyes warmed from worry to pleasure, and he put his hand on mine again.

"I like the sound of that," he said softly. "So, do you think we need to trace back our trees and find out where they all meet? There's that fella on PBS who does that on TV for folks."

"No." I shook my head. "Not family in the bloodline sense. Chosen family." He said nothing, so I continued, "I've told you about the family I grew up with. We're not close, never have been. And that's just what it is. That's been the way of it for a lot of queer folks who aren't accepted or supported at home. But we still need family. And we find them along the way.

"It's the people you think of first when something great or terrible happens. The first people you want to share that with, the people you want to be around at the holidays. The ones who aren't afraid to call you out, and the ones who forgive you when you fuck it up. They're the ones who make you feel at home." I looked up at Mina. "Maybe something you've never felt before, is home.

"So, that's the kind of family we are, Nelly. You, me, all of us now." He nodded but had tensed back up. I figured he was missing his own family and thinking about his daughter and granddaughter at the diner. I wanted him to enjoy this family right now, though, so I said, "It makes it a lot easier to have 'the talk,' you know, about the birds and the bees, I'll tell you."

He laughed along with the rest of the group and seemed to shrug off the melancholy.

I looked over at Byron, making eye contact again. "I'm sorry for my behavior last night, guys. I have no excuse. Y'all took care of me too. Thank you for that."

"Could've let you keep making a fool out of yourself and waited till you passed out or ralphed. Wouldn't've been much longer." The nods around the table made me wince, and Cleo grinned. "Or the first time."

"Oh, stuff it," I muttered.

"It wasn't like it was trivia night or there was karaoke or anything," he continued in between mouthfuls of egg piled on toast. The bottle of hot sauce sat at the ready.

"Sounds like a story," Nelly said to my groans and everyone else's laughter.

Well, everyone but Byron, who was still looking at me. Our eyes met in acknowledgment of the conversation we had yet to have. With the rest of the table recounting my exploits, I opened my mouth to say something, but he shook his head a tiny bit. *Later,* he mouthed to me, and I nodded. I tuned back in. This wouldn't be the time or place for Byron to open up, anyway.

". . . And she goes, 'Yeah, and *Moby Dick*'s about a whale, fucking SparkNotes over here,' and almost falls out of the chair she's standing on." Cleo's laughing so hard, he can hardly get the words out. "So, she sits, then throws herself back over the chair all dramatic—and doesn't fucking move again. That's the position she passed out in."

Enjoying himself, Cleo provided the full dramatic reenactment.

"You carried her up that night too," Johnathon reminded him, grinning. "And Nan tagged in to finish the game." The grin faded a bit. "She was great to have around. I miss the hell out of her."

Murmurs of agreement went around the table.

"Mina here told me some about her last night," Nelly said. "She sounds like a great lady."

I snorted. I couldn't help myself. "Lady, my ass," I said. "She didn't have time to be a lady. She was always working on some new recipe or project or interest. She was a dreamer and schemer," I said, softer. It felt nice, remembering her with these guys. They'd known her—well, everyone but Nelly. I looked around the table. "You guys remember her latest?" Most of them shook their heads, scraping up the last bites from their plates. "Oh, man, okay. So, she had started really getting into salt, right? Different kinds of salt from different places in the world. Pink salt, black salt, Dead Sea salt. She wanted to figure out their differences in taste and the different ways you use them and write a cookbook about it. Okay, awesome, go for it.

"Well, instead of focusing on salt, she went down a rabbit hole into minerology and started looking at crystals and chemical compositions of this stone and that. She found out there's a bunch that are naturally found around here, so she went out and got a gold-panning kit and a rock tumbler so she could make the stones she found all smooth and pretty." I shook my head. "It's still boxed up. She never followed through on it, of course. Another venture abandoned along the way. Not in a bad way," I said quickly. "Just that she tended to go all-in on projects for a couple weeks, and that would be it."

"Man, she could've made a hell of a cookbook," Johnathon commented.

"Don't I know it."

"Do you have any of her recipes?" Nelly asked as he lay his silverware on his plate.

"I do. They're all on flash drives. She had a little lockbox for them. I haven't looked at them," I admitted.

He patted my hand. "They'll keep."

We finished up. Chairs scraped and dishes were passed as we cleared the table. I hit the restroom while one of the guys wiped down the table and someone else started the dishwasher.

In the bathroom, I stared at my reflection as I washed my hands. I looked terrible. My eyes were darker than they had been for a little bit now, as if the color were weighed down by grief. My skin looked tired, my hair looked dull—everything did. I wasn't one for vanity, but shit, I could slap some moisturizer on and wash my hair, at least. I splashed some water on my face, mentally promising myself to take the time for a proper shower tonight, then rubbed it dry with my shirt and went back out.

I was the last one ready, so I refilled my mug, eyeballing the whiskey-to-coffee ratio, and took my spot back at the table. "All right, what did I miss last night?" Everyone looked at Byron. "I remember you said something about a quest," I prompted him.

"You said you seen a bird—a large, white one—that had come from the ashes, and then it was gone, and Nelly stood in its place," Byron recounted. "Sounds like a phoenix to me."

"You had a quote. What was that?" I demanded.

"'When heaven shall call her from this cloud of darkness / Who from the sacred ashes of her honor / Shall star-like rise, as great in fame as she was, / And so stand fix'd.' I can't remember where it comes from. It's a play, I know, but I can't place it," he admitted, then grinned. "I've done a few."

"Yeah, it's familiar," I muttered, trying to keep the lines in my head. "Where's my notebook?"

"I put it back behind the bar last night," Mina said. "I'll grab it."

"What else?" I asked, my fingers itching to take notes and start working on this new piece of the puzzle.

"Well, white animals are often used to signal the beginning or correct path of a quest. That's been common in folklore for a long time, and now you can see it in a lot of video games too."

"Why's it always gotta be white?" Johnathon muttered quietly, getting a nod from Byron and an elbow from Cleo.

"And *Harry Potter*," Mina said when she returned with my notebook.

Grateful, I murmured a thank-you as I opened it to the next blank page. "By, can you give that to me one more time?"

He spoke slowly, watching my scrawl pace him so I could get the content and cadence.

"'Shall star-like rise, as great in fame . . .' oh my fucking God, I know this!" I looked up to everyone staring at my sudden excitement. "It's *Henry VIII*! Of course! I should have figured that last night! Fucking Shakespeare."

Kicking back in my chair, I assumed my thinking position, hands behind my head like a little hammock, tipping my chair back a little with one foot.

"The legend of the phoenix is believed to have transcended culture, age, and country. Homer wrote of it in *The Iliad*. Mina, you brought up *Harry Potter*, and yes, absolutely. Depending on the text, the phoenix represents—um—hold on a sec." I closed my eyes to better rummage through the snippets of literature and poetry. I had always felt like my brain was a bit like an attic used for storage, which really meant throwing things up there that you didn't want anyway. I had all of it tucked away into a very specific system, a delusional filing scheme that I could never explain but relied on completely. "Well, the cycle of life, death, and rebirth—the birth of the new from ashes of the old. Some texts have likened it to the resurrection of Jesus Christ. In *Henry*, he's talking about the newborn queen. So . . . power? Authority figure, maybe? I'm having a hard time seeing any parallels to the religious theme." I opened my eyes and sat the chair back down, scribbling in my shorthand and symbols. "That doesn't fit for me, and I don't think it fits much for Nelly either. White bird, red herring?" I jotted it down as I spoke and circled it, then looked up to confirm and found him staring at me like we hadn't just spent some thirty – odd hours in each other's pockets. "What?"

"I knew you had books, but I didn't realize you were a damn librarian," Nelly said, then looked across at the guys. Johnathon and Cleo shrugged in sync, while Byron had the faintest smile playing around his lips.

"I read books and I know things." The *Game of Thrones* reference went over his head. "Okay, what's next? The white animal, symbol of a quest, most common in Celtic mythology and folklore, but again, also mentioned in the Bible. White bird, dove, peace, joining, harmony. Can't say I'm feeling much of any of that. The phoenix isn't often portrayed as white, usually red and gold, as it's associated with fire and flames . . ." Tapping the end of the pen against my teeth between thoughts, I scribbled and paused, then scribbled and paused again. "I've gotta do more research."

The table, which had been silent until that moment, became a chorus of groans and audible exhalations. Cleo slapped the table with one hand, causing the nearly empty coffee mugs to jump.

"Pay up!" he hooted.

"What the hell?" I asked, bewildered.

Mina rolled her eyes as she reached into the pocket of her jeans. "We may have taken bets on how long it would be before you said you needed to do more research. Cleo nailed the eight-to-ten-minute slot."

"I might know you a little bit." He grinned.

"You guys are fucking weird, you know that?" I muttered. "Anyway, the thing is—"

Nelly, who had been subdued since the librarian comment, spoke up quietly. "I'm not sure how much time we have."

We all turned.

"What do you mean?" Mina asked, touching his hand on the table.

He smiled a little sadly. "I don't know exactly. Just sort of a feeling I've got in my heart, in my gut. I don't know how long this . . . whatever it is—reprieve, I suppose—is going to last." He turned his hand over to hold Mina's. "I'm sure going to miss you all."

"What happens after?" Byron asked.

Nelly shrugged. "Don't rightly know. The last I remember was going to bed like I had every other night. That was six months ago. I don't have anything in between."

"White light? Pearly gates?" Johnathon prompted.

"Nothing. No hellfire or brimstone either," he said with a weak smile. "I don't know what that means for the beyond."

"Maybe you didn't get to the beyond yet. Because of whatever's going on here?" Johnathon asked. "Like purgatory, but not like Dante. More like a rest stop on the highway, something not important or memorable until we figure out how to get you to the end."

"Another thing—why you? Why Nan? No offense," Cleo added. "But how many people die every day? Every week? How did you, Nelly, end up at Del's?"

"A phoenix is reborn from the ashes, a new life begins," Mina murmured. Her eyes were pointed skyward, the way they did when she was working on a tough crossword puzzle.

"But unless you're Benjamin Button, you wouldn't be a new life, right?" Nelly shook his head. "You died, and not only that, you died the same day as Nan," I said. "And—I noticed this, and this is weird, when we saw Jack at the diner yesterday. He has the same funeral card as I have, only his has Nelly's picture and name and birthday, and mine has Nan's. But the birthday—the month and day—are the same, just the years are different. And you guys have the same initials too. NSM. I mean, she added the S on, but for the name she was born with. And lots of times, hyphenated names don't use both initials, just the first." I remembered the frustration of trying to get our new names set up at the bank, and what our usernames could be. Taking both names had been a pain in the ass, but especially now, I was so glad we did it. "Holy shit," Johnathon breathed.

Mina stared back and forth between Nelly and me. "Well, that's gotta be it. That's how you're connected. It's right there in plain sight."

"Is it?" I asked. My head was starting to hurt. I rubbed my fingertips against my forehead, trying to relieve some of the pressure. "This is all so . . . fantastical. I'm not sure I'm seeing what you're seeing, Mina."

She shrugged. "Maybe I'm wrong. Maybe there's nothing. But maybe there is. Here, take a new page." She used her chin to gesture to my notebook. "Write down everything you can think of right now that might connect Nelly and Nan. So far, you've got birthdays, death days, initials, and you." I scribbled these down dutifully. "What else?"

"Um . . . we both had wives," Nelly said. It went on the list.

"Both were cremated," Cleo suggested. Added.

"Lived in the same town." This time from Mina.

"I sold your houses," Johnathon said softly.

"Wait, wait, go back." The brain tickle was back and I ran with it, barely registering that I'd cut off whatever Nelly was about to say to Johnathon. I drew quick arrows, connecting my shorthand chicken scratch. "Cremated, same town—that means same municipality, which means the same coroner. Holy shit. And same flashy lights, paramedics and cops and shit. Asshole," I couldn't help but mutter. "And what, do you want to bet same funeral home? There's only the one in town. Nelly, where did you go?"

"It's not a damn salon you're asking about, Del, for fuck's sake. Take a breather," Mina admonished me. "Nelly, honey, you okay? You want some water?"

"No, no, quite all right, thank you. It's a bit odd, but I'm following right enough. Now, let's see. If everything went according to plan, it would have all followed my Annamaria's guiding light, so . . . I can't quite get the name of it, but it's the old plantation house by the river that got turned into a funeral parlor."

"Random Funeral Home." I nodded. "That's the one. Same as Nan."

"What if . . ." Byron said slowly. My eyes met his across the table, and we shared the same horrific thought.

In the roar of the silence, I heard the distinct flutter of wingbeats.

"Holy mother of God," I whispered. "No, no, that doesn't happen. It can't."

"What? What can't happen?" Johnathon demanded.

I stared at Byron, dumbfounded, so he took it upon himself to answer.

"What if Del hasn't had Nan's ashes all along, but Nelly's? What if she got the wrong ashes?"

There was a beat of disbelief at the table before reactions erupted. The chorus of "No, impossible!" and variations on that theme flew around as I looked at Nelly, the calm at the center of the storm. He had a ghost of a smile playing on his face.

Byron was trying to quiet everybody down when Nelly started to chuckle softly, then louder until we all stopped and sat. He laughed harder and harder, inexplicably, much like I had in the diner. I couldn't fathom what was so funny, yet I found myself smiling, then joining him as he hooted, roaring with laughter until we had tears in our eyes.

The rest of the family looked at us with varying expressions of pity and confusion.

Nelly recovered first. "Well, it took until I died, but I finally went home with the wrong woman." He wiped his eyes. That sent me into fresh peals of laughter, and Mina snorted out a laugh of her own.

"That's not supposed to be possible," Johnathon insisted. "There are safeguards—regulations—on that sort of thing to prevent exactly this."

"*Exactly* this?" I asked.

"You know what I mean." He waved a hand. "Taking the wrong ashes home."

"Hey, who are you calling wrong? I've been Mr. Right before, I'll have you know." Nelly feigned indignity.

"Never had one of those before," I responded, and the two of us dissolved into giggles again.

"I don't know how you two of all people are laughing at this," Johnathon said.

I raised my palms, shrugging. "What else are we going to do? This is all ridiculous. Insane nonsense. It literally makes no sense."

"My Annamaria used to say you either laugh or cry, and I've always been one for laughter," Nelly added.

Mina nodded in agreement.

"But this isn't supposed to happen," Johnathon pressed. "So how did it?"

"I guess we have to talk to the funeral home and find out," I said.

"And how are you going to do that? Nelly walks in and says, 'Oh, hey, I was cremated here, but I took the wrong bus home'?" Nelly stifled a new chuckle. Johnathon shook his head and continued, "That's not going to work. If this is really what happened, you're going to have to find a way to prove it without them finding out that you're, well, *here*."

"Well, now, I think I might have something that can help with that, at least," Nelly said, patting his chest before reaching into his jeans pocket. He pulled out a tarnished silver disk, almost like a nickel that had been flattened by a passing train. I recognized the stamp of the name along the top curve as the funeral home where Nan had been cremated, accompanied by a twelve-digit number.

My gut felt suddenly hot, like I'd swallowed a ball of molten glass.

"Where did you get this?" I asked him, my throat tight around the words.

"I woke up with it yesterday. It was stuck to my foot," Nelly said. "I wasn't sure what it was, but now—"

I pulled out my wallet from my back pocket. I took out the funeral card with Nan's picture and birth and death dates; behind it was the simple navy-print-on-white card and a picture of the same metal token. Every muscle tensed as I leaned over the table, putting the cards and metal disk in the middle of the table. Everyone else leaned forward. I took a deep breath and looked around the table.

"I was given this card with a picture of the token they put on Nan when she was . . . cremated." I couldn't stop myself from thinking *when Nan was burned up*, but I held it in. "They do it to make sure the token with the ashes matches the token in the picture. They match it before and after the, um, procedure. That way, no one goes home with the wrong ashes. These should match if I've had Nan's ashes." I looked down, but the numbers swam in front of me. I shook my head to clear my eyes without success. "I'm sorry, I can't," I admitted and gulped the remainder of my coffee to ease the pain.

Johnathon leaned over me. "May I?" I nodded.

He slid the token and card in front of him. It took him approximately six hours of stretched-out silence before he said, "No. Hold on. Here, Cleo, you read that." He slid the card over to his husband. "I'll read this one, number for number. I'll start. One, eight."

"One, eight," Cleo echoed.

"Zero, three, zero."

"Zero, three, zero."

Was this what it was like to play bingo? Waiting for the next number, hoping you knew it, praying it was the same on the ball as it was on the card?

"Nine, eight, one."

Cleo's voice was suddenly quiet, and he tapped the token as he spoke. "Nine. *Four*. One."

CHAPTER FIFTEEN

Random Funeral Home had been converted from the main buildings of a small tobacco plantation on the outskirts of town. The land along the river had been parceled off for conservation, and the bike trail ran right through. The shacks that had once held over a hundred of enslaved people had long been torn down; a monument stood at the east end of the trail that detailed the history of the people and property. Last year, another monument had been erected at the west end, bearing the names of nearly seventy people who had been forced to serve on the plantation. The Black Lives Matter chapter at the local high school had gotten a grant to have the genealogy traced; it had taken three years to find fewer than half of the people believed to have been there. The kids had raised half the money for the monument and had been matched by the town.

Both the main building and crematory had been made of brick, the second having first been used as a carriage house. The outside of each building bore a large plaque detailing all this history. When I'd first come to make the arrangements for Nan, I hadn't been able to leave easily, knowing she was there. I'd wandered around the property, letting myself become absorbed in the history. Since then, I'd read up on it further on sleepless nights. It seemed a fitting place—and a peaceful one—for a house of death. So many had suffered on this land. The transformation into funeral parlor made it seem like a place where sorrow and suffering could coexist across decades.

We pulled up the curve of the driveway. I parked the truck under the second set of pillars in front of the main building; the driveway was wide enough for at least two cars to pass. We got out, and I was halfway up the steps before I realized I was walking alone. I stopped and looked back at a reluctant Nelly, who was patting his pockets. He fished out the half pack of American Spirits and lit up as I walked back down the marble steps.

"This is the last place I saw my Annamaria," he said, smoke curling around him in the still air. "She was all laid out, her favorite dress and her hair all done up. You would've thought she was sleeping." He took another hard drag. "It had been a long time since I'd seen someone lie dead, and it weren't nothin' like I remember." His hand shook slightly. "The friends I lost over in the war . . . when they died, they looked it. No question they were dead. No question." I was impatient. This was the closest we'd come to finding out what had happened, and I didn't really feel like waiting for Nelly to have a smoke break.

Then again, I understood. Six months ago, I'd seen Nan here, covered from neck to toe and her face with enough makeup and who knows what other mortuary magic to make it look as if she, too, were sleeping. I had put her glasses on; she couldn't see without them, so she only took them off when she slept, and I couldn't keep looking at her, thinking she might wake up.

I came back down the steps and leaned against the bed of the truck, next to Nelly. The humidity in the air seemed to pull down the smoke from his cigarette.

"She wasn't cremated?" I asked and immediately admonished myself. "Sorry, that's too personal. I wasn't trying to intrude."

Nelly shook his head. "Catholic to the bone. She wanted to go in one piece. Pope even said it was okay, but Annamaria? No sirree." He sighed, looking up at the building as he took another deep drag. "I didn't want to be laid out like that. I was for the fire. I wanted to be planted with her, though." He paused. "I don't remember anything like that happening. I don't remember feeling the fire."

"Well—" I felt as if I needed to tread lightly. Even after everything so far, I wasn't sure how convinced either of us were that he was, in all actuality, dead. "Once someone is dead, they stop feeling. No one . . . remembers."

He looked at me with a sad smile. "You know, they say that. They do. And I don't remember anything about it, but I can't help but wonder." He looked back at the brick building, its stately white pillars standing in stark contrast to the faded red. He sighed, took a last drag of his cigarette, and flicked it away. "Best get on with it, then."

We walked up the steps. Nelly hit the silver panel, and the heavy, white doors clunked once, then opened smoothly. We stepped into the foyer.

The double doors on either side of us were closed. A young woman in a boxy suit jacket and blond ponytail looked up from the computer. In an instant, her face moved from unhappy to desperately pleased; I assumed it was due to seeing a couple of people still upright and breathing.

My mind wandered momentarily. Did Nelly breathe?

"Good afternoon!" she said a bit too cheerfully for a funeral parlor. "How may I be of service today?" Her voice carried an elongated flatness that said Minnesota, or maybe one of the Dakotas. Midwest, anyway.

"Good afternoon. I was wondering if we might have a word with Mr. Teasdale," I asked, finding his name within easy reach in my memory. "I'm afraid we don't have an appointment."

Crestfallen, she still nodded graciously. "If you would come this way, you can be comfortable while I go see if I can fetch him. There's coffee and sweet tea in the carafes," she said, opening the side door near her desk. Both Nelly and I hesitated. "Oh, don't worry, there's no one in there today," she said. "You won't be bothering anyone."

Her eyes swept over to the room and back, gesturing us in. I could see the thickness of her mascara and suddenly realized that she had been crying at some point before our arrival. When our eyes met, I saw hers were frightened behind the barest sheen of tears.

I had only a second to wonder before she walked away, the click of skyscraper heels dulled by the thin rug that nearly spanned the foyer. Nelly cleared his throat quietly, and we walked in.

It was the main viewing parlor, empty as advertised. Without speaking, I knew we were standing in the same room that he had last seen his wife and I had last seen mine. I felt the hot punch of grief, and my body absorbed the jolt of memory viscerally. I bit back an audible cry. I felt myself start to sink, one hand over my mouth as my knees gave way. Familiar enough with grief's need to overwhelm not just my heart but my body as well, I didn't fight it.

Suddenly, I found myself leaning, held up by thin arms of surprising strength, a grip I hadn't encountered before. Nelly was holding on, holding me up.

For some reason, I thought of my baseball coach from way back, when I was young enough to not have switched to softball yet. What was his name? All I could remember was calling him Coach.

"There now, steady as she goes. There's a girl," Nelly said.

Soothed, I stayed right where I was, my head dropped on his shoulder. My arms came up around him slowly, holding on tentatively. He was solid, real; he felt like what I imagined any seventy-something-year-old old man would feel like to hug. I didn't want to hold on too hard for fear of breaking thin bones, and still he gripped me tight. It was the first time any more than our hands had touched. I remembered with a jolt that he was dead. He felt solid, warm.

After some moments, I lifted my head and we both stepped back just a little. "You all right now?"

"Yeah, thanks. Thank you," I said. "How many daughters did you say you had?"

He blinked in surprise, then laughed. "Two. Two girls and a boy, and eight grandkids between 'em, all girls but for one. We're surrounded, I tell you." He smiled.

"You remind me of my baseball coach," I said, stuffing my hands in the pockets of my jeans. I didn't know what else to do with them.

"Is that a good thing?" I nodded. "Yeah. Yeah, it is. He was . . . steady. He never flipped out on us for a bad play or a miss or anything. Even when some kid lost a batting helmet, he took it in stride. You couldn't shake him," I said, finally looking up at Nelly. "Yeah. You remind me of him a lot. Mina too. Y'all don't shake."

Just then, the door opened and the funeral director walked in. "Folks, I apologize for the wait. I'm sorry, my assistant didn't get your names, Mr. . . ." he trailed off, looking at Nelly.

Before he could answer, I jumped in, holding my hand out.

"Mr. Teasdale, I'm Del Montgomery-Shaw. You . . . took care of my wife, Nan, a few months back." He shook my hand, turning his attention to me now. "This is a friend of mine, Nelly, uh, Jones. He's a friend of the family," I explained. I didn't want him looking too closely. "Is there somewhere we could sit and talk? Somewhere that isn't, well, this room." I shrugged apologetically.

The director was all dignified sympathy. "Of course, of course, Mrs. Montgomery-Shaw. Come right this way. Mr. Jones, is there anything I can get either of you to drink? Some tea, perhaps?"

"No, thank you," I declined as we walked down another hallway to a small office, which was made to feel much larger with its vaulted ceilings and wall of windows facing the garden. The neat shrubbery created pathways marked with stone, and ornamental trees no taller than I was stood at precise corners. For a second, I thought I saw a flash of white wings in the cascading branches, but nothing appeared as my eyes continued to search.

"What can I do for you today, ma'am?" The funeral director took his seat behind the desk, folding his tall frame into a seated position while he gestured to the wide leather-topped chairs intended for Nelly and me. I remembered I had thought of him as looming at first, back when I had first met him, and had thought his height and profession overpowered his gentle tone and manner.

"Well, we have a bit of a mystery on our hands," I said, glancing at Nelly. He nodded and kept quiet, and I began to tell the story we'd agreed upon. "I was going through some paperwork when I prepared to move, you know, cleaning house. I found the card you had given me with the picture of the token and the number on it." I pulled it from my back pocket. "You said you did that to make extra sure the right families went home with the right ashes."

I still couldn't bring myself to call what was left *cremains*.

He nodded slowly. "Yes, ma'am. Similar to dog tags used by the military, we use fire-resistant tokens for identification purposes."

"I don't think it worked this time," I said, keeping my eyes on his.

"What exactly do you mean, Mrs. Montgomery-Shaw?" The starch in the words implied the level of insult I had just barely levied against him.

"I don't think I have my wife's ashes, sir," I said evenly.

Ramrod-straight in his chair now, he tapped a couple keys, and I could see the screen of the computer light up his face slightly as it woke up. He reached over and slid the card toward him with two long, bony fingers, and I wondered if all funeral directors began to resemble skeletons. I watched him look at the card, screen, keyboard and back, painstakingly punching in the numbers. *18-030981-0128.*

His face settled into satisfied lines that he worked quickly to hide as he turned the screen toward us.

"Here it is. Nanette Sue Montgomery-Shaw, identification tag one, eight, dash, oh, three, oh, nine, eight, one, dash, oh, one, two, eight. We use a combination of the current year, date of birth, and date of death to make sure there are no duplicates. You picked up your wife's cremains, Mrs. Montgomery-Shaw," he said, masking the righteous face but not the tone that so clearly said, *I told you so.*

"I'm sorry, sir, but I don't believe I do. The identification number matches what I have on the card, but—" I put down the hammered piece of metal, the edge of it catching so it snapped against the desk. "One, eight, dash, zero, three, zero, nine, *four*, one, dash, zero, one, two, eight."

The funeral director snatched it up, peering closely at the disk, then back at the screen. The flush that had begun to creep up his neck suddenly faded, the brown skin of his cheeks going tawny. I saw the slightest tremble in his bony hands. He mumbled something under his breath I couldn't quite catch, but it clearly wasn't meant for us to hear anyway.

He cleared his throat gently.

"Mrs. Montgomery-Shaw, Mr. Jones—first, let me extend my deepest sympathies and utter incredulity that this may have occurred. Rest assured that we will investigate thoroughly, make any necessary corrections post-haste, and make every effort to bring about a resolution quickly." He spoke stiffly, delivering a script he had filed away for this purpose with no experience in delivering it. "If I may ask, how did you find the identification tag?"

Even after all the extraordinary events of the past two days, I still felt embarrassed about this part. "I, uh, bumped into it and it spilled."

Mr. Teasdale frowned. "The lid should have kept the cremains in place," he said. "It should have been secured when you received it."

"Well, the lid was loose. My fault," I said quickly. "Totally my fault. But when it fell, the tag came out."

"I see," he said, clearly not seeing. "And if I may ask, why was the lid loose? Did you receive the urn in that state? Or did you have concerns about the status of the cremains at the time?"

I hunched my shoulders. "No. I popped the latch so it wasn't entirely closed." He looked at me in surprise, as did Nelly. I guess I'd left that part out before. "Nan was claustrophobic, okay?" I said defensively. "It didn't feel right to leave her all sealed up like that."

The funeral director sighed slightly, an antiquated schoolteacher when a student wouldn't listen. I'd been on the receiving end of such sighs before, and it only put my back up further.

"Mr. Teasdale, are you able and willing to help me get Nan back or not? It doesn't matter if the lid was loose or if I scattered the ashes or put them in the damn fireplace. I still walked away with the ashes of someone else's loved one. I'm sure that's not the sort of publicity an organization like yours needs."

"Of course, of course," he said, placating me. "We will do everything we can to right this most egregious wrong. And," he stressed, "we will take further precautions to prevent such an upsetting violation from ever occurring again. If you could kindly give us a few days, I will personally follow up on this matter and notify you the moment I am able."

I took one of his business cards from the holder on the edge of his desk and scribbled down my name and the number to my cell and the bar. "If you don't reach me at the first one, try the second. You can leave a message with whoever answers."

He stood and walked us out in silence, the blond startling when the door to the main lobby *thunk*ed open. "Thank you again for bringing this matter to my attention. I will follow up as quickly as is realistically possible. Mr. Jones, Mrs. Montgomery-Shaw, I hope you have a pleasant and peaceful day."

The doors shut in our faces before we had even turned around from the formal exit, the dismissal complete.

We walked down the steps and silently took our spots, where we had stood prior to entering the building. This time, when Nelly pulled the pack of cigarettes out of his pocket, I held my hand out for one. He placed one in my hand, eyebrow barely raised. He lit his, took a drag, and lit mine from the end of his. "He was a cooler customer than some of his corpses, I reckon."

I had chosen that moment to take my first drag and coughed out a laugh, which devolved into me hacking until tears ran from my eyes.

"Not much of a smoker, huh?" Nelly asked with a low chuckle.

"Can't—fucking—stand—it," I choked out. "Don't get it. It does not feel good. Just felt like the thing to do." The coughing slowed enough that I gingerly took another drag before giving up and stamping it out on the wheel of my truck. "I don't like him." I flicked the butt toward the brick steps.

"Can't say I do either," Nelly agreed. "But still and all, we need him right now. Just gotta play along a little longer."

I waited a beat, then shot Nelly a grin. "Over my dead body."

He let out a hoot. "I thought the bit about bad publicity was a nice touch. You don't lose your tongue when your temper is up, that's for sure."

I winced a little, remembering how devastatingly sharp my tongue had been when I'd turned it on him the night before. Was that only so long ago?

"Now," he said, dropping the cigarette and crushing it under the sole of an old pair of sneakers that were only fit for mowing the lawn—and apparently for those folks who magically showed up without a stitch on in someone else's house. "What's next?"

"Next, I think we go back to the bar. Get some lunch, update folks. I still need to talk to Byron."

Nelly nodded. "All right. So, you gonna let me drive?"

I snorted as I swung up into the driver's seat. "Not on your life."

I hit the gas as he hooted again.

CHAPTER SIXTEEN

It was nearly noon by the time we got back to the bar. I realized it had unofficially become headquarters; I didn't want to be bringing this home, putting these worries into the apartment. I had just settled into my new place, and I wanted to have some space free from death and overwhelming memories.

We had gotten out of the truck when my phone buzzed. The display showed a message from Justine, and I felt a hot punch of excitement and shame.

"Hey, Nelly?" I stopped outside the door of the bar. "I, uh—I'm going to take a quick trip back to the house and grab a few things, new clothes for both of us. Give me a chance to clear my head a little, you know?"

"Sure thing. I'll let Mina know you won't be having lunch here. She promised to make sandwiches." He patted his stomach, and I laughed a little.

"Enjoy. I'll be back later."

"See you when we see you, Del." He waved and went inside. I tried to squash the guilt about lying to him as I hopped back in the truck and headed straight for the diner.

There were three cars in the lot: two out-of-staters and the beat-up Subaru that Jack refused to have painted or touched up in any way. *Character*, he liked to say. I parked next to it and went inside.

Justine looked up from the table where she was chatting up some of the travelers and caught my eye. She tilted her head back in the direction of the office and wiggled her eyebrows. I nodded in thanks and headed around the counter and toward the back, touching her shoulder briefly on the way.

I could smell the bacon on the flattop. Remembering Nelly's comment about sandwiches made me remember I was going to miss lunch, and I had a sudden yearning for a BLT. I grabbed a notepad off the counter, scribbled it down as an order, and laid it on the pass-through. Either Amy or Wendy—whoever was on—would get to it when they got to it. I knocked on the office door and, at Jack's grunt, walked in.

I'd never been in it, but had always imagined his office would looked like what I imagined an old-timey private investigator's would. I wasn't entirely wrong, but the room in front of me looked like if he had no appreciation for antiques or organizational systems. Piles of magazines and papers were stacked on the floor, on mismatched leather chairs, and on the gorgeous desk, legs carved and ornate. All it was missing was a typewriter and an ashtray with a still-burning cigarette.

"Got a minute?"

Jack eyed me and nodded. "You still look like crap," he said, his voice gruff.

"Aw, thanks, Jack. You look lovely this afternoon. The green really brings out your eyes," I said and shut the door behind me.

He barked a short laugh. "Smartass. So. You were looking for me this morning." He put the papers he had been leafing through aside and folded his hands on his desk.

"So," I responded. "How do you know Naylor Saltalamacchia Maltby?"

Jack averted his eyes and let out a long sigh. "I was afraid you were coming to ask me that," he said. "I had to come in to get away from Mary for a bit. I finished telling her the story this morning. She didn't take too quickly to it—oh, she's all right, just a little shook is all," he responded to the look on my face. "It's a secret I'd kept a long time. We're not supposed to have any between us." He looked off as he finished speaking, and I waited. The silence dragged out a minute before he sighed again. "He hasn't told you?"

"I haven't asked him. We've been trying to figure out some other things. Like what he's even doing here."

"Yeah? You figure that out yet?"

"Working on it." I tilted my head. "You changing the subject?"

He scratched his chin. "I don't know as it's my story to tell." I waited. "Okay, okay. Not all mine, though."

He pushed himself up from his chair and walked over to a low bookcase full of cookbooks and coffee-table books his grandkids bought him. The top was covered with pictures, the frames jockeying for space—Mary smiling, twin babies wide-eyed and drooling, an old dog with its muzzle going gray being hugged by a little blond girl. He picked up one, a young boy in a T-ball uniform, and slipped the back off. He pulled a small three-by-five photo out of the frame. He took a long look at it, then handed it to me wordlessly.

I held it gently. It was old—old enough to be from a time when pictures had a thin white border around the edge. The colors were no longer bright but dingy from time and touch. Two men were grinning, standing next to each other, clasping other's shoulders. They were much younger but unmistakable: I knew I was looking at Jack and Nelly.

Both wore the dress whites of the US Navy, and the hope shined so brightly out of them, it could have been used for military propaganda. *Join the Navy, see the world, make friends, have a great time.*

"You served together. I didn't know you were a veteran, Jack. I'm sorry."

"What're you sorry for? It was a long time ago, before you were born. Nothing more than a history lesson for you." He took the picture, laid it back in the frame, and replaced the backing. He set it down exactly in the place and angle it had been, a deliberate motion that spoke of repetition; he had pulled out the old photograph before. He came back to the desk and sat.

For a moment, he seemed older than I'd ever seen him as he lowered his stocky but spry body down to the chair. He pulled a hand over his hair, smoothing it back. "I didn't talk about it much. Folks knew, of course, but we didn't exactly find a warm welcome when we came home. And that was before things really even got ugly over there. I did my best to forget it.

"It was more than just serving together, Del. It was brotherhood. Salty— Nelly—and I," he amended, "we were close, close as brothers. Brothers-in-arms." Silence fell. The midday heat pressed against the windows, the rattling whine of cicadas filling the quiet space. Finally, Jack spoke again. "We lost touch when we got home. We had promised we wouldn't. I tried to keep that promise. I wrote to him a couple times, but there was no response. I don't know if he ever got the letters. I never saw or heard from him after the day we disembarked.

"Then, six months ago now, another guy in our unit called me to tell me that he died. I looked up the information for the funeral and found out he'd been right here all along." He looked down at his hands folded in his lap. "We'd been living in the same township for eight years. Never ran into each other, not once." He looked back up at me. "I can't help but think there's a reason for that."

"It's not a big town," I said by way of agreement. "He never came in here?"

"No. And not to toot my own horn, but I thought we'd seen just about everyone there is to see in this town at least once."

"Had you seen the two women in here before? His daughter and granddaughter?"

He looked off into the distance, rubbing his chin. "I think so," he said slowly, then shook his head. "We see so many people here. Hell, we've employed half the high school's graduates at one point or another. If Salty wasn't with those ladies, I'd have had no way to know them from Adam."

We were quiet a moment. From outside the office, we could hear the sounds of the kitchen: Wendy's giggle over something maybe Amy or Justine said, the chirp of the bell, the slap of the doors between the kitchen and the counter.

Jack stood abruptly, sending the top layer of the stacks of papers closest to him floating to the floor. "How can you be so calm about this? What the hell is going on, Del? Chrissakes, you've got me sitting here, talking about him like an old war buddy who isn't somehow back from the dead." He raked a hand over his hair again, holding it there as he closed his eyes. I watched as he took a deep breath, then began pacing around the office. "'Of all the gin joints in all the world,'" he muttered. "He's out of my life for, what, fifty-five years, then suddenly strolls into *my* diner after I wept at his goddamn funeral six months ago? *Now* he's back to haunt me?"

"Haunt you?" I asked, turning in my chair to follow his progress around the room.

"Huh?" He looked back at me. "Oh. I don't know. You know what I mean. Why is he here? *How* is he here?" he demanded. "You figure that out yet?"

"Starting to. A little," I admitted. "Would ya sit down already? You're making me antsy, walking around like that." He waved that off like he would a nagging fly, but he came back to the desk and dropped heavily back into his chair. "Okay. I'll tell you what I know—or think I know."

I walked him through it from the beginning. I held up a hand when Jack began to interject, and he subsided so I could continue.

"So, best as we can figure, he's here because A," I concluded, ticking off the possible reasons on my fingers, "there's some wrong he has to right in order to cross over, and B, he needs his own ashes to do that somehow. And at the end of it all, I'll have Nan's ashes, for real this time. I hope."

Jack stared at me, then shook his head again. "That's one seriously tall tale you got going on there, girl."

"Look, Jack, you can believe me or not. I'm telling you what we feel like might somehow be a possible scenario for all this to happen. I mean, the funeral home confirmed—very begrudgingly, I might add—that they did, in fact, mix up the ashes. And that's a whole other thing that isn't supposed to ever happen but did. So, really, the theme just continues." I shrugged. " 'There are more things in heaven and earth, Horatio.' "

"How long do you think he'll be here?" Jack asked softly, staring off again in another sudden change of mood.

"I don't know. He doesn't either. He says he doesn't think it will be long, but I don't know what that means. Maybe we don't have long to figure it out before it's impossible to fix, or maybe we're a lot closer to figuring it out than we know, or something else entirely. Who knows?" I was getting tired; I wanted time to process all the new information. "Listen, I'm going to head out, back to the bar. We're sort of using that as home base for this—what do you call it—*quest*, if you will. You're welcome to join." We both looked toward the door at the sound of Justine's voice coming through clearly as she shouted out the completion of my order for pickup. "But if you wouldn't mind keeping the details quiet, at least for now."

That finally pulled a smile from Jack, albeit a small and sad one. "As a church mouse, Del."

CHAPTER SEVENTEEN

I thought about Jack's story the whole way back. Something was missing, my mind kept insisting. Old war buddies who lost touch didn't have the hard, cold reunion Jack and Nelly had at the diner. Granted, I had stepped out for some of it, but I hadn't been gone long enough that I hadn't gotten the whole vibe of what was going on. There was something there, something deeper that neither had been at all forthcoming about.

When I got back to the bar, it was quiet. It could have been any other Monday. I paused—it was Monday, right? I had to check my phone.

It wasn't. Tuesday, July 10. Not that it mattered, exactly. I felt the cold, quiet whisper of depression circle me like a breeze, reminding me that one day was the same as the next, that none of that really mattered anymore. I didn't need to keep anyone's schedule but my own, and my days looked the same. Weekends and weekdays didn't matter—holidays, even. The whisper took on weight, settling on my shoulders as I thought that the holiday season wasn't so far off. I was going to be alone for Christmas. I went behind the bar and poured a double, knocking it back to dull the pain that gripped my heart.

Last year, I had almost convinced Nan that we didn't need to spend the holidays with family, an awkward situation on both sides of that particular tree. For mine, it was pretty simple: decline the offers made out of obligation and get through the stiff conversations the day of, my mother and sisters and I "meaning to" and then "forgetting" to send each other our addresses for presents we never even bought. It was all a fucking charade with them. Why should this year be any different?

For Nan, though, the holidays were still a special time. She still believed in magic; she was my optimist. She always thought that maybe, just maybe, this would be the year her family might be better. The year they'd be accepting of her, of me. They wouldn't be just polite but kind and warm.

It was always a disappointment. I hadn't heard from them since I'd told them there wasn't going to be a service at this time, and I would let them know when I was ready. Gloria had snapped at me that she was grieving her daughter and needed the closure, that her daughter needed to be returned to God so she could rest. I wasn't sure who she thought would rest, herself or Nan, but I had told her she was free to set up a service in her church and do whatever ceremony she needed. Nan had wanted to be cremated and have her ashes spread, so whatever Gloria needed to do to feel better that didn't include going against those wishes was fair game. I never heard if she did anything or not; if she had, I certainly was not invited, lesbian heathen that I was.

We hadn't been able to avoid going for Christmas, but I'd gotten her away from Boxing Day to New Year's. We'd both had to work New Year's

Eve and we were used to that; she'd make brunch in the morning and we'd toast to the old and the new then. That year, the time between shitty family and holiday double pay was magical.

We had rented a place in Vermont, up in the mountains. It was supposed to be a twelve-hour drive, but with the dark, unfamiliar roads and lack of any real highways, we ended up spending the first night in western Massachusetts at a motel. Our destination was a little outside of the ski-resort range; it was a small cabin heated entirely by wood stove, with a backup heating system "for the pipes," we were told. We bought our groceries on the way in, extra batteries for the portable radios, and sweatshirts made for tourists that read *I'd Tap That* over a silhouette of what I assumed was a maple tree.

Our Christmas presents to each other had been this time away, where cell phones were left in the car and one entire bag had been packed with books and games. We played cribbage and strip poker and never turned on the TV for more than music. We sank into the garden tub full of bubbles until we were overheated and pruny, stoked the fire and made love on every piece of furniture. The memory of her muscled arms and soft curves splayed out in the armchair as I knelt between her legs, her head thrown back and my hands on her thighs in the firelight, made me tingle and bring my hands to my own hips.

Byron cleared his throat and met my shocked gaze with one eyebrow cocked. "Am I interrupting?"

"Uh, no. Sorry. What's up?" I leaned on the bar and tried to stop my face from flushing. "Where is everyone?"

"Out and about. Johnathon went to the office for the afternoon. I think Cleo is meeting with one of our distributors. Mina and Nelly went for a drive, not sure where."

"And you're here at"—I checked my watch—"one in the afternoon. Why?"

He shrugged. "I was already here and knew you'd be coming back." We both looked down at the empty glass in my hands. "Coffee?"

I nodded and bit back the sigh. There wouldn't be anything but coffee in it. Byron poured from the full carafe into two thick mugs, added sugar to one, and slid it over. He came around the bar and took the stool next to me. We sat in silence a few minutes. He didn't move a muscle, and I wondered if he was feeling the tension between us. One could never tell with him.

"Been a rough week," he said.

"It's been two days," I replied.

"Yep."

I let out a short laugh, then sighed a little. I closed my eyes and lifted the hot mug to my forehead. "Byron, I'm sorry. I was an asshole. To everyone, but you and Nelly most. You didn't deserve that."

Now he nodded. "We're okay. Are you?"

"By, no, you—" He held up a hand and turned on his stool to look at me.

"I what? Need to realize that my best friend is having a shit time? Yeah, got that. You made an ass of yourself. Not the first time either. That's not on me. That's on you to figure your shit out. Have you called any of the numbers I've given you? Talked to anyone yet?"

I opened my mouth to retort and shut it again. I hadn't done anything with the list of grief counselors and groups he'd given me but tossed it somewhere in the living room.

He shook his head and looked back at his coffee. "You don't have to apologize to me. I thank you for recognizing you were an ass, but you don't have any amends to make with me. We're good. But goddamn, girl, you need more than whiskey to get you through. I wouldn't be saying that if I didn't love you."

I still couldn't speak. For him, that was nearly a soliloquy. I wasn't sure what I was more taken aback by his declaration of love or him calling me out for relying on whiskey.

He reached over and put one hand on my arm. His short fingers were callused from work and riding endless miles. His deep brown hand nearly matched the color of the bar, eclipsing my neon tan.

"Del . . . I don't think you know how much you've come to mean to me." Startled, I looked up at him, and his dark eyes widened an instant before he leaned back and laughed. "Whoa, relax. Ha." He rubbed a hand over his braids before dropping it back on the bar. "I can hear it now. Sorry. I'm not coming on to you, promise."

"Oh, Christ, By, you had me going for a second." Laughing now myself, maybe a little nervously, I put a hand to my chest.

"Whoops." He grinned, but it faded quickly. "What I mean is—there's no not-weird way to say this. I feel like we've gotten a lot closer since Nan died. And I wish she hadn't. Goddamn, do I wish Nan were still here. But—and—whatever—I'm grateful to be here with you and you trusting me enough in this quest."

This time, I held my hand out and waited for him to lace his fingers with mine. "I feel terrible because you're right, and I hadn't really noticed. I sort of started leaning on you because you've been right here, steady as a fucking rock."

"I'm going to be right here, Del. I'm not going anywhere. You're family now, as much as Cleo has been for almost twenty years."

"Family. There's that word again," I murmured. "It keeps coming up."

"We've been family a lot longer than this whole adventure," Byron said.

"No, I get that, but literally—the word. I feel like it's been a largely unspoken thing with us, with Mina and Cleo and J." I gave his hand a squeeze and let go, standing up. I went behind the bar and grabbed a couple bottles of water. "This *is* my family. I walked away from my blood years ago and found my chosen family. I've never looked back." I paused and took a deep drink of water to start to balance out the caffeine. "It was the best thing I could have ever done."

"Do you think that has something to do with this?" he asked.

"Maybe? Like I said, it seems to keep popping up."

"What do you know about his family?"

"Huh?" Byron's question threw me off track.

"Well, you're talking about your family. Nan was family, too, but we know that. What do we know about Nelly's family?"

I blew out a breath. "Not much? I mean, he's told me all about Annamaria, and we met his daughter and granddaughter at the diner, and that didn't go well. Um . . . I don't know. They were angry. Thought somebody was pretending to be Nelly, playing a trick on them. The younger one left, but the older one—Jackie, the daughter—had some words to say."

Before he could answer, the back door shut audibly. Nelly and Mina came in, Nelly taking my seat next to Byron and Mina joining me behind the bar. She bumped her hip against mine, and I grinned and let myself lean on her for a moment.

"How was your drive?" she asked me, putting an arm around my shoulders. "Settle you out?"

I looked up and met Byron's eyes and the hint of smile in them. "Something like that. More questions than answers, but yeah. It was good. Where did you guys go?"

"Home," Nelly said quietly. "I wanted to see the old place."

I felt Mina's fingers tighten on my shoulder, a wordless warning to tread lightly.

"How'd it look?" I asked, keeping my voice neutral.

He shrugged. "All right, you know? They took down a couple of chestnuts—had to be done, but still a shock to see stumps where there was shade once. There was a big fence, and I couldn't see if her garden was still there."

I turned and grabbed a couple more bottles of water, passing them to Nelly and Mina.

He turned the bottle slowly in his hands. "It looks good. It just . . . doesn't look like home anymore," he said. "The whole street looks different."

"Town put a cul-de-sac down in between a couple'a houses, got about eight or nine of those McMansions back there. Ugly as sin," Mina muttered, shaking her head.

"Well, now, that might be, but they're easy to sell. That's what Vicky said, at least."

Something clicked, and my focus sharpened. "Vicky—as in your granddaughter, Victoria? The one from the diner?"

Nelly nodded. "She works in real estate."

"With a firm, a realty company, or . . .?" I let the question hang, though I was impatient as hell.

Nelly scratched his chin. "You know, I'm not sure. I want to say with some folks downtown. Might recognize the name if I heard it." He shrugged. "Then again, might not."

"It wouldn't be Lawson, would it? Lawson Realty?" My spine was tingling.

Nelly sighed. "I'm sorry, Del, truly I am. I just don't recall. Why? Is that important?" He looked between the three of us.

Wordlessly, Byron slipped his phone out of his pocket, tapped a few times, then laid it faceup on the table in front of us. I saw the call going through and leaned forward. Johnathon answered, and Byron stepped in.

"Hey, man. Question for you. You got anyone there who goes by Vicky?" He looked up.

"Uh, why?" Johnathon asked.

"Might have a connection."

"Hold on. Let me go pull up that file." The line was quiet for a second, then Johnathon spoke again.

"Sorry, had to get into my office and shut the door. Yeah, Vicky Millar. She's a newer agent, been here. . . shit, a year or so."

Nelly's eyes sharpened. "Vicky, as in Victoria? She's young, roundabout twenty-five? She's a pretty girl, got brown hair and brown eyes, like her mother . . ." Nelly trailed off on the description. "On the quiet side?"

"Yep, that's her. Twenty-six years old last month, graduated University of Maryland, bachelor's in business administration with a certificate in marketing. Why are you asking? Does she tie into all of this?" he asked in a hushed tone.

"That's my girl," Nelly said proudly. "That's my granddaughter."

Johnathon let out a low whistle as the four of us at the bar grinned at each other. "Well, shit. How about that," he said. "The granddaughter of one of my first sales now works for me. That makes a nice little circle."

"What did you say?" Nelly asked, his tone sharp. "What do you mean, your first sales?"

"Johnathon, I think you'd better come by, if you can," I said quickly. "We're here at the bar, minus Cleo."

"I can slip away for a late lunch. I'll be there in a few minutes." With that, he hung up.

Nelly's face had settled into something akin to anger. If I'd learned anything about him these past days, it was that he wasn't one to jump to conclusions. "What's going on?" he demanded. "You're not telling me something." He pointed at me. "Del, what are you hiding?"

"Nothing. I mean—no, nothing. I just remembered something Johnathon said last night, and I think you should hear it from him. That's all. No secrets." I held up my hands, palms out. "Truly. And in the interest of that, I went and saw Jack Mason a little bit ago."

Nelly pushed back from the bar and stood so abruptly, I thought the barstool would topple over. "That was your drive? That's how you were going to clear your head? You made me think you were going back to your place, that you needed some time alone. You knew where you were going, and you didn't tell me. You were going straight to see Jack. How's that for no secrets?"

"Yes. I'm sorry. I wanted to go alone—I wasn't trying to be deceitful. And I did need some stuff from the house, and thinking space, and time alone. I need that sometimes, and that I won't apologize for." I could feel my temper rising. I desperately wanted another shot to settle it back down.

"You had no right to go to him."

Mina held up her hands for peace. "All right, step it back. Nelly, honey, come sit." He shook his head and continued to pace. "Suit yourself. Okay. Now, Del. Maybe you should've said where you were going, but you're telling us now, and it's not like you've had much chance before, seeing as we've been in the door all of ten minutes." I nodded. She moved her gaze to Nelly and raised her eyebrow. "And you—this is the first I've seen you mad, so I'm inclined to let you ride that wave." She held up a finger to me to silence any coming protest. "What's on your mind, Nelly?"

He kept pacing. "You think it's so easy, sitting here like you know what it was like. It's different now. It was different then. You have no idea. No idea how it was." His voice shook. "And then you just—just go and see him. At his diner. He got his diner," he said, now half to himself.

"Nelly, I do know. Jack told me." I paused a moment as his face drained. He stopped in his tracks and swayed in place. Byron was the first up and caught him, murmuring something to him as he led him over to the booth from yesterday.

No stool for the unsteady, I thought, remembering vaguely when he'd helped me in a similar situation. Nelly sat heavily and looked up at me.

I hurried over with another bottle of water for him and twisted the cap off. "I didn't mean to shock you. Shit, I'm sorry."

"What did he tell you? What did Jack say?" He grabbed the bottle, heedless of what spilled, and drank quickly without breaking eye contact.

I shrugged off the remnants of anger in his tone. "He told me you served together in the Navy. He showed me a picture of the two of you in uniform on the boat."

"Ship." The correction came in unison from both Byron and Nelly. Surprised, I looked from one to the other.

By said nothing, just fetched a towel from the bar and dropped it on the spilled water.

"Is that all he told you?" Nelly asked.

"Yeah. Um . . . said you guys lost touch after you came back, although you had promised each other you wouldn't. He called you guys brothers-in-arms."

Nelly laughed mirthlessly but seemed to relax and get his color back. Whatever he would have said then was delayed by Johnathon's arrival.

"I got here as quick as I could—oh, shit, Nelly, you okay?" He knelt in front of the man who had gone from spritely to angry to seeming his age for the first time, all in the span of minutes.

Nelly looked up, and something like regret moved across his face.

"You," he said quietly, looking directly at Johnathon. "It was you who sold my house."

Johnathon straightened and quickly pulled over the closest chair. "I did. You were one of my first clients around here. I didn't think you recognized me at first."

"You sold my house."

"Yes, I—"

"You never came. I asked you to. I asked you because it was important. You said you would, but you never came." His voice trembled slightly.

Johnathon was quiet a moment. His face was down, staring at the spot on the floor between his feet. No one else spoke. I had never heard silence in the bar like that before. I could make out the clink of newly frozen ice in the machine.

When he finally spoke, we all strained to hear.

"You're right." He cleared his throat and sat up straighter. "You're right, Nelly—Mr. Maltby—and I'm sorry. I should have come to see you."

After another brief silence, Nelly asked, his voice pained, "Did you even look?"

Johnathon nodded vigorously. "Yes, sir. I remember where you said to this day. In the red metal toolbox, under the tray. I looked. There was nothing—no toolbox, no envelopes, no pictures. I looked around the garage but I didn't find anything. I figured maybe someone in your family found it, and—"

"The entire point was for them not to find it!" Nelly snapped. "It's not enough that they sold my house out from under me, sent me to live in that damn home without my wife or my own coffeepot or my picture books or my movies, and then visited even less than they did when I was in my own home. Oh, and that's a fine kettle of fish." He pushed up from the table so that for a moment, he was looming over Johnathon. "I am going for a walk. I need to clear *my* head"—he glared at me—"and I can surely say I won't be ending up at that damn diner with goddamn Jack Mason!"

On that declaration, he stormed out the front door, leaving it banging in his wake. I began to move toward the door to follow him, catch him by the arm, something—when I was stopped by a hand on my arm instead.

Mina shook her head. "Let him go. He really hasn't reacted much, you know. He's taken a lot of this . . . quest alarmingly in stride. Let him walk off some of his mad."

I looked helplessly at the door.

"What's the story with him and Jack?" Johnathon asked.

I shrugged. "Other than what Jack said, I don't know. They served together, promised to stay in touch, and didn't."

"There's more there," Byron murmured.

I nodded. "I thought the same, but I don't know what that is. Not yet, at least." Once again, I looked toward the door.

Mina patted my shoulder. "He'll be all right. Why don't you distract yourself with getting ready for work? You're on the early shift tonight."

My mind still on Nelly, the dead man walking, I went upstairs to wash up for work.

CHAPTER EIGHTEEN

Nelly didn't come back until happy hour was in full swing. Tuesday was trivia night, so the place was hopping. I was three deep at the bar, mixing and pouring out drinks and shots. There were a bunch of folks who were trivia regulars, a couple newcomers I could see, and the usual week-night crowd. People had patterns, whether they realized it or not. The same drinks, same tables—or deliberately not. One kid—I ID'd him every week; he looked like a child to me, but he was just a baby-faced recent college graduate—was working his way through the menu. So far, he wasn't a fan of vodka or rum but really enjoyed the spritzer selections.

I liked to think about my clientele as characters in a book. I could match them up, intertwining backstories with some of my favorites. Spritzer guy was Zaphod Beeblebrox, on the hunt for the best drink in existence. Jane Eyre was quiet and reserved and had impeccable posture. She sat at a different table than Mr. Rochester, an assistant professor at the university. He was broody and seemed to have more of an aloofness than bars usually brought out in people, particularly as the hours wore on. I wanted to think that he looked over at Jane now and again when she made an excitedly louder response than usual, but I couldn't be sure.

Steinbeck had his hand in too. We had a guy who I thought of as Doc, an older gentleman who always wore a suit jacket and pressed jeans. He took up a table right in the middle, closest to the emcee. He liked his gin and tonic with a twist of lime and had a very kind smile that turned giddy halfway through his second round. I fancied him to be a marine biologist, whiling his retirement days away on the river. Mack was our resident frat boy, enjoying the summer before law school, loud as hell and boisterous but always polite. He haunted the bike shop next door, asking questions, wanting to learn about it. I wondered when he'd realize that he didn't actually want to be a lawyer.

And what literary collection would be complete without Shakespeare? We had our Romeo, of course, a dreamer and poet living off his parents' wealth, my sworn rival in anything related to literature. I paused for a second, wondering if that made me Juliet. I made a face and rolled my eyes as I filled another order and caught sight of Nelly coming toward the bar.

Roy was close to finishing his second beer. I made eye contact with him and tilted my head toward Nelly. He nodded and fished out his wallet, dropping the cash and slipping off the stool to block anyone else. He held a hand out, and Nelly, though surprised, shook it. Roy settled his cap on his head and wound his way out through the throng of millennials.

I saw Nelly watch him leave, his hand on the stool, before taking it and turning to me.

"What was that about?" he asked, pitching his voice above the din.

"Oh, Roy's been coming here for years. He figured out I was keeping an eye out for you and wanted to make sure you had a seat if you wanted one," I said, pulling two draughts of Fat Tire, the house favorite. "You okay?"

Nelly nodded. "Could do with a beer." "What d'ya like?"

"What you've got there is fine." I slid over the finished pint and pulled another. The crowd noise swelled, then quieted as the trivia emcee brought up the chalkboard and took the mic. I finished a handful of orders, wiped down the bar, and then leaned over.

"I've got a fifteen coming. I can take it now and we can step out," I told him.

He nodded, and I turned to catch Byron's attention. I flipped up the pass-through and led Nelly out the back.

The sun was still high, the day hot and hazy. "Jesus, Nelly, were you walking in this for two hours?"

"Not so much. I found the park a couple streets down." It was only a half mile away, another popular spot on the bike path. "I sat there a while, watched the world go by." We sat at the picnic table in the parking lot, facing out. I let my upper body fall between my knees, rolling left to right, working out some of the stiffness from tending bar. "If I did that, I'd stay a pretzel," Nelly commented.

I rolled back up and saw him grinning.

"Yeah, well. It helps," I said. I wasn't sure what to say or how to bring up the earlier developments.

He sighed and looked off into the distance. "Guessing you want to know what my little conniption fit was about."

I smiled a little at the term. "Might help me not piss you off again."

He huffed out a breath. "I don't like secrets. I'm tired of them. And we've been keeping them, you and I. It's a hard habit to break. I've had a lot of practice," he said, drawing out the words. He sighed again and pulled out the pack of cigarettes. I saw he only had a few left and made a mental note to pick some up. "I know you don't have long right now, and I'd rather not start telling you then stop and start my way through it. It's not an easy thing," he said, finally meeting my eyes.

"Fair enough. I'm on till eleven," I said. "Bar'll be busy enough then, I think, to want to get out. There's an IHOP not far from here."

Nelly smiled. "I know," he said. "And I could go for pancakes."

"Figured as much."

My shift went by quickly; it always did on trivia night. I hadn't worked it when Nan was alive, preferring to come in with her and play. Since then, though, I didn't know if I could sit and not keep myself busy. I still got to shout out answers from the bar, since the emcee had about a snowball's chance in hell of hearing me over the crowd. I cashed out my register as the crowd mostly dispersed, then leaned my head on Byron's shoulder a quick moment.

"Tired?" he asked.

"A bit. I'm about to take Nelly to IHOP."

"Ah, that's why you didn't want anything." Byron had offered me a margarita earlier when the color hadn't matched what the customer had wanted. I rarely turned down those kinds of gifts, but tonight I had. I'd kept my intake to a shot and a small glass of beer, splitting one of our new Pilsners from a local microbrewery into two flights and keeping the leftovers for me. Flights were one of biggest sellers and always ended up in the bartender's favor. You couldn't go wrong.

"Yeah." I stuffed my tips in my pocket and held out a hand for a fist bump.

He caught it instead, gave my bunched fist a little shake. "You good?" he asked, looking in my eyes.

It felt good to smile at him and mean it.

"Yeah. Yeah, I'm good right now. Are you?"

It felt even better to get that slow smile in return.

"Sure am. Go on, now."

With one more wave, I slipped out of the bar and back to the office, where Nelly had again dozed off in the chair, a magazine opened to custom wooden taps. I nudged his shoulder, and his eyes opened.

"Wasn't sleeping."

"I didn't say you were," I replied, holding out my hand to help him out of the old, decrepit chair.

"Needed to rest my eyes so they could handle the dancing ladies," he continued. I gave him a little snort.

"Sure, sure. Still up for pancakes?"

We pulled into the parking lot not ten minutes later, the streetlights brighter than the muted neon we'd come from. We settled in at a booth with plastic menus and bad coffee.

"Yes! They still have it!" I dropped the menu on the table with some extra flair. The waitress wasted no time.

"What'll it be for ya?" she asked, pen and pad at the ready.

"I'll take the cupcake pancakes, please, with extra icing and the syrup on the side," I said not at all excitedly. Like an adult, one who understood that dessert wasn't a meal substitute, and not the walking sugarplum fairy.

Nelly laughed. "I'll take the blueberry, please. And if I could get a side of those little sausages?" The waitress scribbled it all down and moved on. Nelly looked at me. "How many cavities have you had?" he asked suspiciously.

I grinned. "One ever. Fuck the dentist."

"You've got a hell of a sweet tooth, I'll give you that." His smile faded. "Guessing I can't avoid this any longer." I said nothing. "I didn't recognize your Johnathon. He looked familiar, but I couldn't place it. Figured it out this morning."

"He sold your house a bunch of years ago," I prompted. I remembered what Johnathon had told me but felt like I needed to hear the story in its entirety from Nelly. I felt a little twinge, like maybe I was being dishonest by not disclosing that, but he kept talking.

"It wasn't my call. I'd been in the hospital—I'd fallen down the damn stairs. I hadn't been able to get anyone's attention when I fell, and I must have fallen asleep or something. I don't know, a lot of that part is hazy." He waved that off. "But the rest of it . . . I had gotten my girl Jackie to go away and leave me be with him—Johnathon, I mean, this man I'd never met before, and who was selling my house without a care. I wasn't even allowed back in my own damn house, that I'd bought and paid off my goddamn self. My own house, and I couldn't go in. It had been a battle just to go see it one last time.

"I finally got Jackie to leave me be for a moment, and boy, did I seize that. I asked Johnathon to make sure he got something out of the house before anyone else did. There was a packet of envelopes that was very dear to me. Old letters, love notes, pictures. Promises. I'd kept it hidden, secret, for years. Decades. They were in the bottom of my toolbox, under some sandpaper. No one knew they existed, not even my Annamaria. It was all from before she came into my life. It was a different life, a different me. It's the one thing I kept from her—she never knew. The kids didn't know. And I didn't want anyone to know now either. So, I took a chance. I told this stranger where I'd kept it and asked if he could bring it to me. You used to be able to tell the measure of a man by the grip and the look in his eyes when he shook your hand. And his told me I could trust him to do this.

"I waited days, weeks, who knows. Time at Twelve Elms was endless. It went by in shifts. This nurse, that one, wash and change and wheel you down for a lukewarm meal. Every so often, they'd shave your face and trim your hair, have a bingo or casino night. You had to let go of reality to make it in there. We weren't demented, we'd just given up." His eyes were focused somewhere in the distance. "I don't know how long I waited, or when I gave up exactly. But he never came."

In the pause that followed, our pancakes arrived. It suddenly felt like too heavy a moment for cupcake pancakes at midnight in a brightly lit IHOP.

After a minute or so, Nelly broke from his reverie and noticed the pancakes. "So, that's that," he said, unrolling the silverware and cutting into the stack.

I followed his lead. "What happened to the letters?" I asked before I dug in.

He shook his head. "I don't know. I thought maybe one of the kids ended up with the toolbox, but I guess I gave up there, too. I assumed someone threw them away," he said, his voice tightening as if someone were squeezing to keep him from crying out.

"Who were they from?"

He was quiet a long moment. "Jack Mason."

CHAPTER NINETEEN

I knew it.

My heart jumped hard in my chest, pulse pounding. I knew there was more between him and Jack than just service buddies. Brothers-in-arms, I thought, had a whole different meaning in this light. I forked up more pancakes, knowing Nelly was watching for my reaction. The waitress stopped and refilled our coffee, asking how things were while I (of course) had my mouth full. I nodded, and Nelly smiled quickly and said they were just fine. She finished topping off our coffees and went to seat a couple who had clearly come from some much swankier date. Their formal suit and evening dress looked out of place in the harsh light, and I fleetingly wondered if it was prom, though they'd clearly had that last dance a couple decades ago.

"You don't seem surprised," Nelly finally said. He slowly started back in on his pancakes.

"Should I?" I asked. "You said it had been so secret."

"You should have some sort of reaction, at the very least," he retorted. He almost sounded angry. "Something to say about it. Love letters from a man."

Ah, I thought. There it was.

"Should I be surprised because it's Jack? Or because he's a man?" He sort of grumbled at that, one shoulder moving in a half shrug. "Nelly, I've known I was queer since I was fifteen years old and I saw Winona Ryder in *Girl, Interrupted.* Do you think I'm going to clutch my pearls finding out that you had a relationship with a man in the Navy?"

"Things were different then," he said, shifting uncomfortably.

"I'm not saying they weren't. But I know my queer history."

"I wish you'd stop saying that." He looked around again, gauging the distance between the other diners and us.

"Say what?" I asked, baffled.

"That word. *Queer,*" he mumbled.

"Okay," I said, not by way of agreement but trying to make the bridge. "You just told me yourself that your old flame was Jack Mason."

"Yes, but I married a woman. I had children, a family. It wasn't like that. *I* wasn't like that. It was a mistake," he said, his brow furrowing. Stubborn old man, I thought, watching him make quick work of his pancakes now, as if finishing the meal would end the conversation. "I'm not—I wasn't— like you."

"What do you mean, like me? Gay?"

"It was just different, okay? It was one thing in the Navy. It was an entirely different thing out of it. I left that behind. It wasn't like it is now. That was no kind of life for a man back on land."

"So, you were a sea queen," I said.

Nelly fumbled his fork, and it clattered against the plate. The over-dressed couple glanced over between giggles and murmurs. I wondered how much champagne—it had to be champagne, with that dress, unless they'd gone full Gatsby with gin rickeys—they had on board and hoped they weren't driving.

"How do you know that term," Nelly asked, his voice so low, it was nearly a hiss.

"I told you, I've read up on my queer history. It's what I do," I said with a cocky grin. " 'I drink and I know things.' "

"You learned about sea queens in a book," he said, doubt soaking his voice.

"Yeah. I've got it at—at the apartment. Somewhere. Can't remember the name off the top of my head. It'll come to me." I was slowing down on my sugar-coated dinner.

"Okay, smarty-pants. What do you think you know?"

I grinned again. "That a challenge?" His stony expression didn't change, and I sobered up. "All right. There is a significant history of gay men in the military, most visibly in the Navy. It was possible to be oneself at sea, amongst no one but other men. It was a safe place for a time. It happened outside of the Navy, as well, on merchant mariner vessels and more commonly on cruise ships. Relationships developed, sometimes with one man acting in a role similar to a wife or mistress, which doesn't say anything, but they didn't have the language we do now for roles in same-sex relationships. The term was also used, to a lesser degree, to refer to men who had those relationships at sea and nowhere else, similar to the 'lesbian until graduation' phrase you hear now.

"Over the years, laws changed, and it became illegal to be gay in the military at all, even legislated as a defense directive that became known as Don't Ask, Don't Tell under Clinton's first term in office. That was repealed in 2011, though the stigma lingers, even in the Navy. But the history is there. So, no, I'm not surprised that a man who joined the Navy in the— what, early sixties, assuming from your birth date—had a relationship with a fellow sailor."

I had no sooner finished my discourse, along with my pancakes, than the waitress dropped the check on the table and moved off without a word.

"It sounds to me," I continued, draining the last of truly terrible coffee left in my mug, "like this has not only been a secret, it's also something you carry a lot of shame about, which is interesting. When I mentioned that I had a wife, I know it got *my* back up, waiting for your reaction. You were fine. You've been completely unfazed at my relationship and all my friends—Cleo and Johnathon, Byron. You haven't met Angie yet, but between us all, we make up the whole damn rainbow, or so it seems."

"Different," he muttered again. "Things were different in 1963."

"I get that, Nelly, I do. And I'm not trying to negate or minimize any-thing you've experienced or felt about it at all, I hope you know that. I'm just trying to understand and figure out what's going on, here and now. Your history and your past have something to do with it, or I don't think you'd be here."

He nodded, then pushed his half-finished plate away and patted his pockets. "Need a smoke," he said, his voice gruff.

I went up to the register at the counter and paid, then came back to drop the cash for the tip on the table. The fancy couple were feeding each other eggs and toast. When we walked out, I saw a black sedan idling in the front row with a livery plate. So, they weren't driving. Good, I thought, as Nelly lit up and leaned against the tailgate.

"Here," I said, motioning him forward a bit. I dropped the creaky gate and boosted myself up to sit, legs dangling as I leaned forward with my elbows on my knees. Nelly stood, slightly hipshot, looking off in the distance and taking a drag. For a moment, the years faded away, and I could see him as Jack must have: young and vivacious, handsome with that quick laugh.

"There's nothing wrong with being gay, or queer, or whatever. It's a part of who you are."

"It's a part of who I was, maybe," he said. "But I haven't been since then."

"No? Were you still attracted to men?" I asked gently. For a while, there was nothing but the faint hum of the highway and the chorus of crickets to break the silence.

"Once I met my Annamaria," he said slowly, "there was nothing for anyone else. It was only her for me."

"Do you want to tell me about before her?" My legs were swinging back and forth, working off the sugar rush from my dessert dinner.

He was quiet again, another extended pause. He finished his cigarette, flicking the butt toward the grate in the dip in the parking lot.

"I put it out of my head. Daddy died while I was at sea, maybe six months before my tour was up. Mama had been wasting away since. I couldn't stand to watch. Her sister nursed her until she died. I took off, stuck a pin in the map, ended up in Santa Fe. I sold cars, if you can believe it.

"One evening, I got home to a bundle of letters, forwarded from Mama's sister. She had stayed in Ohio, at the house. In a crazy moment when I didn't give a damn about anything but Jack, I'd given him my address. We had promised to keep in touch, had sworn it to each other," he continued quietly. "I didn't hold up my end. That night, after I got the letters, I went back out and bought a bottle of whiskey. I took it back to my little apartment and stayed up all night, going back and forth between the whiskey, cigarettes, and letters. I didn't even read them. Not that night."

I could picture him: drunk, a half-burned cigarette in one hand, touching the letters and holding them, knowing this man he loved had written them just for him. I pictured him crying, whiskey tears leaking from his eyes.

"The next Friday, I went to the local bar, met a gal. We hit it off okay, danced some, talked some. I hadn't done that since high school. I told her what I did and told her if she was interested in buying a car, I'd make sure she got a good deal." Nelly pulled the last cigarette from the pack, cupped his hands, and lit it. Blowing the smoke out slowly, he continued, "I went home, determined to burn the letters. It was the only way I could move on from this—this madness that I had fallen into in the Navy. But I wasn't in the Navy anymore, and it was time to man up, settle down, start a family. Only instead of burning them, I read them." He went quiet again. I said nothing, letting the crickets fill the silence. "We had loved each other fiercely. It was more than a need, more than two hot-blooded American boys on a ship halfway across the world who needed somebody.

"Jack loved me. I loved him. I read those letters, the four of them, until I knew them by heart. His script was so neat, so crisp. He'd put a little spray of dried, pressed flowers in the last one. Tiny blue flowers. In the letter, he said they were called 'forget-me-nots.' And I didn't forget him, ever." A sigh trembled out with the smoke. "But I didn't write back either. I thought about it—about what I could say, what response I could possibly give. There was no way for us to be together, as he had dreamed about in his letters. The man was a poet when he wanted to be. Talked of moving west to the mountains, where a man could be himself, a Montana sky that was big enough for us to carve out a piece for the two of us. I knew it could never be, but oh, how I wished I could join him in that dream. I couldn't ignore the letters. I just didn't know what to say.

"Then, a few days after I met the girl at the bar, she came to the dealership with her sister. She was a firecracker of a girl—that was Annamaria. And I was sunk." He laughed now, a little wondrously, tears still on the edge of his voice. "She was all fire and flame, bless her. Told me I wasn't going to try to sell her sister a car from the back seat, not if she had anything to say about it." He shook his head. "She was a pistol. Dolores ended up dragging her out of there, but not before they took a test drive. A week later, Dolores came back to buy the car with her father. While he was kicking the tires, she told me the telephone number was on the paperwork and that I should call her sister, who couldn't stop talking about 'that salesman.'"The rest, as they say, is history. I courted Annamaria for about six months and asked her to marry me. I never told her about Jack. Whenever the topic of my service came up, I avoided it. One time, I even yelled at her for nagging me about it. I went out and got drunk, stumbled home. She cried. I almost broke down and told her, but she grabbed my hands and kissed me, apologizing for bringing up such painful memories that made me so upset. She promised she wouldn't ask any more about it, that it must be too hard to remember, and she wouldn't do that to me.

"I let her think that for the rest of her life—for our lives, together. I never told her anything about Jack, about some of our shipmates. 'The war,' 'my service,' anything about it became code in my head for Jack. We moved away from Santa Fe. She wanted to live between the mountains and the sea. We ended up here in Virginia. She liked the history of the place—it was the teacher in her. When we moved east, I left no forwarding address. If Jack wrote again, I never received it. I kept the letters, with the pictures and little flowers, tied up in a little bundle of bank envelopes and hid it. I kept it with my books when I went to night school for the insurance company that gave me a job, then the toolbox in the garage. It was my man space, as she called it—she didn't need any part of what went on in there. So, I kept it there, hidden.

"Then she died. Gone, just like that. It took a long time to accept that. At some point, long afterward, I took out the letters and reread them. I remembered every word. The flowers—most of them were still intact, if you can believe it. They were like the most delicate memory, ready to turn to dust. Holding them made me feel clumsy. I wondered where he was, what he was up to. If he'd found somebody, and who would that be? What would that be like for him? I wondered if he remembered me with any fondness or at all.

"One day, there was a story in the newspaper. A couple of out-of-town-ers had bought up that old restaurant—a pizza joint, I think. And there he was. Jack Mason. Older, much older than in my mind, God knows, but I recognized him even without the caption. I couldn't believe it." For the first time in his story, he looked over at me. "I felt like I got hit by a freight train. The memories crashed into me. It shook me to the depths of my soul. I couldn't believe it," he said again. "Here, right here, where I had settled with my Annamaria. Here was Jack, more than fifty years later." He stopped there, looking lost in thought.

"What did you do?" I asked softly.

His eyes still faraway, he answered, "I had to see him. I had to know if it was still—still there, you know? There I was, flabbergasted, and it was like something inside me opened up and was pouring out. I had to know if it was the same for him. I knew he'd married, from the article, but all I knew was what they'd printed in the paper. I ran upstairs to get dressed. I wasn't paying attention—moving too fast, you know. I missed a step on the way down."

"*That* was your fall? The one where you ended up selling the house and moving into the nursing home?"

What timing, I thought. There had to be something about that timing.

"Under duress," he said indignantly. "The kids wouldn't let me live alone anymore."

"They were worried about you," I said. "It must have scared them. Nobody found you right away."

"Pah." He waved that off. "Sure, it's hazy. I know I hit my head. My memory hasn't been quite the same since, at least about right after the fall. But I was fine," he insisted. "I could have stayed there. They wouldn't let me. Getting old sucks, Del, don't let anyone tell you different. You get treated different. Like a little kid, even by your own family. Especially by your family. Like you can't make your own decisions, like you don't know what you want, like you haven't lived your whole damn life doing what needed to be done. They see a moment of weakness, and they turn the tables on you. I might have been slower than I was, but there was nothing wrong with my mind, ever, I tell you that.

"Anyway, with all that—losing the house, the kids visiting less—I eventually made my peace with it. I figured the man upstairs didn't want me running into Jack Mason again. We had our time, and we were done with it. I had broken my promise to him, kept him a secret from my family. I've never been wildly religious, you know. I wasn't nearly as good a Protestant as Annamaria was a Catholic, but the way I saw it, that was the price we had to pay for the sins we'd committed together. I'd already figured it would be the one secret I'd take to my grave. There was no way to fix any of it, not the promise or the secret or the sin."

"What would you have said?"

"To Jack?"

I nodded.

He looked away again and sighed. "That I never stopped loving him. That I was sorry I broke my promise. I was sorry that I got scared and didn't make things right. That I hoped he'd found happiness like I had, even if it was different than what we'd once dreamed about together. It just wasn't in the stars for us."

He lifted his face toward the sparkling night sky. Even the bright lights of the IHOP parking lot and neon signs from the building couldn't dim that shine.

"We learned how to read the stars together," he said softly. "We had shore leave once, somewhere south—Panama, I think. We spent the night at the beach, away from the water, up in the dunes where we wouldn't get caught. The stars were falling that night. It was the July Phoenicid meteor shower. We came together that night as lovers—it wasn't the first time, but it was special, and it felt like it could never end. It was one of the most beautiful experiences of my life. In that moment, no other world existed than what we made between us. Too close for there to be room for anything else."

"Wait, wait—did you just say the Phoenicid meteor shower? Phoenicid, as in *phoenix*?" I asked, bolting upright.

Nelly looked slightly alarmed at being jolted from memory and back to the present. "Yes. It's named for a small constellation in the southern hemisphere."

"There's a phoenix *constellation*?" I was incredulous, my heart pounding. I jumped off the truck, pacing in the parking lot.

"Yes, I—oh my. Oh, well, now." The realization had hit Nelly too.

"We have to tell the others," I said.

He nodded. "Let's go."

CHAPTER TWENTY

We got back to the bar a few minutes before closing time. The front lot was empty but for two cars, Cleo's Jeep and another I didn't recognize, which wasn't unusual for a Tuesday night—Wednesday by now, but whatever. The university was in its summer semester, so plenty of folks from trivia likely had to be up and at class early enough to warrant skipping last call. I pulled in and took the spot next to Cleo. The other car, a blue Volkswagen sedan from earlier in the decade, sat on the other side of the Jeep. Empty, I noted as we hurried inside.

Byron was wiping the bar while Johnathon tapped on the screen for the cash register, closing us out. Cleo hummed to himself as he flipped chairs onto tables as easily and efficiently as righting hurdles on a track field. The music was off, and there was no occupant who might've belonged to the VW. I didn't see Mina, but I figured she'd be in the office, so I called to her.

"You want to join us? I think Nelly and I got something," I shouted.

Byron shushed me a little. "Got someone in the doghouse. She's up in three."

"Blue VW?"

He nodded.

"Gotcha." I paused a minute, shoving my hands in my pockets. "You, uh, wanna pour?"

Byron took a long look at me, apparently deemed me sound enough, and pulled the glasses up. Mina came out just as Johnathon finished on the register. He printed the last batch and handed her the envelope, which she walked back and tossed on her desk from the doorway before joining us at the bar. Cleo, still humming, strolled back. Johnathon raised an eyebrow at him as we all took a seat at the bar. Byron passed out the shots.

"Okay, so. I think Nelly and I might've figured something big out tonight. Something that ties all this together." Suddenly a little nervous, I looked at Nelly. He looked, if anything, a little pale under the blue lights. "You want to tell it, or should I?"

He shook his head and said, "No, you—" His voice broke a little, and he cleared his throat. "You go ahead," he said calmly.

"Okay. We know Johnathon was the one who sold Nelly's house. It was one of his first sales. Nelly wasn't really on board with the plan, but his kids railroaded him into it—the whole, 'You can't live by yourself, you just fell, it's too dangerous,' yadda-yadda bullshit. Nelly ended up at the nursing home, Johnathon sold the house. Okay.

"Before the sale, Nelly asked Johnathon—the one time they met—if he could grab something out of the garage without anyone noticing and bring it to him at the home. Johnathon agreed but couldn't find it, and so he never went to visit Nelly."

"I should have," Johnathon said, regret heavy in his voice. "I am sorry about that, Nelly."

Nelly reached over and patted his hand. "It might've been for the best," he said.

"There's more. A big, whole lot more." I threw back my whiskey. "Way before that, Nelly served in the Navy. Guess who with?" A pause for dramatic effect. No one spoke. "None other than our own Jack Mason."

There were some murmurs now, Mina mumbling something about never having known about it.

"But here's the kicker. They didn't just serve together." I stole a quick glance at Nelly, who nodded. I leaned over the bar, and everyone leaned in to hear more. "They were in love."

A collective gasp went up, and then Cleo, the sweetest heart of us all, made a soft little noise mostly reserved for kittens and ducklings.

"When their tour was up, they went their separate ways, promising to stay in touch, but they didn't. Nelly here moved away from his childhood home, ended up in Santa Fe. Well"—again, I paused, enjoying myself, the whiskey warming me—"just like *Titanic*, Jack didn't let go. It was the other way around. Jack had been writing to Nelly, and the mail finally caught up to him in Santa Fe. Days later, Nelly met and fell for Annamaria. They married and moved away, and the trail for Jack's letters to find Nelly went cold. The newlyweds moved here, settled down, had two-point-five kids and a picket fence. As for our esteemed Rose—Annamaria—Nelly never mentioned Jack to her or anyone else.

"Then Annamaria died. It took some years, but one day, he finally looked at the letters again. He had kept them secret and kept them safe this whole time." Byron lifted his glass at the nod to Tolkien. "Not long after he reread them, he opened the morning paper to find a story about these two folks from out west who showed up in town and bought the old pizza shack. Who else but Jack fucking Mason," I continued, hitting the bar with my hand for emphasis. "So then, Nelly literally went running to get ready to see his old friend, his secret lover. And what did he do but biff it and fall down the goddamn stairs.

"Hurt and dazed, that's how the kids found him, and that's where the pieces of the puzzle all fall together," I said, lining a couple empty shot glasses up like a setup for three-card monte. "Here's Nelly's story about Jack, ending with his fall"—I brought the front glass around to the back—"and here was his life in the nursing home, starting with the sale of the house, a result of that same fall."

"Holy shit," Mina murmured. "Well, that all lines up together perfectly, doesn't it?"

"There's still more!" I exclaimed, barely able to contain my excitement. Everyone leaned in: Byron and Johnathon curious, Mina a bit skeptical, and Cleo dreamy. Nelly remained silent and still. "It turns out, one of the pivotal and most romantic nights of their relationship happened during a meteor shower. Specifically, during the July Phoenicids. A quick Google search on the way over says this meteor shower happens twice a year and is best seen from the South but can be seen as far north as—you guessed it—Virginia, and it comes from a constellation known as the motherfuckin' *phoenix*." I slapped a hand on the bar to punctuate that revelation.

Silence.

I waited impatiently for some response. Byron got there first. "Phoenix. Queer love." He ticked them off his fingers. "Missed opportunities. Family connections. Birth and death dates. Holy shit," he said, shaking his head in amazement.

Johnathon piped up, "And for those of us who don't think in bullet points?"

Cleo laughed and patted his husband's hand. "I think I got it." He got up and went around the back of the bar, gathering our empty shot glasses toward him with one hand. He placed two on the bar about six inches apart. "Here's Nelly and Del, both married to amazing women"—he added two more directly next to each glass, almost touching—"that they love deeply, who die unexpectedly." He flipped the glasses over and pushed each pair together, a perfect fit. "Then Nelly dies on the same day as Nan." Now he laid a straw over the glasses that represented Nan and Nelly. "They end up cremated at the same place, and the ashes get mixed up."

"Switched at death, as opposed to birth," Mina added.

"Exactly. Okay. So, the ashes are all tucked away until Del's clumsy ass—"

"Hey!" I protested. "I was drunk, not clumsy, thank you very much."

Even as I spoke, I looked around for the whiskey bottle for refill.

"Okay, fine, until Del's drunk ass knocks the ashes out. Now they're exposed, and maybe it's that exposure that awakens the phoenix"—he pulled a saltshaker over—"which gives way to Nelly. Del takes Nelly to the diner, where they run into Jack Mason"—another shot glass, standing alone, and straws connecting to each of ours—"and they have a capital *P* past. Then they come to the bar, where Nelly and Johnathon reconnect unknowingly." Another glass and straw, this time from me to a new one for Johnathon. "And as it turns out, Nelly's granddaughter is J's employee." Now a straw from Johnathon and one from Nelly to a new glass for Vicky.

"And what about everyone else?" Johnathon asked.

Cleo shrugged. "I don't know. This is how it all connects in my head."

"It wasn't quite what I was thinking, but close enough," Byron said.

Cleo grinned and leaned in for a high five. "I got you, man!"

I was only half listening to all this going on. Something about the way the straws and glasses were lined up reminded me of something—something on the tip of my tongue.

I pushed off my stool, and suddenly, it came into focus.

"It looks like a constellation."

Everyone looked at me. Nelly, largely silent until this point, looked back at the diagram, then back at me, wide-eyed. "You're right."

"Do you remember the constellation? What the phoenix looks like?" I demanded.

"No, I mean, it's been a long time since I've had to use that—"

"Never mind," I said, pulling out my phone. Quickly searching, I pulled up a star map of the phoenix. I looked back at Cleo's straws and glasses. Laying my phone on the bar, I adjusted some of the pieces: the angles, shuffling this glass closer, this glass farther. I added a couple glasses around and inside and pulled out some coffee stirrers. I laid them in between the leftover glasses. "Fuck me sideways," I breathed. "This is it. Look." I put the saltshaker away. On the bar now was a close-to-perfect, line-for-line version of the star map on my phone screen.

"Where's my notebook?" Without waiting for an answer, I glanced under the bar and saw it. I pulled it out, grabbed a couple pens from the register, and started to sketch it out.

"Here . . . Nelly, Jack, me. Johnathon, Vicky. This is Nan, one of the stars in the middle. And Annamaria out here."

"What's that one between Del and Jack?" Cleo asked.

"Maybe the diner?" I looked up, saw a nod from Byron, and labeled it.

"There's another star in the middle there, not attached to anything," Mina commented.

"I'm not sure about that," I admitted. "Or these out here. It looks like there's a total of thirteen stars," I said, checking my phone.

"This is amazing," Nelly said, scrutinizing the tableau in front of us.

"Not to put a damper on all of this"—Johnathon gestured—"which is cool as hell, but it doesn't explain how or why it happened, or how to fix it."

"Well, yesterday—Jesus, was it only yesterday? Byron, you said something about a quest as a way to right a wrong that had been done."

He nodded in agreement.

Nelly stood, straightening up. "I need to make things right with Jack," he announced.

"Well, that's not happening till at least daylight," Mina announced. "We've got all this mapped out. I think it's time to sleep on it."

With all in agreement, we disbanded, leaving the setup on the bar as it stood. I stared at it for a couple minutes, then I pulled Byron aside.

"You look absolutely beat. You want to take my truck or crash here or something? I don't know if you should ride home."

He smiled and covered the hand I'd laid on his arm with his own. "Yeah, not a bad idea. I'll take seven," he called out.

"You know where the keys are," Mina replied from halfway up the stairs to her own rooms.

"You know, that office chair might be ugly as homemade sin, but it's comfy," Nelly said.

"Are you sure? There's another couple rooms upstairs. You don't need to sleep in a recliner," I told him.

He waved it off. "All set, but thanks, Del. G'night, all." He disappeared into the office. I heard Cleo and Johnathon call out their goodbyes as they left out the back.

"Go on," I told By. "I'll lock up."

He nodded. "Appreciate that. Good night, Delilah."

His use of my full name made me smile.

"Good night, Byron." I waited until he was upstairs before taking the last lap around the bar, locking the front door on my way. Something caught my eye, and I moved over to one of the small booths.

A black purse lay on one of the benches, where it had been mostly obscured by the shadows. Not an uncommon occurrence. I brought it to the bar for safekeeping, opening it to check the ID before I tucked it away.

My heart thumped. The hairs on the back of my neck tingled as I recognized the picture on the driver's license.

The teary blond from the funeral home smiled out at me from the window of her Kate Spade wallet.

CHAPTER TWENTY-ONE

I awoke to the pounding of a fist on my door and nearly fell out of bed, all tied up as I was in the blankets. I managed a groggy, "Ya," as I disentangled myself. I looked at the clock and realized I'd never set an alarm. The room was light enough that I knew it was at least after seven. Fuck it. Four hours of sleep was enough, right?

Cleo opened the door enough to poke his head in. "Oh, sorry, did I wake you?" he asked, all innocence and none of it feigned.

I rubbed my hands over my face. "What's up?" I stood, comfortable enough around him to not care I was down to a T-shirt and underwear.

He didn't blink, and his eyes didn't stray. "Oh, nothing. I got your text last night, and I wanted to let you know the blond is up. Figured she'll be on her way out pretty soon. I've got her sitting down at the bar with some of Momma's fix—should hold her long enough for you to put this in your face." From behind the door, he pulled out a thick, steaming mug.

"Bless you," I said, every cell of my body grateful. I took it from him and got a couple swallows in before he even closed the door. "Be right down," I called out anyway.

By the time I'd shimmied into clean jeans, brushed my teeth, and pulled my hair back, the mug was empty. Perfect excuse—or, you know, reason—to be back behind the bar at seven thirty in the freakin' morning. I pulled on my ball cap with the bar logo from the night before, deemed myself passable enough, and headed downstairs.

As promised, the young woman was sitting at the edge of the bar. Well, she wasn't so much sitting as collapsed.

Looking at her license last night had told me Alaina Sue Parsons was twenty-four years old, five-foot-four, hair blond, eyes brown. She was wearing the same pencil skirt from the day before, blouse rumpled and untucked, ugly jacket among the missing. There was a nearly empty glass of Mina's fix by her hand, and her head was dropped into her folded arms. I quietly stepped behind the bar and made up round two of morning coffee, grateful for my clear head and for Cleo alerting me about Alaina. I added two shots of whiskey—measured, this time.

"Rough night?" I asked, the way people do whenever they see someone hungover. It gave the poor soul an opening to explain that no, no, of course not, everything was fine.

Leaning on the bar in front of her, I got the full view of her misery when she lifted her head. Her skin had the pallor of the recently drunk, embarrassment riding high in her cheeks. Her eyes were swollen, the makeup cried off again. Smears of mascara winged away from her eyes.

"You could say that," she said. She looked puzzled, as if she recognized me but wasn't sure why. Misery won over embarrassment, overriding the hazy memory of our connection. "My boyfriend got fired yesterday, then told me I was going to have to quit because he wanted to 'sue the bastards.' I need the job," she said imploringly to the glass in her hands. "And I told him I didn't want to quit. Which is a lie, but I don't want to quit because he says so, you know?"

"That's some bullshit," I agreed.

"So, we got into this big fight when I got home because I didn't walk out when he told me to. He was so angry. He punched a hole in the wall, and I ran. I ran out. He's never hit me before—not, like, on purpose, I mean—but he scared me. I got in my car and I left."

"Smart. And you ended up here?"

"I guess so." She turned the glass around in circles, the last couple sips lapping gently against the sides.

"What did you say your boyfriend got fired for?" I asked as nonchalantly as possible.

The glass stopped moving on the bar. Her eyes angled upward to meet mine. "I didn't," she said slowly. I could almost see the last piece falling into place for her. "It was you at Random, wasn't it? You're the one who came back because you took the wrong ashes home," she said much more accusingly than I was expecting her to be.

"Given someone else's family member's ashes in the urn I brought specifically for my wife's ashes, you mean." I was immediately incensed and giving no quarter. "I didn't *take* shit-all, it was *your* place that fucked up. I didn't spend a ridiculous amount of money at your establishment to be taken for a fucking ride. You know, I bet there's regulatory boards you folks have to answer to, isn't there? I'm sure I could give one of them a call, let them know exactly what's going on."

She shrugged. "Go ahead, get them in trouble. If they shut down, I don't have to work there anymore. I might not want to quit because of what my stupid boyfriend says, but I wouldn't care if I never had to walk in there again."

"Why? Is life so hard sitting behind that desk?" I rode the wave of anger that continued to grow inside me, pent-up energy I hadn't screamed at the stars with in a while. I could feel the familiar restlessness in my shoulders, the itch to fight, to swing out at anything in my path. Right now, Alaina was it.

The look she gave me was cutting and drenched in disgust. "Do you have any idea what it's like to be surrounded by death like that every day?"

"Considering my wife is one of those 'surrounding' deaths, yeah, I think I've got a pretty fucking good idea."

She paused as it caught up with her. Her cheeks flamed bright with shame.

"There you go," I muttered, rolling my eyes. "Now she gets it." I took another long sip of coffee. "So, what did the asshole get fired for?"

"He's not an asshole," she snapped, then sighed. "Fuck. Yeah. Yeah, he is." She paused, then nodded to my cup. "Could I get some of that?"

I narrowed my eyes at her. She didn't seem so fragile and lost as she did when I first saw her, either yesterday or this morning. It was harder to stay mad at someone who clearly needed caffeine as much as I did. Either way, I wasn't about to begrudge anybody coffee, and I still had questions for her. "How do you take it?"

"Little sugar, lot of milk. I'm Alaina," she added.

"I know," I said, fixing her coffee. "You left your purse in the booth over there. Found your license, so I knew whose it was." I handed her the mug, and she took a long enough drink to erase the annoyance from her face. "You and my wife have the same middle name."

"Ha, that's cool. Ugh, this is good. Thank you. Thank you," she said again, softer. She raised the mug in a half toast. "Sorry I was bitchy. I'm still pissed, and now I'm hungover."

The thanks and acknowledgment helped to clear the last clouds of rage for me. "I get that. I'm Del," I offered. I waited a minute, letting her boot up a little more. "So."

"So," she replied. "He is an asshole. You're right. I should have paid more attention to the signs. Well, I'm paying attention now." She gestured skyward with her coffee cup. "I just need to get him out. That'll go well," she muttered to herself, then sighed again. "If I'm honest—mostly with myself—he's been putting up some serious red flags. I'm not sure how I let him convince me to ask him to move in, but it's been downhill all the way. I guess he's hard to say no to."

"How did he get fired?" I might have been accustomed to letting people go on about their issues—bartenders are part therapist, after all—but I still wasn't in the mood for story time.

"Teasdale found out he'd been careless with the paperwork. He drove the van for the morgue and hospital pickups. I guess there were parts of it he didn't fill out, or didn't fill out well? I'm not entirely sure. Derek said they were blaming him for not doing someone else's job and that they've have been out to get him, looking for a way to get rid of him. And since he's the one who got me the job there, I'd have to quit, and he'd get a lawyer and sue them."

"And you didn't take too kindly to that," I surmised, topping off our cups.

"Thanks. No, I didn't. I quit my other job, a really good job, because he wanted me to. But I really need *a* job to pay the rent until he can find a new one. I told him that, and he didn't like that. He grabbed me by the jacket and pushed me against the wall. He yelled at me and demanded that I quit. I said no, and he punched the wall next to my head. He punched it hard enough to leave a dent, I think. I didn't really look. The second he let me go, I ran out," she finished, looking off into the distance.

"Fuck that," I said. I felt the anger growing again, but not from the same place. This was different. I realized how wrong I'd been. She wasn't fragile. She was smart and scared and in a bad situation. The guilt churned in my gut a moment. At least I hadn't let my mouth get away from me. Now the need to help was stronger than the anger. "Fuck men."

"Yeah, well. Now I've got to figure out how to get him out." She looked down at her coffee. "Not sure how I'm going to do that." Out of the corner of my eye, I saw Cleo coming out of the office with Nelly. I poured two more coffees and laid them on the bar as they approached. "Actually . . . I might have an idea about that."

By ten, we had a plan, and we were on our way to Alaina's place. I rode with her, with the toolbox from the bar and a bag from the hardware store in the back seat. Cleo and Mina followed separately, Cleo in my truck. We had decided it was better if Nelly didn't go, in the event that someone other than us called the cops; we didn't want to have to explain a statement from a guy who'd died six months ago who was clearly alive, with a defunct social security number and no identification. He'd been dismayed, understandably; the guy loved an adventure. Cleo had dropped him off at my place while Alaina and I hit the hardware store, so he could at least have a change of scenery.

It turned out that she only lived a couple streets down from me. In the time in the car, she proved to be both talkative and witty. She was from way up north in Michigan. She had just finished her bachelor's in sociology at the university and was trying to figure out where to go from there. She'd met her boyfriend, Derek, at the Wawa. I ignored the twist of jealousy and instead commented that was a funny place to find someone, to which she sighed.

"It was like a movie," she said. "I was going up to the register and he turned, bumped into me, and spilled his drink down my shirt. And he was so cute and embarrassed and flustered, trying to clean it up without touching my boobs. He bought my snacks, and we started talking. It was the closest thing to romance I'd ever had," she admitted.

"Then you're dating the wrong people. Look, I'm not trying to be a Debbie Downer, but you said it was like a movie. And meeting like that sort of sounds scripted to me."

She looked over at me, then back at the road. I could see her working through that and watched her hands tighten on the wheel, her eyes hardening.

"You know something? You're right. He's never been charming like that since."

"Let me guess," I said. "He had some sort of story about where he was living that wasn't working and was super hesitant but somehow also persistent about wanting to live with you. Helped you get the job—maybe you didn't want to work at a funeral home, and he got butthurt about you not wanting it, so you took it."

She was nodding. "I had a job. I was a receptionist at a law firm in town. The hours were good, the pay was whatever, and there weren't any dead bodies around me."

"Just soulless ones," I quipped, and she smiled.

"Nah, the attorneys were nice. It was a good firm. There's not a lot you can do with a BS in sociology, I don't think."

"Why don't you go back?" One of the questions I hated the most popped out before I could think about it.

She shook her head. "To the firm? I doubt they'd take me. I mean, I left on okay terms. They were a little confused, since I'd only been there a few weeks."

I leaned back in my seat. There wasn't enough room in the little VW to cross my legs, I discovered when I tried.

"Here we are. His car's not here," she said, a little puzzled, but I could hear the relief in her voice. "I don't know where he is."

She pulled into the driveway of a side-by-side duplex, similar to mine. The lawn was short, and the neighbor's trash cans were at the edge of the street, to the right of a small tree the township had planted a few years ago in their "regrow, re-green, regain" initiative, trying to keep owner-occupied home rates up next to a college town.

"Works for me," I said as I climbed out. I pulled the seat forward to grab the toolbox and the bag. She was unlocking her front door as Mina pulled up in her hybrid, then Cleo in my truck.

The interior was a mishmash of very different personalities. The sofa was a bright teal with gold-and-royal-blue throw pillows; multicolored textile art livened up the white walls and beige carpet. The colors were overlaid with an interspersed blanket of black clothes—mostly T-shirts and some jeans—and more than a handful of empty, half-crushed beer cans.

Alaina muttered to herself, kicking some of the cans out of the way as she made her way inside. "I'm so sorry, it's not usually like this. Ever," she said, clearly disgusted.

"Don't worry. I can tell," I replied. The place read clearly as a young woman's space invaded by a man, rather than a couple who lived together in any sort of actual coexistence. "Hey," I said, drawing her attention back. Her eyes were brimming with tears again. "Let's get to it, okay?"

Mina came in, juggling boxes. She dropped them on the floor in the kitchen, the most sparsely furnished room. "Don't worry, honey, we'll make sure that roach knows he's not welcome here." She tucked her hand into Alaina's arm and grabbed a box. "Why don't we start back here?" she said gently, guiding her to the back of the house. I could barely make out her murmuring to the young woman, then suddenly, "Del, you go on and get started now, okay? Maybe we can be done before the little turd even shows up."

Grinning to myself, I went back to the front and started working on changing the doorknob.

An hour and a half later, after some interesting developments that put me behind, I had finished the knob and dead bolts out front and was tightening the last screw in the back door replacement. Cleo was telling me some story he'd gotten from his distributor yesterday about a flock of turkeys attacking the truck when we heard the front door open. We'd left it open, as there had already been a couple trips back to the cars.

"Alaina! What the fuck!" We heard the crunch of cans as an angry man's voice—Derek, I assumed—came toward us. Before Cleo could move into his line of sight, we saw Alaina stand square in the door, facing him. Good for her.

"Derek, you can leave. You're not welcome here anymore."

"Babe? What the fuck is this? Those bastards are lying! Whatever you heard, it's a fucking lie," he yelled. The words weren't quite slurred yet, but they were off. More than booze on board, I realized. I looked at Cleo and tapped the inside of my arm. *Drugs*, the signal told him.

"After your behavior yesterday, and what I'm finding *now*? You god-damn pig, you liar, you—you *asshole*. Get out. Just get out. I'm packing your shit, and you can pick it up on the curb."

I could hear Mina's coaching in her words and had to smile. Momma Mina wasn't about to let this girl take anyone's shit.

"Now listen—" The threat in those two words had Cleo at the door in a flash. I slid around him to watch the show, vaguely thinking about popcorn.

Derek was shorter than Cleo by at least a foot and had the physique of a high school football player who'd discovered beer when graduation came, and the glory days were gone. Not a fist you'd want coming at you, I mused, glad Alaina had gotten out in time. The wall hadn't just been dented; the drywall had cracked behind it. We'd had to knock the piece out and patch the hole.

"You don't want to be here, man," Cleo said. His normally gentle tone had a steely edge to it we rarely heard. I had to bite back a grin, thinking he'd gotten that— besides everything else—from Mina.

Derek sneered. "Hire a bodyguard, Alaina?"

"My friends are helping me out. Well, actually, they're helping *you* out. Get out. We're done."

"Not by a long shot," the asshole said, taking a step forward. Cleo matched it, and Derek stopped. "Call off your fucking dog and let me in the bedroom. I won't fucking touch you. I'm just going to get my things."

"Your things? The bag full of pills and cash, you mean? All those pre-scription bottles, the little baggies? Those things? Yeah, I don't think so. The police will be coming to collect it, and I'm sure they'll have a few questions for you."

Derek recoiled. He looked at Cleo, then away, his panicked eyes unable to land anywhere, then whirled back to Alaina.

"Stupid bitch! Fucking whore! This isn't over," he yelled, his eyes getting wild as he moved quickly to the front door. "I'm not fucking done with you," he shouted and took off.

I put a hand on Cleo's arm and could feel the anger vibrating through him.

"Not worth chasing," I warned him. "Plus—" The *whoop-whoop* of a siren sounded. "Angie's got him," I said, grinning.

"Attagirl, Angie!" Mina called. "Can we go now? Since the cops are going to get everything anyway. Alaina, hon, grab what you need, come stay at the bar a couple days, then we'll come over and help you put all this to rights."

Alaina, standing poker straight and a little paler than before, finally smiled.

CHAPTER TWENTY-TWO

Angie came to the bar that night.

It was around nine when I saw her making her way up. She was poured into her off-duty clothes, turning enough heads that watched her walk away to warrant keeping an eye out. I was pulling drafts for a table of cyclists who were on their way through. I didn't care what anyone said about light beers and performance; they looked like pints of piss. I'd pull and pass them, but I'd be damned if I was going to try one for myself.

"Nice crowd tonight," Angie yelled over the din.

"Tour de France," I called back, "Stage 5. Coverage goes till ten. It'll be like this another couple weeks."

"I guess that's what you get for being a biker bar," she said, sliding up between two stools.

"Works for me," I replied. She was right; we always saw an influx of people for the Tour and the Olympics. We would show other races—tennis, swimming, gymnastics—but we didn't show football or baseball games. It made for more engaged and far less rowdy crowds, which was nice, especially in a college town. I definitely did not miss bartending the local watering hole by the university, even though it was where I'd met Nan. Nostalgia? Sure. Regrets about leaving? Absolutely not. "What can I get you?"

"Mmm, gimme one of your mojitos, girl. It's story time."

"On it, but story time will have to wait. Hang tight, I've got a break coming." She waved a hand. Once I slid her mojito over, she gave me a little salute and slipped back into the crowd. She'd have no problem finding someone to flirt with for a few, I thought to myself with a chuckle. Not in those jeans.

I found her twenty minutes later, tolerating conversation with a stocky, blond dude with a military haircut. I didn't recognize him, but I could read the boredom on Angie's face.

I leaned down and put my arm around her shoulders. "Hey, man, thanks for keeping my girl company till I could get here." I enjoyed the stunned look from me, to Angie, and back to me before he mumbled something and made his undignified escape.

Angie sighed. "You have such a way with people," she said, then giggled. "I love when you dispatch pesky men. Not that he was so bad—just a guy, but boring." She rolled her eyes.

"How's that mojito treating you?" I asked, grinning.

"Just fine. All right, strap in for this one. And believe me, this is completely off the record," she reminded me with a dramatic sweep of her arm. I, in turn, traced an *X* over my heart and listened.

By eleven, the bar emptied out almost completely. Three booths were still occupied by small groups and couples and there were one or two left flying solo, just a bit below typical for a Wednesday in July. It was a low-enough patronage that we could huddle up, so we did. Byron was off, but Nelly, Cleo, Johnathon, Mina, and Alaina gathered at one end of the bar with Angie. I felt weird that Byron was missing this, but Angie started.

"Oh, you guys aren't gonna believe this. The stones on this fuckin' guy. Sorry, sweetie, I know he was your boyfriend."

"*Was*," Alaina confirmed, emphasizing the past tense. "I feel stupid for letting it go this long."

Mina might have taken the girl under her wing, but she still wasn't one to attend a pity party. She rolled her eyes at her and said, "Girl, you kept that douchebag around just over a month. It's not like you're wearing his ring."

Alaina, a little chagrined, gave her a half smile.

Angie nodded emphatically. "Good thing it wasn't longer. Thank you, by the way, for your cooperation with the investigation."

"Of course." Alaina shrugged. "I'm not letting him fuck up my life any more than he already has."

At this, Mina gave her an approving nod. "Attagirl."

"All right, all right, y'all. Well, that's it for me. I'm back on tomorrow, and 7:00 a.m. comes way too goddamn early."

"Aw, come on, Ange, you're leaving? Now?" Cleo whined good-naturedly, earning a shoulder bump from his husband. He grinned in response and kissed his cheek.

Angie held out her hands. "I'm confident that you'll have all the information you need and none of the gossip with it." She winked at me. "Y'all take care now. Let me know if there's any more fun to be had." She sauntered away.

"Sure, drink's on the house, that's fine," I called after her, and was rewarded by a one-fingered salute without further acknowledgment.

"Okay, so, you didn't hear this from me, and I didn't hear this from anyone." Nods all around. "This isn't Derek's first run-in with the law."

"Shock and awe," Mina muttered.

"Well, I—" I door opened, and a collective groan went up from the group at the new interruption. Byron paused, helmet unclipped, bike in hand.

"I texted him," Johnathon said. The relief must have been evident on my face because he smiled at me. "Just leave it in the booth," he called to Byron. "Get over here."

By shook his head, and I could practically see the group's impatience grow as he took the additional forty-five seconds to efficiently store his bike and helmet and join us at the bar.

"Did I miss anything?" he asked before slipping around to grab a bottle of water. He handed me one without a word, just a gentle smile. I smiled back and took it.

"Not yet. Del's getting to it," Cleo said. "So shut up and let her talk."

"He's been picked up for possession before, but nothing's really stuck. Loitering, too, which netted him some community service, for all the good it did, and that's just what they could get him for instead of actual, factual charges. Anyway." I paused to take a drink. "Once he realized that he was well and truly fucked, charged with possession with intent, he sang like a fuckin' bird. He completely ignored the public defender assigned to him and gave up everything—names, dates and times, all the juicy details. Cops have already picked up his accomplice."

Cleo raised a finger. "Can you back up a second? I'm a little lost. What's he been in trouble for?"

Mina reached over and ruffled his hair. "You're such a good boy," she said to everyone's laughter.

"He's been picked up on drug charges before. Having drugs—possession. Having a *lot* of drugs, like the way he did, with packaging and scales and shit? Possession with the intent to distribute. He was a drug dealer. Or, really, a wannabe." I grinned when Alaina snorted.

Cleo nodded. "Cool, cool."

"Basically, he and this guy up at the hospital had a deal. Hospital guy would make sure he was the one to prep the bodies for transport when the morgue was done, which included him in the custody chain of the personal effects. He thought he was being smart not touching any cash or wallets or jewelry and just focusing on the medications. He was also boning on company time with one of the nurses and snuck her key card when he could so he could get stuff from the pharmacy. That's a much more recent thing, too, and is likely where most of the shit in the duffel bag came from. My 'unnamed source' said they didn't have a genius plan for that yet.

"He'd smuggle out the meds with the bodies, which Derek was responsible for picking up. He would futz with the paperwork and made it look like accidental, crossed-out mistakes in the documentation, instead of actually being altered."

"So . . . what you're saying is I'm here because of red tape?" Nelly said.

"I would say that fraud, drug dealing, and stealing from the dead is a lot more than red tape. Alaina, why did he say he was fired?"

"He said they were accusing him of doing something with the paperwork. That they made it up because they had it out for him."

"No one had it out for him. He was just a criminal." I shrugged.

"Well, I'm so sorry that led to trouble to your families," Alaina said, looking at me and Nelly.

"Well, not so much of a problem for my family, as it turns out," Nelly said. "Just for me and Del here."

The young woman looked blank. "I'm sorry, I don't understand."

"Oh, see, I'm a phoenix," he stated matter-of-factly.

Alaina stared at him, then at me.

I shrugged again. "I mean . . . he's not wrong?" I smiled hopefully, as if this were a totally normal thing to hear. That didn't do anything to stop the staring as if I had three heads. I cleared my throat. "All right, this is really the unbelievable part. I knocked over Nan's ashes, and when the light from outside hit them—in the middle of the night, so you know, moon and star-light—they turned into a phoenix, which turned into Nelly."

"In the flesh!" he added cheekily.

"We've been trying to figure out where Nan's and Nelly's ashes are so we can get them back to the right place."

"And what happens then?" Alaina finally asked.

"Actually, we're not really sure." I looked around the table. Still no help, still no ideas. "And we're figuring out why too. Turns out, Nelly here was, well, 'roommates' with Jack Mason, about fifty years ago when they served in the Navy together."

"Jack Mason? Jack from the diner? Jack and Mary Jack?" Alaina looked incredulous.

"That's the one," I confirmed, though I was surprised she knew them. I remembered then that she'd been a student at the university, so of course she'd know the diner. "They lost touch because Nelly made sure of it. They lived their separate lives. Nelly hasn't been able to think of anything else he left unresolved when he died. Anyway," I continued, "it looks like Nelly and I are connected, too, through more than the power of the funeral home and death and stars and ashes and such. Nelly's granddaughter, Vicky, works for Johnathon at the real estate firm."

"Junior agent. Quite good too," he elaborated.

"Johnathon was supposed to find old love letters from Jack in Nelly's place, which is one of the first homes he sold here. He was supposed to get them and bring them to Nelly at the nursing home he ended up in after he fell down the stairs at his place, when he read in the paper that Jack Mason had bought and opened the diner." I was getting excited. Things really felt like they were coming together, like they were starting to make some sort of fantastical sense.

"Alaina?" Mina reached over and laid a hand on her arm.

She slowly looked up from her hands. She looked pale again, that air of fragility back. I thought, Fuck, she wasn't prepared for any of this insanity.

She took a deep breath. "I'm sorry, I got a little lost. What did you say?"

"I just, uh, wanted to make sure you had all the pieces right. It's a lot to take in, I know," I said, unsure.

"All the pieces right," she repeated. "I mean, yes, you're right. That's what happened. But I'm not sure if Random is really how I'm connected to all of this."

"Okay," I said, baffled. "What else could it be?"

She smiled and raised her glass. "I'm Jack Mason's granddaughter."

PART FOUR:
FLAMES AND FIRE

CHAPTER TWENTY-THREE

My jaw dropped. Byron's eyebrows shot up. Cleo and Johnathon grabbed each other and gasped, while Mina let out a breath full of obscenities. Nelly went as pale and gray as the first lights of dawn.

"Why didn't you say something?" I demanded finally.

She gave me a baleful look. "This is the first I've heard of any of this. I suppose I could have introduced myself this morning, 'Hi, I'm Alaina, Jack Mason's granddaughter.' That would have been a normal thing to do."

"Smartass," I muttered as Mina hooted and clapped her hands together. "I thought his family was back in Minnesota or Montana or something?"

"Michigan—and yeah, most of them are. We came to visit Gammy and Pappy when I was in high school, and I fell in love with the place. The river, the woods, they're all so different than back home. I love being so close to the mountains. Plus, the weather is way better. I came here for school," she said with a shrug. "And I want to stay. Gammy and Pappy don't have anyone else nearby, and they're old. Sorry," she said with a look over at Nelly. "I wasn't trying to be rude. I just mean they're going to need more help with getting by, eventually."

"Pappy," Nelly tried the word out, almost imperceptibly. I reached over and laid my hand over his, tan over liver spots.

"You okay?" I asked gently.

"Yes, yes, I'm all right. Alaina—" He paused to clear his throat. "You love your grandparents, of course. Your grandfather. You have a good relationship?"

"Yeah, they're the best. They bought my books every semester, and I'd make sure I got to the diner at least once a week. They always made sure I brought donuts back when I was living in the dorms."

"And how do you feel about him now? I know you only just found out, but aren't you ashamed to know that he and I were—were together?"

She looked puzzled. "No," she said, her voice trailing up on the answer. "Why would I be ashamed?"

I bit the inside of my cheek to hold back the smile and glanced over to see Byron doing the same. "Well, I—uh, well, that wasn't something men were supposed to do back then," he finished, looking over at a grinning Johnathon and Cleo and blushing.

Alaina smiled. "I'd wondered. He talked about someone he knew from the service, just one guy by name. He called him Salty. My dad said it was good old boys' tales, nothing more. But that was literally the only name he ever talked about, so I wondered if they were more than friends. So— you're Salty?"

"He talked about me," Nelly said. "He talked about me to his family. And I never even mentioned him to mine." His voice broke. "Excuse me," he said, pushing away from the bar. He walked quickly to the office. We all watched but followed Mina's murmured directive to let him go. He shut the door quietly, and we didn't see him the rest of the night.

By closing time, we had worked out a plan. Angie had to follow up with Alaina and was already going to take her statement in the morning, which would lead her back to the funeral home. She could do whatever she needed to do with her investigation without involving Nelly, and it would still be truthful beyond a doubt. Alaina would wait until the day after to tender her resignation and was going to contact the law firm she'd left in the meantime. She also mentioned that her grandfather had given her a standing offer for a job at the diner, if she ever needed something to tide her over. Between the ditching of the ex-boyfriend, the criminal issues surrounding his departure from the funeral home, and having some sort of safety net, she felt comfortable leaving a job she hated and hadn't wanted in the first place. She would come along with Nelly and me when we went to the diner.

Mina gave me the next two nights off. I didn't like to miss the almost-weekend pay (especially the Tour de France tips), but the timing didn't give us much choice. The next appearance of the July Phoenicids was slated to peak on the thirteenth, and the clock had tipped past midnight, so it was already the twelfth, albeit long before dawn. Nelly had been feeling like there wasn't a lot of time left since this whole thing began, and now with the way everything was lining up, it seemed like he was right on the money. If the stars were indeed connected—and at this point, I thought, how could they *not* be—that was likely a time of great import.

We had all parted ways. Byron and the boys had headed home, and everyone else had bunked down for the night. Alaina was already upstairs by the time I finished the last checks and rounds. I peeked in on Nelly, sacked out in the office, a box of tissues on his lap instead of a magazine this time. Content that everyone seemed to be where they should but wishing I could be of more comfort to Nelly, I headed up myself.

As I brushed my teeth, I looked at my reflection. I looked older; the months of grief had aged me by years. Watching the mirror copy my every move, I wondered if death was like an alternate universe, one we couldn't access until we were gone. Whatever lay beyond was through the looking glass, and death was the password. I wondered what we looked like in that place, if it existed.

These were the things that had first made me doubt the existence of heaven. What age were we after we died? The age we had been when we took our last breath? Our favorite? Did we revert to being children who were also married and divorced and had kids and all the adult stuff? The late-hour wanderings of my mind turned, of course, from what I used to wonder in the abstract to a specific individual.

How old was Nan, wherever she was? Did she even know she was elsewhere? Nelly hadn't known he was dead when he came back. Was Nan going to come back? The thought made me lower my toothbrush and stare into my eyes, over my own foamy, open mouth. Was I going to see Nan again?

I looked like shit, I thought. I didn't want that to be the case. If I was going to get to see her—I felt my heart race a moment—I wanted to look good for her.

From the other side of my brain, I thought, Oh, maybe I shouldn't look too good. I wouldn't want her to think that I'm over her. Fuck knows I'm not.

I nodded emphatically to the woman in the mirror, spit and rinsed. But I also didn't want her worrying about me, if that was something she was even capable of anymore. I splashed some water on my face and resolved to pick up one of those face masks at the local drugstore, the kind advertised to rejuvenate your skin overnight, or something to that effect.

You're beautiful, Nan said. The memory played out in my mind, projected onto the mirror like it was a movie screen.

I have goopy, pink paper all over my face. So do you, I muttered. We had discovered these magical, pseudotherapeutic masks the Christmas prior and nearly bought out the two drugstores to fill each other's stockings.

Yeah? You're gorgeous. My beautiful wife, she said, a smile in her sweet voice.

You don't even have your glasses on, I reminded her, smiling myself.

I don't need them to see how good my wife looks. I watched in the mirror as she came up behind me, sliding her arms around me. We began to sway.

Careful, I murmured to her, eyes closing, content.

Why? she asked, her head bowed to my shoulder, pressing kisses all the way up to my neck, leaving a wet trail from the mask she still wore.

I can't kiss you with this mask on, and that's all I want to do. That's all? Her mouth stopped, and her eyes met mine in the mirror.

No. I grinned a little wickedly. *Not by a long shot.*

She moaned a little and pressed her body flush against mine. I'd been sneaking my hand up between her legs and now fumbled with the zipper on her jeans, caught between us. *Yes, find me*, she whispered. *Find me, Del.* My body jerked with that feeling of falling that suddenly awakens you as you're trying to sleep, breaking my reverie, washing the memory from the mirror. I stared, my face still dripping, the water running. I turned the tap off, hands shaking a bit. That almost hadn't felt like a memory, but like it was happening—or rather, like I was both watching and participating. It was hard to explain. I finished undressing and crawled into bed. It was not going to be easy to fall asleep, I thought, not with what had just happened. I turned off the light, rolled over to stare at the wall for a while, and finally fell asleep.

The morning dawned softer; clouds had rolled in, dimming the bright announcement of the sun's early rise. I checked my phone for the time only to roll my eyes and wish I wasn't getting used to this schedule of a rough four hours. Just needed some coffee. I threw on fresh jeans and an Over the Rhine festival T-shirt, laced up my boots, grabbed my hat, and headed down.

Everything was as I'd left it a handful of hours before. I jabbed the button on the coffeemaker, staring at it as it rumbled awake and began to drip. I heard a sound and looked up to see Nelly coming out of the office. He was still in one of Nan's flannels, and I felt a pang at seeing the plaid I'd only seen on her before. He came up to the bar and slid onto a seat. "Mind if I get a cup of that?" he asked, nodding at the slowly filling carafe.

I managed to grunt out enough of an affirmative answer that he said nothing more. We watched the coffee brew in silence until it beeped. I poured two mugs. I dumped my sugar and a couple ice cubes in, downed half, refilled, and eventually carried them over to the bar for the last addition to mine.

"How're you doing?" I asked. Last night had been such a short time ago, but I felt like it had been ages since he and I had spoken.

He shook his head and took a sip, then a gulp of the coffee.

I stared. "Do you even feel heat?" I demanded.

"Huh?" Nelly looked totally alert, drinking as if the coffee wasn't molten hot.

"How can you drink it down that hot, that quick? I have to cool it to get it down fast enough," I said.

"I guess I hadn't noticed, now that you mention it." He looked pensive, studying the cup. "I mean, yeah, it's hot coffee. But not too hot to drink."

"And it was ninety-something out yesterday, when you went for a walk and sat around outside." He shrugged. "I don't rightly know, Del. I felt like it was hot, but it didn't bother me overly much, now that I'm thinking about it."

"Interesting," I murmured. I wondered if it was because he wasn't really alive. Or, I thought with a shudder, if it was because he'd been cremated. How could anything be hotter? My mind wandered to heat maps I had seen on TV and the paranormal ghost-hunter shows that talked about energy fields and heat signatures. I wanted to ask more, but he finished the coffee and sighed. I sipped mine and tried to drag my attention back. "Sorry, squirrel moment. How are you feeling?"

He set the mug down and pushed it around in little circles, oscillating it over the bar. "It's a hard thing to know that he spoke of me, told his family about me. Not everything, of course, I'd never expect that. Then again, I never expected he'd mention me at all. And what did I do in return? I buried him in my mind as surely as if he'd been dead, for so many years."

"How many signs have there been, Del? How many of these connections are there? Is anything random? Is anything by chance? What have I done by ignoring him for so long?" His eyes were pained as he now gripped the mug as if to steady himself.

I took a minute to refill his mug before replying. "I don't know," I said slowly. "We've definitely uncovered a lot of connections. You to Jack, you to Johnathon, you to Vicky to Johnathon to me, Jack's granddaughter to the funeral home that switched you and Nan. But really, Nelly, it's all centered around you and Jack."

"I didn't do right by him. I never did. I can't go back and fix that, Del."

"No," I agreed. "But maybe you can make it right from here and now."

"Time's running out," he said, to which I nodded.

"I think so too. We all do."

"Is that what you talked about last night, after I left? My apologies on the matter, it was—it was too much. I couldn't contain myself."

"Nelly." I reached out for his hand. "You don't have anything to apologize for. Okay?"

He nodded.

"All right. Here's the plan." I brought him up to speed in the quiet of the bar. "We're going to the diner today, you and me and Alaina."

"Today," Nelly repeated unsteadily. He swallowed down more coffee. "When?"

"I guess . . . when Alaina is up?" I shrugged. "We didn't want to make any detailed plans for you without you."

"So, going to see my former lover to bury the hatchet is a fine decision to make without my input, but I get to decide if we go before or after tea?" The unbridled sarcasm in his voice came as a complete surprise. Before I could gather my thoughts to answer, he held up a hand. "I'm sorry for that," he said stiffly. "That was uncalled-for."

I tried to give myself time to answer in a more appropriate way, but the words leapt out. "Yeah, well, I wouldn't know anything about doing that," I snapped back.

Tension crackled in the air between us a moment. It broke as he grinned, leaned over the bar, and clapped a hand on my shoulder twice.

"I tell you what, Del, I think we'd've gotten along just fine, whenever we might've met. You meet fire with fire. I like that. I like that," he said again, giving my shoulder a little shake.

Just then, Alaina made her way down. I turned to pour another mug and put the milk up for her as Nelly greeted her and the two chatted like old friends. I felt as if something important had passed between me and Nelly at that point, some sort of deeper connection. I tucked it away as I heard Alaina laugh a little.

"No reason to wait," she said to him kindly. "You've already had your whole life to guard that secret and regret it at least some. I don't think he will take it badly. I think last time you caught him off guard, is all. I mean, he was expecting you to already be dead, not tripping over him in the diner."

Nelly, who was a little paler than he had been before, blew out a breath and looked up at me.

"All right. No time like the present, I suppose."

CHAPTER TWENTY-FOUR

We took my truck, Alaina graciously taking the middle seat. We stopped at my place long enough for Nelly to get a clean shirt; Nan had some polos tucked in the dresser. I pulled out the one she liked least, a forest-green color. She'd only kept it because I'd loved it on her. The deep pine brought out the green flecks in her hazel eyes; she said she felt like a Christmas tree about to be cut down. I remembered the last time she wore it. It must have been the fall before she died, after some argument that didn't matter in the slightest. We had each taken our time away to cool off—not much, less than an hour. She'd said she hoped the shirt would do, since she didn't have time to get me flowers. The tears shed, plus the shirt, made her eyes look like the softest moss. It had always drove me nuts that she was such a pretty crier.

The lot was empty when we got to the diner. I could see Justine's car sticking out a bit from the back, and the neon sign read open in the window. Nelly had been uncharacteristically quiet on the way over, not even attempting to meet Alaina in the middle on things she was chatting about. I figured he was worried about talking to Jack again. I couldn't blame him; I wouldn't even know where to begin.

I turned off the truck. No one moved.

"How're you doing, Nelly?" I asked him as gently as I could. He glanced up at me, his hands clasped together in his lap, trembling slightly.

"Well, I'll say one thing. If you were on fire right now, I wouldn't be able to draw spit to save you." He looked worried, more so than I'd seen him look.

"I'm sure it'll be fine," Alaina assured him.

"Has he said anything about me? Oh, heaven, what must your grandmother think? Has she been a good match for him? Did she make him happy? Oh, listen to me!" With that, he threw up his hands, then covered his face.

"I haven't talked to him this week. Honestly, I've been kind of ignoring it. Things with Derek were starting to show and I didn't want to stop in because they'd know something was up. And yes," she continued, laying a hand on Nelly's arm. "He's been very happy. My grandmother's name is Mary. They've had a long and beautiful marriage—they had their fiftieth anniversary celebration last year."

"He always wanted this diner, you know," Nelly said, patting her hand.

"Really? He's said that as long as I can remember, but you've known him a lot longer than I have. When's the last time you guys actually talked?"

Nelly paused. He looked out at the diner for a minute, but the look in his eyes made it clear that he was seeing much farther away. He let out a breath. "Not counting the other day, it's been fifty-five years." He shook his head. "It's too long. Maybe it's been too long, and this is all for nought, dredging all this up now. What's the point?"

"You recognized each other. You haven't seen each other in over fifty years, haven't spoken, but you both recognized each other. You said you saw the picture when the diner opened in the paper. That's what had you running to get ready, and you fell," I reminded him. "And Jack knew you immediately when he saw you. I mean, he'd been to your funeral. That says something."

"He recognized you too," Alaina added. "He has your obituary on the fridge at the house."

"Surely not. Really?" Nelly looked up, his eyes sheened with tears and nerves.

"Yes." She leaned in a little. "And don't call me Shirley," she quipped.

Nelly laughed, the tension relieved, at least for the moment. Once again, he looked toward the diner and sighed. "I guess there's nothing left to do but go in."

Pushing the door open, he went out. Alaina and I followed, and together, we walked into the diner.

The bell jangled. Before it had even quieted, Justine stood before us, arms folded. "I was wondering when y'all would decide to grace us with your presence. Come in, come in. Here, now, I've got coffee poured for you, just the way you like it. Alaina, sweetie, good to see you." She offered her cheek for Alaina to kiss and then patted hers in turn. "You're a good girl. Now you, honey," she said, looking at Nelly. "I'm guessing you're the reason Jack's been in such a state these last days. He's shut up in his office, doesn't want anybody bothering him, but I reckon he'll let you in. I'd put dollars to donuts you're the only one, though. So, you go on and scoot. Take your coffee, now—go on." She ushered Nelly toward the back office.

Turning back over his shoulder, he shot me a nervous look. I smiled at him and made the same shooing motion as Justine. He nodded, straightened his spine, and rapped on the door, a little syncopated rhythm. The door opened quickly.

"You remembered," Jack said by way of greeting.

"So did you," Nelly replied.

Jack looked through the window at all of us watching. "Go about your business, the lot of ya," he said. He looked back at Nelly. "Well, come on in."

Nelly did so without a second's hesitation, and the door shut with a click.

Justine sighed and turned to me. "Now, you. It's your turn."

"My turn for what?" I asked, baffled, almost fumbling the cup of coffee she pushed into my hands.

"Some answers. Jack's been stingy with the details and all in a tizzy since you walked in here with that sweet man. He's barely told Mary a thing," she added, nodding her head toward the back of the diner.

"Well, now, Justine, that was before. I have quite a bit to add," Mary said. I whipped around to see her at her booth.

"Shit, I'm sorry, I didn't see you there. Good morning, Mary."

She smiled. "Good morning, Del. Alaina, dear, lovely to see you as always." She looked back at Justine, who made no secret of listening intently. "Why don't you pull the shades, Justine, and turn off the neon. Go ahead and lock the door. Put the sign up. We have some family business to discuss."

I helped with the shades, as the whole front face of the diner was windows. Justine hung the laminated sign that said closed — we will be back when we are back and not a moment before." She grabbed the coffeepot, hissed a whisper to signal Amy and Wendy, and within a couple of minutes, we were all gathered in the last two booths.

"Del, I'd be obliged if you'd start. How did this man come to find you? What do you know about him?" Mary tilted her head slightly. I remembered in that moment that she had also been a teacher. Nelly and Jack had both married sharp, smart women.

On the way over, Nelly had agreed to letting me bring everyone up to speed on the events of the past few days. So, I did. I told the women around me about knocking over the ashes and about the phoenix that had appeared right before Nelly did. I told them how it was Jack who'd made us realize that Nelly had died months ago, on the same day as Nan. I told them about the web of connections we had discovered. I said nothing more about Jack and Nelly other than their shared Navy service, and that they'd lost touch.

They were certainly the most animated people I had shared this with. My story was peppered with gasps and "oh my goodnesses" and "no ways." Justine jumped in at the places where she, too, had entered the scene.

"So, what now? You've got his ashes, the poor dear, and you need to find Nan's. What happens then?"

I shrugged. "I'm still not sure, but time is running out."

"How do you know?" Wendy half whispered, her eyes wide and round beneath her Volunteers ball cap.

"There's a meteor shower tomorrow, a small one. We're about as far north as you can be and still see it. Since it was the starlight that made the ashes glow, we're thinking we need the starlight on both of them—both of their ashes, I mean—to set things back right."

"Why is the meteor shower important?" Amy chimed in.

I hid a smile, along with the sweet secret of two men in the sand dunes. "It's called the July Phoenicids, and it's called that because it comes from the constellation known as the phoenix." The three younger women gasped in unison. Mary said nothing. "We can't be sure, and we definitely don't know exactly what will happen—if anything does happen. But that's our best guess," I said with another shrug.

"How are you going to find Nan's, um, ashes?" Wendy asked quietly.

The bubble of excitement that surrounded me from telling the story and feeling like we'd solved the mystery (or at least most of it) popped suddenly. I could feel myself deflate as I leaned forward, hunching over my nearly empty coffee. "I don't know."

Raised voices came from the office; the six of us turned as one toward it. But as quickly as they had risen, they subsided, and we all turned back to the table.

"Well, Delilah, that's quite a tale." Mary let a hint of a smile touch her lips. For a moment, she reminded me of Professor McGonagall toying with a student, her wordplay sharper than a sword. "I believe I have some details that might beat it, though."

We all leaned in. Mary took a moment to compose herself, her eyes closed. She breathed in deeply through her nose and exhaled sharply. She opened her eyes and looked at each of us.

"I want you to remember, times were different when Nelly—also known to some as Salty—and Jack were in the Navy together. For many, it was a lot harder to be who you were, for fear of hellfire, exile, or worse." She paused a moment. No one uttered a sound. The air conditioner behind us hummed. "I've learned a lot about my husband this week. I've learned that he had a love before me, one I had never known about and only briefly suspected. It was a strong love, wild and passionate, and it ran deep. Deeper, perhaps, than either were ready for. For, you see, Jack's love was Nelly."

Hearing Mary tell it, in her usual beautiful style, was enchanting in a way that hadn't existed with Nelly. When he had told me, and when Jack had, too, it was raw, full of emotion and need and loss. Mary's narrative, by contrast, conveyed the details with so much poetry and romance that the story was steeped in longing, reminding me again of *Titanic*.

"They met on the ship in 1961 as bunkmates. They took meals together, trained together, cleaned weapons and ran drills together. They became close, as people often do when they find themselves far from home and in tight quarters. Over time, they grew closer still in ways convention deemed forbidden. They weren't the only couple onboard—there were those who knew the Navy to be a more tolerant and forgiving arm of service, where some men looked to others for the purposes of pleasure and comfort. For Jack—I cannot say for Nelly, as I do not know him—but for Jack, what they shared was more than a willing body to lie beside in the night. He loved deeply and said he knew he was loved so in return.

"They were out before the US became entrenched in Vietnam. When their respective tours came to an end and both declined to reenlist, tears were wept and promises were made. Each went his own way with the agreement that they'd stay in touch and somehow figure things out. But the world was less kind to men like them then, and especially to men of a certain age during the long years of the Vietnam conflict, whether they were sent there or not. Jack wrote letters to Nelly, posting them to the only address he knew. He sent them weekly for more than four months until they started coming back unopened, marked as 'Unable to Forward, Return to Sender.' He knew then that whatever the two had while together, they could never share apart. It took him some time to allow his broken heart to mend enough to let love in again."

She paused here and took a long sip of her coffee.

"It wasn't until his death that I realized the sailor about whom my husband had so many stories had been, perhaps, something more than a friend. Jack received a call from another sailor he had served with, alerting him of the death of his 'brother-in-arms.' The obituary didn't appear until two days later, the day before the funeral was scheduled to be held. There was no wake, no viewing. Jack was devastated. He spent days shut up in the office here, only coming home after closing. He dressed for the funeral in silence. Knowing they had been close, though not the extent, I gave him his silence and space. He spoke to no one after the service, declined to pass condolences to the family. He took me home and finally said he needed to go and raise a glass to his friend. I don't know where he went that night, but he did not come home till morning—nor, in that state, did I expect him to. That was when I began to wonder if there were more than ship tales between them. But he came home the next day, clear-eyed but no less burdened. He never spoke of Salty again. That is, until now."

Again, Mary paused and drank, fiddling with the handle of the mug. The women and I sat wide-eyed, entranced with her story.

"Months went by, and I forgot the strangeness about Jack in those brief days until this Tuesday." She looked toward the closed office door. "When Justine came in with the message that old Salty was here, Jack's face paled as if he'd seen his ghost. I saw his hands shake on the ledger before he stood. Once on his feet, he seemed overcome with anger or some similar passion. The door crashed open, and I came out to see what commotion was to come. Most of you were there for the rest. Well, after he left with you"— Mary nodded briefly at me—"he went back and shut himself up in the office again. I remembered with sudden clarity the grief he'd endured and the solitude he'd imposed on himself when he first learned of his friend's death. This time, however, I'd have my answers."

She smiled in the way that women do when they know their way through the minefield of your mind and were not giving away their strategy.

"I made sure he came home, and when we got there, he tried to shut himself in our room. But this time, I was ready. I pulled out a bottle of bourbon and poured two glasses. I sat him down at the kitchen table and told him, 'Jack, I've loved you over fifty years, and I'm not going to stop now. Tell me the truth about that man.' And he did. It was in fits and starts at first, but soon he was telling me a tale of passion, one of lust and love and need and secrets. He told me he had believed they could be together, somehow, forever. They'd move somewhere, somewhere out west, where there was enough space between neighbors to hide. They could watch the stars turn together and grow old, never needing anyone else. Nelly had little to no family, and Jack had run off to join the Navy as soon as he could and never looked back. There wouldn't be anyone to miss them or find them out. Nelly had agreed to the plan—which had been much more of a dream—when he and Jack were lying together in sand dunes in some faraway place. Jack told me how the stars fell that night, and how they had sealed the promises the two men made.

"But as time passed, in the light of day and as their tour of duty ended, Nelly spoke more and more of his longing for a family. How Jack was a dreamer, and a crazy one at that, to think this plan could possibly be. How could two men make it in such a world? Jack argued that times were changing, that people were changing, that attitudes toward women and war and sex and love and taboos were evolving. It was still a few years before the Summer of Love, but the winds of change were certainly blowing. Nelly wasn't convinced and felt that they were both too much in love with each other to listen to reason. He was the one to ask for some time apart. He promised Jack that he'd write, that the two wouldn't lose each other. Jack promised him back and kept it. Until the letters came back. And now, here we sit, waiting for the dead to make peace with the living," Mary finished.

None of us spoke. I wiped my eyes, Wendy sniffled, and Justine grabbed a paper napkin from the holder and blew her nose.

Finally, it was Alaina who broke the silence. She leaned forward with both hands on the table, palms up and open. Mary placed her hands in them, and the two leaned in toward each other.

"Thank you," Alaina said, her voice thick with tears. "Thank you for always being the amazing person you are. There's no one in this world with a bigger heart. Thank you for sharing—and for staying."

Mary smiled a little at that. "Even if I had somewhere else to go, I wouldn't leave your grandfather, darling. I'm not afraid of the world. I know the magic I've got in that man."

"And Nelly couldn't—or didn't," I finished for her. "Either way, he didn't see any option but letting go."

Mary nodded. "And now I'm grateful for that every day, because if Nelly hadn't let go, he wouldn't have found his way to me." She broke hold with one of Alaina's hands to take mine. "I'm also grateful to you for bringing him back."

"Me?" I asked, surprised. "I didn't bring him back. He just showed up."

"You brought him here, to the diner. You brought him back to Jack."

"I didn't know it, though."

Mary tilted her head. "Why does my gratitude offend you?"

I gaped at her. "What? No. It doesn't offend me, it's just—it's not needed."

She smiled again at that, that same wily, womanly smile. "You have it anyway, Delilah."

I couldn't keep from fidgeting under her gentle maternal gaze. "Um. Thanks. I mean, you're welcome. Damn it, Mary."

She laughed. Just then, the office door opened, and the two men, those brothers-in-arms, stepped out.

CHAPTER TWENTY-FIVE

"It's time to go, Del," Nelly said, his voice gruffer than I'd ever heard. I looked at the time; the neon-rimmed clock above the office said it was nearly noon. The morning had slipped away while we had sat, rapt under Mary's storytelling prowess. I wanted to ask if he was sure, if he wanted more time, but there was a look of both resolve and relative ease on his face, so I nodded.

We said our goodbyes quickly; Alaina elected to stay at the diner for a bit so Nelly and I could go on. I got to the door and was flipping the lock when I happened to look over and see Nelly in the middle of the aisle, Mary standing in front of him, both of her small, frail hands in his. He murmured something to her that made her nod and smile; I watched as Jack laid a hand on her shoulder. He watched his wife kiss his friend's cheek, the first and only time. The two men shook hands once more and held on; the moment spun out.

Justine and the girls had already moved back into the kitchen. Alaina was pulling up the shades. The bright, hot sunlight broke the men from their shared spell, and each slowly let go of the other. Nelly walked away, and as we stepped out, he took his last long look at Jack.

We were silent as we got in the truck. I didn't know where we were going but didn't feel as if I could ask at that moment either. Instead, I drove to the Riverwalk. I parked the tree in the lot by the bike path, shaded by sycamores and pawpaws. From there, I could see the funeral home in the distance. The heat shimmered up from the pavement on the bike path, emanating in a column over the chimneys on the crematorium. The whining drone of cicadas occasionally faded long enough to make out the rumble of machinery inside the brick walls.

I heard some bird call out that I hadn't ever heard before. I looked but only caught a glimpse of white disappearing into the foliage. I turned the truck off, rolled the window down, and waited.

Finally, Nelly turned his faded blue eyes away from whatever memories were conjured before him. He looked at me a long time before he spoke.

"I owe you, Del, a debt I won't have the time to repay, not that I think I ever could."

For the second time in as many hours, I felt surprise cross my face. "You don't owe me anything, Nelly. Of course not."

"You brought me to Jack. You brought me to—to the only man I ever loved. And not well enough, at that." His voice still held tears and a deep tiredness I hadn't heard before. "Not nearly well enough," he said, more to himself, again gazing out the window. He patted his shirt pockets.

"Here," I said, reaching in front of him to grab another pack from the glove box, along with another lighter. He nodded his thanks before pushing open the door and getting out of the truck. I did the same and followed him off the path and into the grass to sit on one of the painted benches.

He drew on the cigarette as he sat, looking out toward the river, away from the funeral home. I wondered if he realized where we were.

"I don't know what to say," he said. His knee bounced, keeping the ash from collecting at the end of the cherry.

"You don't have to say anything."

"Jack and I—"

I put a hand over his. "Nelly, whatever you and Jack talked about is yours. You don't have to share any of that with me. I'm not going to pry. All I need to know is where we're going next, and when you're ready." I hoped the earnestness I felt for him to maintain his privacy was conveyed.

"You're not going to ask?" he said, looking at me in surprise. "You little inquisitive thing, you?"

I shrugged. "I wasn't a part of your relationship. That was for you and Jack. Whatever passed between you—or didn't—is none of my goddamn business."

The silence stretched out between us, broken briefly by the strange call again. A breeze, no more than a breath exhaled, whispered through the dark green leaves above us. I looked up again, hoping for another glimpse of the bird.

"I appreciate that more than you know. I lived a long time in secrecy over him. I've never shared any of this before you. What I will tell you, though, is that between the two of you, there's a heaviness that's been lifted off my heart. I never knew the weight of it until it was gone. And it wouldn't be gone but for you giving me a chance to talk to Jack again."

Now I had to wait for my own tears to leave my throat before responding. "I'm honored to have been a part of your story, Nelly. I'm glad I could help bring you two back together—gladder than I have words for."

"I know we have to finish this. I know time is running out this time. I can feel it." Nelly looked up to the sky, the bright blue above us obscured by dark leaves and twisty branches. "But I still don't know what comes next or how to get there."

"We need to get your ashes—or, not yours, but Nan's." My heart tripped, and every fiber of my body went stock-still as I was overcome by a sudden realization. "Wait a minute. What if she's doing the same thing? What if she's out there searching for answers too? If you're back, maybe she is! Why didn't I think of this before? Fucking moron!"

"Slow down," Nelly advised.

Shaking my head, I pushed off the bench and paced.

"What if—what if she's out there right now, trying to figure this out on her own? Not knowing she was dead . . . what would she do? Where would she go?" My eyes snapped back to Nelly. "Our place. Our home. She would have just gone home. Come on!"

I rushed around to the driver's side and jumped in the truck. I yanked on my seat belt, reversing out of the parking spot before Nelly could even buckle his. "Del, slow it down! Give me a damn minute here!"

I looked around wildly for oncoming traffic and gunned it out on the road.

"Damn it, Del. You don't know she's there. No sense killing yourself to get to her anyway. She's already dead."

"So are you," I muttered. What had he known? Nothing. He had known *nothing* when he'd appeared. "Okay, look. You thought you were still at the nursing home, where you last remembered being. You thought you were waking up like normal. What if when you came back, she did too? We have to find her. What if we've been going about this all wrong?"

Nelly gave me nothing but silence in response. I felt like I was on fire, my heart and mind racing. What if I actually *could* see her again? What if I could hold her, touch her, one more time? What would I say? I ignored the cold seed of doubt in my theory; I let myself blaze with what-ifs, my grief raging wild and burning with an irrational hope. But what even *was* rational anymore?

The radio was off, but my ears rang and my chest hummed, as if a tuning fork had been pinged within my lungs. Looking over quickly at Nelly, I said quietly, "What if our premise was wrong? What if by finding you both and righting *that* wrong brings you back?"

I looked over again and saw Nelly close his eyes.

"Jesus, Del, I don't think I'm ready to think about that." He shook his head emphatically. "No. No. I'm not discussing that right now. I won't go down that road."

I wanted to press. I wanted to tell him it would give him a chance to be with Jack, to see him again. To see his family, maybe get out of the nursing home. Even as I thought it, though, logic mounted its defense, and the dark seed of doubt I was trying so hard to ignore grew. I kept my whirling thoughts to myself.

In short order, we pulled up to the house.

The driveway curved downward like it always had; from the street, it looked deceptively long. I held down the shudder of grief I felt at coming home to a place that was no longer home. There was a little tricycle on the front step and one of those fake-wooden playgrounds standing in the yard. The plastic slide and accents were still shiny. Two crossover SUVs—one gray, one bright blue—sat at the bottom of the driveway, outside a wide ring of little white lawn flags. My stomach sank, but an irreconcilable hope pushed me forward and I headed down the driveway.

The truck rattled down, my body naturally shifting with it from years of practice. There might've been new curtains in the windows and kid stuff scattered around, but going down the driveway almost felt like coming home. Nelly kept a tight grip on the Jesus bar while he tried to warn me one last time as I parked and jumped out; he sounded resigned, as if I were a child who wasn't listening.

I ignored him as I ran up to the door and knocked. A young kid with white-blond hair ran up and pressed their face to the glass, blowing their cheeks out against it and making a raspberry sound. I regarded the child quizzically.

A moment later, a young man appeared, around my age and height. He opened the door, scooping up the child in the same move.

"Afternoon," he said with an easy smile. "How can I help you?"

I felt all the energy leave my body. The impetus that had pushed me here deflated with staggering abruptness. "I used to live here," I said blandly. "I was . . . just driving by and thought I'd stop and see if y'all were liking the house."

"Oh, you're the previous owner! I'm sorry, I know we signed the paper-work, but I'm forgetting your name." His smile turned a little sheepish.

"Uh, it's okay. It's Del. Anyway, I wanted to make sure you were happy with it."

"Yeah! Yeah, we're thrilled. Especially with Michelle due in October, we needed the extra space. And Jacky here loves the yard, don't ya, buddy?" He jiggled the boy on his hip. "We put up the swing set for his birthday last month and the electric fence for Dasher." I heard a bark from behind him. "Whoops, there he goes. Do you want to come in? He'll jump, but he's friendly."

"Ah, no, no, thank you. Okay. Well, I'm glad you're enjoying the place. I gotta get going." I backed away. "I hope you guys have really happy times here," I said sincerely. "Nice to meet you."

"You too! I'm Alex, by the way. Stop by again sometime!" he said.

I nodded and turned to go down the steps.

"Bye-bye! Bye-bye!" the toddler yelled.

"Aw, Jacky, that was nice," I heard the man praise his son, and the door shut. I quickly walked back to the truck and jumped in. I stopped and lay my head on the wheel for a moment.

"She's not here," Nelly said.

"No. And you're right. I don't think she's around either."

"What makes you say that?"

I stayed where I was, head down, eyes open, staring at the odometer. We had stopped between eight – and nine-tenths of a mile. Almost to the next. "I just . . . feel it. There was nothing of her there. Nothing left. And the guy—Alex," I remembered, "didn't say anything about anyone else coming around lately."

"Did you ask?"

I shook my head. "Wouldn't need to. Talkative sort."

"Unlike some of us," Nelly joked, straight-faced.

"What's your daughter's name again?" I asked suddenly.

"Jackie. I mean, Jacqueline, but we rarely called her that. Only when she was in trouble, really." He smiled.

I looked back at the house for a minute before putting the truck in drive and giving her a little gas to get back up the driveway. "And she was your first kid?"

"Yeah," he answered, looking at me, puzzled. "Why?"

I paused another moment to turn onto the main road. "My dad wanted me to be named Elvira, as in the Oak Ridge Boys. That was his favorite song then. My mom refused, said it wasn't pretty enough. Her name's Bobbi and she hates it—she wanted something girly and pretty for a girl. So, he proposed Delilah. That way, he could still sing the song to me, just replacing the name."

"You have a fine name, Delilah. Though I think Del fits you well too."

"Did you name your daughter after Jack Mason?" I was too busy watching for traffic to catch his reaction well, but when I did look, his face was wistful.

"Well, now, I might've done that with some purpose, then. But that was near fifty years ago. After a while, Jackie was just Jackie. And Jack never stopped being Jack, for me."

"Is she anything like you remember him to be?"

He shook his head. "Not a whit. Just as sharp, to be sure. But if that girl ever had a fanciful notion in her head, I didn't hear it. She was never one for anything but practicality. She was always quite proper. Never sure where she got it from," he mused with a half laugh. "I had the most won-drous bouquet of beauties, I always knew that. Have I told you about that?" I shook my head as he continued, "My bouquet of beauties. Annamaria was a wildflower, fiery and red, who didn't care much for staying where she was put. Jackie was my cool one, as picture-perfect as a pale rose. Melanie—she was in the middle—was my petunia, sweet and easy and unassuming. Our last, Steven—well, he was like clover, quiet and steady. It was Annamaria who assigned all those. She used to doodle them on their lunches. But Jackie, yes, she's a cool one. She was in real estate, too, until she met her husband. Adam was a stockbroker, a client of hers. It was like one of those movies you see on the womenfolk channel on TV. Romantic, elegant, sto-rybook romance, you know."

"'Womenfolk?'" I raised an eyebrow, and he laughed.

"You know. The Lifetime channel or something, the one next to the Home Shopping Network."

"Uh-huh," I said, and he laughed again. "So, she's the eldest, smart, and likes things in their proper place."

"That's her," Nelly affirmed, looking out the window as we drove back toward the diner.

"She wouldn't like finding out about Jack. Especially if she made the connection that Jacqueline and Jack are derivatives of the same name." Nelly, again, was silent. "And she was the one at the diner that first morning. She was angry with you."

"She said I was dead to her, and that it was a dirty trick," he answered, his voice quiet.

"Do you think she found out?"

He looked up at me, blank, then his eyes went wide. "The letters. Johnathon never found them. What if she did? Oh, heavens, it's all gone to hell now. What if she found them, Del? She'd be so angry. The letters—they didn't have dates on them. Not the year, anyway. What if she thought I was unfaithful to her mother? She'd never forgive me." He rubbed a hand over his face. "Oh, mercy, mercy me. What do we do now?"

"I say we make that our next stop."

CHAPTER TWENTY-SIX

Nelly directed me left and right until we reached one of the fancier neighborhoods. This was old-Virginia money, no new cul-de-sacs or McMansions here. I pulled up to a large, perfectly symmetrical brick facade with neat black trim and an impeccable green lawn. The front door stood on a brick stoop with a wrought-iron railing and a brick walkway to the driveway. The stoop was flanked with rosebushes, blooming a silver white and perfectly pruned. It didn't scream money, but said it in the low tones meant for after-dinner brandies in the parlor.

"Must be thirty years she's lived here now. It was the last house she sold—to her husband. She quit working when she became a wife. She was good too. I never understood that about her. Kids, sure, I get it." He shook his head. "It made her happy, though, so we never said anything, though my Annamaria had plenty of thoughts about her daughter being at the beck and call of a man without her own career."

"I think I would've liked your wife." I smiled at him.

His hands were clasped tight, and his brow was furrowed with worry.

"Oh, you would have. It was impossible not to. Unless you got on her bad side." He chuckled briefly. "A fighter and a lover, she was. You don't have quite her temper, I don't think, but you have the same fierce love. It pours out of you," he continued as I took this in silently. "When you're with your family at the bar, at the diner. You've a big heart, a good heart." He reached out and took my hand in both of his. "I'm glad you're here, for whatever we find behind that door."

"Nelly," I started. The air in the cab of the truck hung heavy with inevitability. "Whatever happens, I'm so glad I had a chance to get to know you."

He shook the hand he held and patted it again. "Me too, Delilah," he said, smiling. "Well." He looked up at the house, then back at me. "Once more into the breach, eh?"

With that, he pushed open the door and stepped out. I followed, and we headed up to the black doorway with its brass knocker. With a single bracing breath, he pressed the doorbell. We heard the chime faintly, and within moments, Jackie opened the door.

Her hair was loose today, a soft sable reaching to her shoulders. She wore cropped linen pants the color of tropical sand, paired with a spring-leaf-green sleeveless top in deference to the midsummer heat. She was barefoot and had a French mani-pedi, along with a thin gold chain around her right ankle. I remembered her smooth, attractive face from the diner. I watched as it moved from the careful composition of greeting a stranger through shock and on to restrained anger as she took in the sight of her late father standing before her.

"What are you doing here? This isn't a joke. I am calling the police and reporting you for impersonating a dead person. This is harassment, and I will not tolerate it." Her voice was steady and clipped. She whirled around and moved to slam the door in our faces, only to be stopped by Nelly's hand.

I figured by this time, I shouldn't have been surprised by the strength in the man, frail as he seemed in appearance.

"Jackie, please. I'm not impersonating anyone. It's me. It's Dad, my little rose." His voice was soft, pleading.

Slowly, she turned, her face pale. The anger in her eyes was now mixed with doubt. The door swung wide open, though neither moved. They stared at each other, and somewhere in the house, a clock chimed the quarter hour. Somewhere outside, I heard the strange bird call I'd heard outside the funeral home.

"It can't be. That's impossible," Jackie said after some minutes had passed. "I-I'd like you to leave now."

"Jackie, you know it's me. Look at me. C'mon, baby, you remember me."

Suddenly, her dark eyes snapped with fire. "Don't you 'baby' me. You—you have no right." Her voice shaky, she spun on her heel and marched away. Nelly looked at me, and I shrugged.

We followed her into a large sitting room in shades of ecru and tan, with rare, cerulean-blue accents in the pillows and the sash on the curtains. She paced in front of a mantle that held silver frames with photos more posed than candid. I recognized the granddaughter, Vicky, in her business headshot.

Jackie turned quickly, and I almost fell back a step, such was the force in the movement. "How, then?" she demanded of Nelly. She had yet to acknowledge me or even look my way.

"Heavens, Jackie, I thought you'd be a little happier about seeing me," Nelly gently chastised. "After all, I hear I look pretty great for a dead guy." He grinned quickly as Jackie rolled her eyes and flung up her hands.

"Always a joke with you. Always a damn joke. Well, I'm finished laughing. Why are you here? *How* are you here?"

Nelly shrugged, holding his palms out. "*How* is a long story, and I don't know as I could do it justice, or if you'd believe it. *Why*—now, that's relatively easy." He put a hand on my shoulder. "This young lady's name is Del, short for Delilah Montgomery-Shaw. Ring any bells?"

"No," Jackie responded, coldly appraising me. I suddenly felt underdressed in my jeans and tank top. "Should it?"

"Well, now, not necessarily. Her wife passed away, you see, the same day I did. And Random Funeral Home took care of us both—the viewing, the cremation, and what have you. Do you follow?" Receiving nothing but a stony glare in response, he went on, "Well, it turns out the ashes you took home weren't mine, and the ashes Del took home weren't her wife's." Still nothing. "They got switched."

Finally, Jackie shrugged an elegant shoulder. "And what should it matter? You're both dead. You said it yourself."

"Mercy, Jackie rabbit, when did you get so cold?"

"Don't call me that!" she shouted, her cool composure stretched to breaking. "And I am who I've always been, which is more than I can say for you!"

"Now, honey—"Nelly reached out—to comfort her, I suppose. The strength was fading from his voice.

She recoiled as if a snake had risen in front of her.

"No. Don't you dare. Don't you come a step closer. I know what you are. I know what you did. I found the letters, *Dad*." She spat the words out. "I know about the affair."

"Affair? Honey, there wasn't any—"

"Don't you lie to my face anymore! You lied my whole life. All those years, looking at you and Mom like you were these perfect paragons of what a marriage should be. And it was all bullshit! You cheated on Mom," she accused.

"No, I—"

"With a *man*."

A warm breeze stirred the cool room, though the front door was closed now. Nelly's face, already pale from the tongue-lashing he was receiving, lost all remaining color. Still, he kept his feet and most of his composure. "If you would just listen—"

"Get out. Get away from me. Stay away from my family. I don't care if you're a ghost or a spirit or what have you, I won't have you ruining our lives with these—these indiscretions!"

"Jacqueline Ramira Maltby, you will sit down at once and listen to what I have to say," Nelly's voice boomed out in an unexpected timbre. His face flushed with righteous indignation, and his old body stood straight and proud.

His daughter promptly sat in an ivory-damask high-back chair, her back stiff and straight as a board, her eyes flashing.

"Thank you. Now. Yes, I had a relationship with a man. But it was no affair, young lady, and you'll mind your mother's memory. I never stepped out on your momma. I cherished that woman more than my own life. I buried my past and a piece of my soul so I could give my Annamaria the rest and all else that I had. And I have never, would never, and will never dishonor her or her memory in such a way. You should be ashamed of yourself for thinking that," he admonished. "Now. What have you to say for yourself?"

Jackie rose slowly, her eyes on Nelly, hands trembling as she pushed up on the arms of the chair to stand. "I want you out of my house. Take yourself and your justifications and your lies and get out. Do not come here again. I have washed my hands of my father." She advanced toward us, a lioness staring down her next meal.

We backed up in response. Her anger was palpable as she marched around us and flung the door open.

"Rest assured, Jackie, I won't be back to bother you again. But we need the ashes from the funeral home, and I'd like my letters, too, please."

"I threw them away. The letters, the ashes, every reminder of you that I could. They're gone, and so are you. Get out. Get out!"

With this last yell, we were left with no choice but to step back outside. As soon as we crossed the threshold, the heavy door slammed, effectively sealing off the house and any hope we may have found. I heard the bolt click into place. The cicadas resumed their whining, and the pained cry of the mysterious bird cut through the drone like a knife.

CHAPTER TWENTY-SEVEN

I was too much in shock to know what to do but blindly step down onto the walk.

Nan was gone. I hadn't had her ashes all this time, and now even that last vestige of her was beyond me. I felt a hollowness and a burning all at once, like a tree struck by lightning that smolders from the inside out. I found I didn't have the strength to take another step and simply sat on the stoop.

Nelly sat beside me. His uncharacteristic silence told me he didn't know quite what to do either. He rested his arms on his knees, somehow managing to appear casual at a time of such tension. The air hissed with it. I sat stiffly, hugging my elbows. Every fiber of my body was on full alert, ready to bolt. I gripped my arms together to keep myself from taking off, running into the street, running away into the distance. I'd run so far, I'd disappear, I thought. Just let me fall off the map.

The air was so hot, it rose in waves from the pavement until it threatened to swallow me up. The burn in my lungs and legs would finally be overtaken by the fire inside, and I'd disappear in a puff of smoke. All this madness, pain, grief—it would all be over if I could run right into the sun.

A tear splashed on my knee, breaking my reverie. Nelly was looking at me, his face quizzical, a study of sadness and confusion. He was about to speak when we both heard a soft cough coming from the driveway.

Vicky stood in the open garage, her arms crossed and shoulders tight. She jerked her head, gesturing toward the yard with a pointed look at the house. Nelly stood quickly and began to follow her, but after a step, he looked back and saw me sitting still.

He reached out a hand. I looked up at him, not sure if I could move.

"Nothin' left to lose, Del," he said softly. "Come on."

I put my hand in his, using the other to push myself up off the stoop. My bones felt like they might shatter at the slightest impact, but I followed tentatively.

Vicky walked around the side of the garage, out to the dense trees that separated the properties. The span of trees was only maybe twelve feet wide, but it was enough, with the kudzu and English ivy that clambered over every tree limb, to keep the narrow path hidden from sight of either house. Vicky said nothing as she led us down the path. The foliage was so dense, even the birdsong was hushed.

Still, I could hear the same cry from above.

Within a couple minutes, we came to a clearing. I dimly remembered something about dances and fairy rings but couldn't quite catch it. Besides, this wasn't natural; this had been cleared to serve as the dooryard to what looked to be a fort of some kind. The crude lashings that held branches together was definitely the work of a child's hands, but the sturdiness of the structure made me think there had been some help along the way. Nelly took a step into the clearing, toward the fort, then looked at Vicky, who looked away and rubbed her arm.

"I still come here sometimes. I think we all do, actually," she said. "Mom's so angry. She's so sad and so angry about things, and Dad's never home. Kyle's headed off to California in a week or so. I need to get away sometimes."

Nelly lifted a hand a little, and when Vicky didn't respond, he took another step toward the fort. Still nothing, so he closed the distance, resting his hand upon the thatched branches of the roof.

"It's, uh." Nelly cleared his throat, his voice thick. "It's what it's here for. What it's always been here for." He looked up at me. "I cleared out a little circle like this for the kids back home. The kids helped me build it. They wanted a tree house, but I wasn't too keen on letting them fall out and bash their heads open. So, we compromised." He looked back and stroked the sticks. "When the grandkids came along, I did it all again. Here, and for Melanie's brood up in Richmond. Stevie and his wife are out in California, so that never quite materialized. It's always been a good spot. Over there"— he gestured with his chin—"you take that little deer path and you'll be in the backyard in ten feet. Vicky took us the long way."

"You can get here from the street, so you don't get caught at all," she said. "My, um—well, I guess it's okay to tell you. My friends and I smoke weed back here sometimes. But we never leave anything," she hurried on, as if reassuring Nelly. "Nothing burning, no trash. It's not really partying or anything like that. I wouldn't do that. I wouldn't do that here, Pops." Her eyes shined with tears. "Is it really you? Can I—can I touch you?"

Nelly opened his arms, and the smartly dressed woman raced into them like a child. Her arms came around him, clinging as if he would slip out of her grip.

"I've missed you, Pops." Her voice was muffled by tears and Nelly's neck. He held her tight.

"I've missed you, too, sweetie." I couldn't tell what she said next, and I guess Nelly couldn't either. He pulled her back a bit. "What's that now?" he asked, still holding her arms. "I couldn't make it out."

"I couldn't do it, Pops. I couldn't let her do that to you. I was so mad at her, I came back when I knew she'd be asleep and . . ." she trailed off, trying to burrow back in.

My heart was pounding. Nelly pulled her back a little harder this time.

"What happened, Vick? Come on, let's have it."

She hung her head, an apologetic child. "I went through her trash."

Nelly's wide eyes met mine over her head. "You did what now?"

Vicky nodded and sniffled, rubbing a hand under her nose. She took a shaky breath. "She had a bunch of your stuff from the house in the basement. After.... After you died, she put the rest of it from the old folks home you were in down there too. We went through some of it when we were getting ready for your funeral. This is weird to talk about, isn't it?" She looked up at Nelly, then me, then back to her grandfather. She didn't wait for an answer, but continued. "It feels weird. Anyway. She found the letters. I didn't see them, she wouldn't let me read them, but... She put your picture albums and your letters and your Navy stuff and your—your ashes, your urn, in a trash bag and threw it out all at once. So, I got it out." Her voice trailed up on the admission and she shrugged. "And I hid it."

"You—" Nelly let out a hoot of laughter and was quickly shushed by Vicky. "You rascal. You always were my favorite," he added.

She smiled. "We're all your favorite, Pops. You tell everyone that."

"Yeah, well, I mean it this time." Again, the old guy winked at me.

I couldn't move.

"You—so—Nan's not gone?" I managed to get out.

Vicky shook her head. "If you mean the ashes Mom threw away, then no." She stepped back and straightened her outfit, brushing her hands over the wrinkles only to stoop down and open the little stick door. She reached in and pulled out two grocery bags. She stepped over and handed me one of them. "The urn isn't even broken," she said. "Mom threw it at the wall, but it just sort of . . . I don't know, bounced. Huh. Weird. The lid's not all the way on," she said, looking down at the black stone top. She reached for it to set it right, but I put my hand over hers to stop her.

"It's okay," I said. "It's perfect, just like that."

CHAPTER TWENTY-EIGHT

The morning of July thirteenth dawned hazy, the buzz of cicadas heralding the heat to come. The Phoenicids were set to peak. The decision had been made to close the bar for the day due to a death in the family. The message went out on social media, and the overwhelming response was condolences for the unnamed, undefined loved one. A couple of folks made comments about this being a bad idea for a bar—why not host the wake there? Others quickly stepped in and talked about the family who owned the bar and how everyone there was very close, so of course it would be closed. It made me feel good to think that our patrons and community had our back; it wasn't known as "the bar a couple of gay guys owned" but rather a family-owned and – operated place. It meant a lot to be recognized that way, even if it was via Facebook comments.

When Nan died, Mina had asked if I wanted to close the bar for the day. I had declined; there was no service at that point, and I needed to get out of the house, away from the space where she had last been. I needed the bar open to remind me the world kept going on around me, that I hadn't died alongside her, even though I felt as if I had. The bar was such an important representation of my family, it became almost a person to me. I needed it to be there. Our clients, circulating in and out, were the very air she'd breathed, the money exchanged was the blood that had flowed through her, and our staff was the heart of it. I needed that. I'd taken the time off that was also offered not to grieve or whatever, but to pack and sell the house.

There was nothing that didn't remind me of her: something she had touched, commented on, picked up, taken down. Things she'd used, things she'd worn. I didn't throw anything of hers away; I couldn't bring myself to. My stuff, on the other hand, was more pitched than packed, except for the books. I needed them around me too: old friends, the stories I'd read ten or twenty times; new guides I'd never needed to read before from Joan Didion, Megan Devine, Marie Kondo. I put everything of Nan's into the "sentimental" category and touched it as little as possible. It didn't spark anything but sorrow, but I didn't feel like I was in any place to make a decision either way.

Her cookbooks, with their notes and marginalia, had taken up a full thirty-gallon plastic tub; her clothes from the closet took half of one, with her sneaker collection finishing it off and filling another besides. Her two suits were hung in protective bags; her cuff links and hats, ties and tiepins, handkerchiefs and belts were all carefully tucked away. Her family hadn't wanted any of her clothes, only the things they'd given her and items that had been passed to her already. I found it easy to think unkindly of them, more so than I had before; they were angry, yes, and grieving, but also seemed all too ready to completely disconnect from me. Their baby was gone—might as well toss the bathwater with it.

I woke up with all this turning over in my head: family, what it means to different people. I wrestled with the idea of informing them I hadn't been in possession of Nan's ashes, but now I was. Should I tell them about what amazing things had happened these past few days? Would they even care? Since my brain did nothing but snarl at these questions, I opted for coffee first and another opinion before deciding whether to reach out or not.

It was seven, and Mina was already pulling a mug out for me when I got downstairs.

"Morning," she said. "Hope you got some rest. I slept like shit. Gonna be a long day, girl."

I nodded, gratefully accepting the mug, already doctored for quick consumption, if not complete. I downed half and responded as I reached for the whiskey, "Didn't sleep much or well. I don't know what to expect, and you know I don't like that."

Mina leaned over the bar with her tea, black as my coffee. "I don't think any of us do."

"Byron, maybe?" I posed the question with more hope than actual belief. "He was the one who figured out the quest part."

She shrugged. "Maybe." We drank in companionable, if heavy, silence. Eventually, she turned, put the electric kettle back on, and fished out a new tea bag. "Gonna miss that guy," she said, and I could hear both the affection and sadness in her voice.

"He's something else, isn't he? When he first showed up, I couldn't believe it. Not only that he was, you know, *there*, but that he was this funny, I don't know, grandpa. Like the things he said, and the winking?" I laughed. "I thought I'd lost my damn mind. I kept waiting for him to pull out a pipe or a monocle or something."

"Never had either one of those," Nelly said, coming out of the office with a cheeky smile.

"Well, I never had a grandpa that I knew either," was my retort. He rolled right over it.

"Had a nice pocket watch, though. It was supposed to go to Cooper, my oldest grandson. Wonder if it did." He sat next to me at the bar. "Mina, my dear, would you mind pouring me a cup?"

"Of course, honey. Here you go." She offered the mug and her cheek, pleased with the buss. "You know . . . if you get where you're going and you get the chance to, I guess, return, you stop on by."

"Are you inviting me to haunt your bar?"

Mina grinned. "Sure, why not? There's a selling point for ya."

Nelly laughed. "I hear paranormal business is all the talk these days," he said. They continued chatting and laughing. There were nearly twenty years between them and they had known each other less than a week, but it didn't matter. There was love in every touch, kinship in every laugh.

"I'm not telling Nan's family about this. Any of this," I said suddenly. Mina and Nelly turned toward me.

"Is that your final answer?" Mina asked dryly.

"There's no point. They wouldn't get it." I looked from one to the other. "They haven't had shit-all to say to me. I can't see them accepting any of this outside their church stuff either. They'll say it was demons or some-thing. I don't want that. I don't want any of this week, I dunno, sullied by people who aren't gonna get it."

"Good," Nelly said. I looked over at him. "I don't know about you, but they don't sound much like family to me." He motioned me over to him, and I tilted down to put my head on his shoulder. He patted my back. "You, on the other hand—now, that's family."

I felt tears rise in my throat again, but before I could say anything, we heard a ruckus coming from the back door.

"Why they always have to announce themselves so loudly, I'll never know," Mina muttered as Johnathon and Cleo came in.

"Boys will be boys," Nelly said with a wink.

"Guys! We found it!"

"Found what?" I wondered out loud.

Johnathon looked excited, and Cleo looked like he was about to burst. "There's a small gorge about an hour and a half east of here that happens to be known by stargazers and astronomers for its darkness and unobstructed views. It's the perfect place to catch the meteor shower tonight."

"And the trails are *awesome*. I can't wait to tell Byron," Cleo added.

Nelly, Mina, and I all looked at each other. I felt slightly panicked that this was ending, but Nelly smiled calmly. "Anyone else fancy a picnic?"

I didn't rightly know where the day went. Some calls were made, supplies picked up. Sandwiches were crafted and stacked, watermelon cut and packed. Two bottles of whiskey and one of White Star champagne—it seemed appropriate—were procured. My truck was loaded and the guys' Jeep too. By four o'clock, the rest of the convoy started to arrive. Byron actually drove in his ancient station wagon, wood panels and all; his bike was stashed in the back, I could see, just in case. Alaina rushed in, all aflutter with the good news of a second chance from the law firm. Justine, Amy, and Wendy all arrived in Justine's minivan. Vicky came alone.

Hugs and introductions as needed were exchanged, diner to bar and bar to diner. I thought it sort of funny and fitting that my life, even without Nan here, still revolved around food and drink and the same great people. Mina called out car assignments, arguing with Justine about who should fit where, and if anyone at all had to take a middle seat. Nelly and I, it was decided, were to go first and alone, with Nan's ashes in the black urn, the seal of the United States Navy prominent on the front. Everyone else would follow, with the girls from the diner in one car, the boys taking Byron, and Mina bringing up the rear with Vicky and Alaina. We were silent as we started out, leading the caravan. It was a good twenty miles outside of town that I finally broke the quiet.

"What're you thinking over there?" I asked Nelly.

He took a moment before responding. "I don't know what's going to happen tonight. I don't know what's waiting for me on the other side of this. But I sure hope it's my Annamaria. I miss her dearly." The light of the day was starting to gild the treetops as the sun sank. "I wonder if we'll see Nan," he said.

"I don't know."

"Do you hope to?"

It was my turn to pause. "I don't know," I said honestly. "It's going to be hard enough letting go of you. I don't know if I could let go of her again, even if that meant seeing her again."

His hand covered mine on the urn, and the silence returned. In a way, we had already said all we needed to each other; in another, there'd never be enough time to ever feel like enough.

Eventually, the hills got a little steeper, and we turned off the main road. The woods were darker under the thick canopy of leaves. The expansive park was protected state property and felt like a world away from Halfway. After about three miles at a crawl, dodging potholes and jutting rocks on what could loosely be called a road, we pulled out into a clearing.

My temper flared when I saw the chain across the posts, keeping us out; it cooled just as quick when I saw Angie get out of her cruiser to unlatch it. We pulled in, followed by everyone else in short order.

The evening felt more like a family reunion than some kind of send-off. I couldn't say *funeral* but was reminded of Lois Lowry's *The Giver,* when it talks about the elderly being "released." I wondered if the people in that village had wondered what it was like on the other side of that release—if they understood it as death or truly believed people were let go, out of the safety and sanctity within their walls. I had hated the book when I first read it in school but had returned to it on my own in the years since graduation.

The night was warm and there was no need for a fire, but we built a small one anyway. Cleo had brought an armful of campfire logs, and he'd occasionally toss one in, watching the sparks fly from the embers. We liberally applied bug spray and set the chairs in a half-moon shape with tiki torches in between, facing the edge of the gorge. Day gave way to dusk; dusk gave way to dark. But for the torches and emerging stars and a couple of burning cigarettes, there was no light. The moon was new and black. You couldn't ask for better conditions for a meteor shower. Angie had turned back a couple cars, sending them further into the park to another, not-quite-as-optimal spot that Johnathon had found.

The conversation died down to murmurs somewhere around ten, if I had to guess. My watch had died again, and most of us had left our phones in the car. Amy had brought along her old film camera and had it draped around her neck.

All of a sudden, the sky seemed to shimmer—not with falling stars, but almost like a ripple across the fabric of the universe. We all fell silent; Nelly had been talking with Mina most of the night and now reached over the arms of the camping chair to mine. I had kept to myself, occasionally chatting with Byron and Cleo.

"I think it's time," Nelly said. His voice was calm and warm.

Angie swore as headlights beamed up the pocked road. "Motherfuckers. Just a minute, I'll get them out of here. Hey!" she called out as she started to approach the car. The engine quit, and the lights went out. A figure stepped out of the car—first the driver, then the passenger. "I need to ask you to move along. This is a private function by permit only."

"I know," a familiar voice said. "That's what I'm here for."

Nelly's head snapped toward the voice. "Jack?" he whispered, no longer calm.

Within moments, Jack and Mary approached the half-moon of chairs, now empty as everyone stood.

"Wanted to come see you off again," Jack said. "Mary too."

"Hello, Nelly," came her soft tones. "I hoped we wouldn't be too late."

"Look!" Justine shouted.

We all looked up as the first trail appeared, crossing a brief inch of sky.

Nelly drew a breath, took my hand, and patted it one more time. "Del, my dear, it's been nothing but a wondrous pleasure getting to know you. Know that I hold every good wish in my heart for you from here on."

My eyes sought his in the dark and caught their shine. I pulled him into a hug. I closed my eyes as his arms came strong around me. We embraced for a moment or two, then let go. I kissed his cheek. "Safe travels, wherever you may go, my friend. I love you." My voice caught on the end.

"And I you." One last squeeze of my hand, and he let go. "Jack."

"Salty." The two men stepped forward into each other's arms and embraced, not as guys so often do, with one arm between and one clapping the back, but as two people who'd shared a love, if not a lifetime, that would remain forever. The two men released each other without another word.

Nelly stepped forward into the clearing we had left in the middle, a good ten feet back from the edge of the gorge, leaving the fire between him and all of us. He opened the domed lid of the wine box that had held his ashes for six months, then lifted the lid off the urn and laid it beside the black stone. I had a sudden panicked thought that we had no real plan other than this—no words, no pattern to stand in, no way to summon or call or divine or *whatever*, I don't know. I suddenly felt unprepared and helpless.

He stood a moment, looking skyward. A star passed by. Nelly didn't move. I felt like no one breathed. Another star, and still he stood.

A sick terror began to creep up my throat. What if this didn't work? Why were we so sure it would? What were we even *doing* out here?

"Jack," Nelly called out quietly. "Del, would you two come here a minute?"

We exchanged a look, Jack and I, and approached slowly.

"What's going on?" Nelly whispered, still looking up.

"I don't know!" I whispered back.

"How did it happen the first time?" Jack asked.

"I don't know, it just sort of happened. The ashes glowed, like—" I heard a gasp from someone in the circle and looked over.

The urn had begun to sparkle inside. I looked back up and watched as a light golden glow began to rise away from the earth and curve toward the sky. It looked like the trail of those fireworks that look like chandeliers, only in reverse. An arrow of light shot down from the sky, platinum white, hitting the carved wooden urn and refracting. Beams of light swirled up to twine around it in sparkling tendrils. The pale gold shifted and danced, ribboning out and curling back into itself.

For the space of a single, thudding heartbeat, a golden phoenix showed its shape, eyes of glittering amethyst. It joined the other in an aerial dance, the long-tailed plumes of sapphire and royal purple as dazzling as the sleek white-and-gold forms. The white one looked at me with its impossibly blue eyes, and I recognized the sound of its wings, the cry I had heard on the wind, as its own. Now on the wind came a sigh—not of longing, but of finding. Not of distress, but of contentment.

The two magical creatures pulled apart, shimmered brilliantly, and then disappeared into the darkness before our eyes, leaving a gentle shower of stars from their silhouettes.

"He's gone," Jack said.

I looked back to where Nelly stood—or had stood. He *was* gone.

I felt a sweet ache in my heart, and I reached my now-empty hand out for Jack's. He took it and gave mine a squeeze and nodded behind me. I turned and looked. Everyone was standing nearer than I thought. I saw

Vicky and Alaina holding hands, and Johnathon and Cleo. Mina and Mary leaned on each other, and Wendy and Amy were pressing their faces into Justine's shoulders, one on each side. Byron stood by with a small smile on his face. Angie stood across from him on the other side of the group, hands on her hips and gaping up at the sky.

I wasn't ready for any of them yet. Instead, I crouched, touching and grounding myself where Nelly had just stood. I reached over and placed the lid on the stone urn, holding my friend's ashes safely, allowing it to fully close over the last whispers of the white glow. Then I shifted, kneeling in front of Nan's ashes.

I hadn't seen her—no image or visage, no whisper of her voice or any other indication. I felt a strange peace at that; I couldn't say why. The golden vision had been enough.

Slowly, I tipped the dome back over, and for the first time, I latched it. The peaceful feeling stayed.

I rose and carried her back to my chair, placing her in it gently. Someone passed me a Solo cup with the effervescent mist of champagne.

Jack raised his first and cleared his throat. "To Salty—to Nelly. May he shine over us for all time."

"To Nelly!" we shouted, holding our cups to the heavens, and then we drank the sparkling wine down as the night shimmered and the stars fell all around us.

PART FIVE:
SMOKE

CHAPTER TWENTY-NINE

JULY 13, 2019 – ONE YEAR LATER

    The sun was still high above the trees, deep and lush with leaves, as I pulled the truck up over the rough road. I was the first one; I had come hours early to make sure of it. I left my pack and everything in the truck and walked up to the spot. The first time I had returned here, I had wondered if I could find where it was—where Nelly and Nan had returned to their rightful places. I needn't have worried. A white burn marked the spot right there in the dirt, in the shape of a small feather. Concentrated around that mark was a hum of power; as far as I could tell, though, it was one of those "if you know, you know" things. I'd seen hikers pass right over without missing a beat and could see they did not hear the universe crescendo around them.

I sat in the grass, looking out over the ridge, reaching over the mark.

It didn't feel as if a year had passed since our fantastic ordeal. Maybe it was the spot, but it felt like time had stood motionless, as if we had just been here. It couldn't, though, not with everything that had happened.

We buried Nelly a week after all the ashes had been returned, laying him to rest in the cemetery where his Annamaria waited for him. It was a quiet graveside affair, without tears, without many words. Mr. Teasdale from the funeral home had offered his services free of charge to complete the interment. He asked no questions about the man he had known only as Mr. Jones, nor about Alaina's presence at the service. His duties completed, he acknowledged me with a small nod and slipped away. Our party had moved from the cemetery down to the bar, where we closed for the day to wake our friend.

Vicky and Alaina, surprising everyone, became a couple by late summer and quickly moved in together. They delighted in telling people they'd met at a funeral. Everyone was happy for them, and by all accounts, Vicky's mother, Jackie, was at least polite, if not particularly thrilled about the match. Alaina had gotten her job back with the firm and was now thinking of law school, and the two had been touring campuses up and down the East Coast. No one heard from the idiot ex-boyfriend—or cared to find out.

Jack and Mary were still plugging away at the diner with the usual crew. There were a couple new things hanging on the old white walls there: a picture of a golden phoenix rising from the ashes that Mary had picked up at a flea market, and two small plaques above one of the booths. Just the size of a business card, each of the plaques simply bore a single name, one for Nan Montgomery-Shaw, and one for Naylor "Nelly" Maltby.

Johnathon and Cleo invested in another property across the street from the bar, the corner shop where the smoothie bar had lasted less than five months. They were being tight-lipped about it, though, for once. Mina wouldn't stop harassing them for details, and even she was getting nowhere with it. Byron just smiled and kept his counsel whenever the topic came up.

I guessed the biggest changes were mine, though. I leaned back in the grass and propped myself up on my elbows. I let my head fall back and eyes close, soaking up the last of the sun as it began to gleam gold. It had not been an easy year, and I treasured these peaceful moments in a new way. One rainy night in mid-March, I'd ended up in the doghouse before my shift even started. Byron refused to work with me, let alone serve me; I'd come to work already smelling of whiskey and completely unable to pour a pint. I had not grasped the fact that my drinking was no longer in my control. I was simply doing what I needed to do to get by. I only vaguely remembered a shouting match, which resulted in me storming upstairs.

In the morning, I'd faced a quiet intervention by Mina, the boys, and Byron. I would be welcome in the bar, they said, but I would not be served, and I wasn't allowed behind it until I figured my shit out. Mina, bless her, didn't shed a tear as she told me she'd hold my job, but her eyes welled when she said she refused to have a hand in me checking out.

I watched a pair of hawks rise from the trees and circle each other in a slow sky dance as the sun continued its descent. Angling up onto my hip, I reached into my pocket and fished out a small stone disk. I flipped it over in my hand, revealing the painted *90* on the other side. Cleo had made it for me when I hit ninety days without a drink. I had quickly found that the traditional twelve-step programs weren't comfortable places for me, so in my usual way, I bought a bunch of books and worked my way through them. At this point, I felt ready to go back to the bar.

I closed my fist around the little disk to stop the bump of anxiety that came up. I'd gotten rid of all the liquor at my apartment and kept no more than a six-pack of beer for the guys to come over. Sure, some of that was exposure therapy. I'd even drank a couple, on different occasions; there was still nothing like a cold beer with a fresh-off-the-grill burger. I wasn't counting those against me, since they'd never gotten me into trouble. It was whiskey, the sweet fire of whiskey, and hard stuff that I could not handle. That all belonged to a past Delilah.

I looked over at the sound of cars pulling in. I checked my watch; I'd been sitting and reminiscing nearly an hour, I noticed, as I got to my feet and dusted off my jeans. Cleo, Mina, and Johnathon stepped out of the black SUV as Byron pulled up to the other side of my truck. Cleo wasted no time and effortlessly set out six camping chairs.

"Wasn't sure who else would need one, so I brought a couple extra. They're in the trunk," he added with a toss of his head back toward their car. He enveloped me in a hug. "How're ya doing, honey?"

I clung to him for a moment, grateful for his presence, his friendship, and just Cleo being Cleo. Then I let go and found myself passed into a hug from Johnathon, then over to Mina. She pulled back and lifted my chin with her fingers. With a narrowed look, she assessed for whatever secret signs mothers searched their children for when worried about them.

"Well," she said, her voice brusque, "I will say this. You're looking pretty damn good, girl."

"I'm feeling it." I smiled. "Actually, I wanted to talk to you about—" "All in time, all in good time. Now go on, get that table open and the things all set out. We've got to give our girl a proper send-off."

Within ten minutes, we had the pop-up tent up and open, the table laden with condiments, chips, and ice-cold sodas and beer in the two Yetis. There was nothing left to do but wait for the stars to come out. I caught a look between the husbands before Johnathon opened his mouth to speak.

"Well, I guess now's as good a time as any," he said.

"For what?" Mina demanded.

Johnathon grinned at her. "Okay, well. Y'all know we bought the corner smoothie shop."

Mina snorted and took a sip of her Diet Coke. "Get on with it," she grumbled. She wasn't used to being left out of the loop.

"We-e-e-ll," he said again, drawing out the word, "Cleo and I have been doing some research into things, and we realized that there aren't really a whole lot of spaces for people to just, y'know, hang out without alcohol. It wasn't till we were missing Del at the bar that we noticed that."

The color in my cheeks rising, I shoved my hands in my pockets. I may have been welcome at the bar to everyone else, but I couldn't make it work in my mind. I fingered the token, with its slight ridge of paint. "You all came over often enough to not be missing me."

Johnathon ignored my grumbling and continued, "So . . . we want to open a new bar. A dry bar."

My head shot up, and I saw Mina's eyebrows do the same.

"There's a courtyard out back. We can make, like, a beer garden, but with no beer!" Cleo added excitedly. "None of the shops are using the space other than their back doors."

"A sober bar?" I said slowly. "What in the hell nonsense is that? That totally defeats the purpose of a bar."

Johnathon's forehead crinkled quickly in annoyance, then smoothed. "Nonsense. Girl, didn't I just say we did some research? They've been around since around 1900 and were a gathering place in the Prohibition era. They're more popular in Europe, but there's a couple in the States. No reason we shouldn't right here in Halfway."

"Plus, think about how much queer culture has centered around gay bars and drag clubs." Cleo shrugged. "Times, they are a'changing, and I think this could be pretty big."

"There's all sorts of fancy nonalcoholic drinks out there nowadays," Mina mused. "One of my old neighbors had a baby shower recently. She was excited for the 'mocktails,' she called them."

"I think we'd get a lot of people in the door," Johnathon added. "Clientele for folks who don't drink for whatever reason. Baby showers, like your friend, Momma. Younger LGBTQIA folks who need a place to gather, a place you can come and hang out, play some games, meet in person instead of only on the internet. We would set it up to complement the Hub 'n Spoke."

"Covered wagon theme, Prohibition propaganda for art. Can call it Temperance," Byron finally chimed in.

"On the wagon," I said with some amazement.

"Who'd be running the new joint?" Mina asked, a small smile on her lips.

Johnathon spread his hands out. "Job's Del's, if she wants it."

I blinked twice. "Me? I'm just a bartender."

"That's why you'd be perfect. You've been a bartender a long time. This would give you the chance to do that without having to dodge shots all the time. You know what makes the bar run, you know how to make drinks, and you know how to get the atmosphere of the place right." Cleo ticked his reasons off his fingers, grinning at me.

I narrowed my eyes. "How long have y'all been planning this, exactly?"

Cleo scratched his chin and looked up at the deepening sky. "Well—"

"Cleo," I said, a warning in my tone.

Johnathon jumped in. "We had been looking for a new investment already, and By came to us with the idea of a sober night at the bar. One thing sort of lead to another, and now . . ."

I turned to Byron, who was standing above me on the slope of the grass, making our eyes level. "This was your idea?"

"Tried to bury that lede," he muttered, then grinned. It faded just as quickly. "Del, we miss you at the bar. And we want you to be okay and healthy. And this seems to tick an awful lot of boxes."

He was right. I sighed. "And you've got a business plan for this and everything? This isn't just out of sentimentality? You think this will actually work?" I asked, looking back at J and Cleo.

Johnathon shrugged. "We can go over that another time, but yes. Cleo's right, I think this is going to be the start of a bigger movement. Everything is all drawn up. We're ready to start outfitting the space. Truth be told, we are open to you having equal part ownership as us. And we don't need an answer now," he added quickly, as my jaw dropped. "We figured it was time to get this all out in the open, and everything seemed to fit today." He shrugged again.

I looked between them all. My family had come up with a business idea that would get me back to doing what I loved, in a way that I could still be all right. I knew the pull of whiskey would never fully go, but that didn't mean I had to stare it in the face every damn day. And who knew? Maybe this would actually work.

"You know… I had wanted to tell you that I'm ready. I was going to tell you today. But this… doesn't really change that all that much. I'm in," I said decisively, and Cleo let out a whoop. He picked Johnathon right up off the ground and gave him a smacking kiss, then gave me the same. Byron stuck his hand out, so Cleo just bear-hugged him instead. Mina accepted a slightly more restrained kiss from her son and reached her hand out for mine.

"Pretty damn good, girl," she said again, as a pair of headlights pulled up the darkened road.

By the time the first stars came out, the gang was all there. Jack and Mary had joined, and Justine, Amy, and Wendy had arrived from the diner. Vicky and Alaina were regaling them with stories from their recent trip to Maine, with its single law school and a house for rent where they'd been chased by chickens. Angie and her girlfriend, Marie-Claire, an anthropology fellow at the university, were in a deep conversation with Byron and Johnathon about origin stories in voodoo. Cleo and Mina were playing gin rummy.

I was sitting apart, watching everyone and the way they interacted and mingled. They had all been here for me; I knew in my bones the love and respect they had for me, and I for them. I hadn't ever wanted a service for Nan. Still didn't. What I wanted—needed, really—was my family there, to be present. They had all agreed to the quiet, simple plan.

As it felt like the moment had come, I didn't make an announcement, just quietly picked up the wine box that held Nan's ashes. I moved over to the mark in the grass, a spot I could find, I knew, if I was bound and blindfolded.

The lid was unlatched, of course. The box had never fallen; the ashes had never spilled again. Still, I hadn't looked at them since the year before, when they were returned to me. I pushed the lid back, opening it all the way, and sucked in a breath of surprise.

Oh, shit, not again, I thought, as I noticed the ashes glowing brightly. Had they been like that the whole time? Why hadn't I checked?

Unsure of what to do next, I put the box down, where we had released the ashes the year before.

The conversations behind me faded out as we all watched the ashes rise, impossibly, in a gentle swirl. For a moment, I thought I caught sight of the edge of a golden wing and a triumphant cry on the air; the ghost of the image disappeared just as quickly. As the ashes were pulled up and up, as if by some invisible thread, they glowed brighter. Then they stopped in midair. The mountains echoed the crescendo that sounded across them, the sky rippled like a dark blanket of diamonds, and suddenly, the ashes shot straight up into the sky.

A breath like a warm sigh settled over me, and I felt all the tension leave my body. Still facing the heavens, we watched as Nan's ashes left our world, and bright stars began to fall.

I picked up the wine box, now empty but for a small metal disk with all the right numbers on it. I latched the cover and thought it was the perfect time to learn how to wire a lamp. It was time to hold onto the light again.